"May 10." Rhys repeated the date.

The memories crushed in from all sides, hard and fast, squeezing his heart with love and regret and grief. Then he understood. The dress, all that hair curling around her shoulders: the woman he'd abandoned in Stovall's at dinner. The one promising date he'd had in years, brief as it had been.

On the worst night of his life.

He dipped his forehead down until it touched hers. Her name was a whisper on his lips, but it might as well have been a shout for all the emotion, the love, he felt for her. "Camile." Then he inhaled the lilac scent of her and realized he'd never hoped for anything as much as he did right then. *Please let her forgive me.*

Dear Reader,

Have you ever done something completely outside of your comfort zone for someone you love? Maybe you've even gone skydiving or bungee jumping or snowboarding just to please your significant other. Or, if you're an introvert like me, the thing could be as simple as attending a social outing. Now you're nodding and smiling as you think about slipping on your heels, fluffing your hair and gritting your teeth as you set off for that party you've been dreading. Ugh. But it's all worth it in the end to see the look on your sweet one's face, right? Of course it is! (Usually.)

After Rhys McGrath made a brief appearance in my last Pacific Cove book, *Keeping Her Close*, I couldn't get the handsome but slightly awkward social recluse out of my head. What would it take to get him out of his comfort zone? Learning to waltz for the girl he adores felt like the perfect motivation, and taking dance lessons from the woman he once left stranded on a blind date was a very fun way to keep him there. I hope you think so, too.

Thanks so much for reading!

Carol

HEARTWARMING

Second Chance for the Single Dad

—

Carol Ross

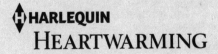

HARLEQUIN
HEARTWARMING

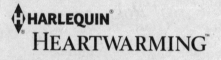

HARLEQUIN®
HEARTWARMING™

ISBN-13: 978-1-335-88962-1

Recycling programs for this product may not exist in your area.

Second Chance for the Single Dad

Copyright © 2020 by Carol Ross

This edition published by arrangement with Harlequin Books S.A.

For questions and comments about the quality of this book, please contact us at CustomerService@Harlequin.com.

Harlequin Enterprises ULC
22 Adelaide St. West, 40th Floor
Toronto, Ontario M5H 4E3, Canada
www.Harlequin.com

Printed in U.S.A.

Carol Ross lives in the Pacific Northwest with her husband and two dogs. She is a graduate of Washington State University. When not writing, or thinking about writing, she enjoys reading, running, hiking, skiing, traveling and making plans for the next adventure to subject her sometimes reluctant but always fun-loving family to. Carol can be contacted at carolrossauthor.com and via Facebook at Facebook.com/carolrossauthor, Twitter, @_carolross, and Instagram, @carolross__.

Visit the Author Profile page
at Harlequin.com for more titles.

For Lisa.

I know I say this all the time, but I *really* don't know what I'd do without you. You're everything a friend is supposed to be, which makes me so, so grateful that you're mine.

CHAPTER ONE

"HERE IT IS," Anne McGrath called out, striding into her brother Rhys's workshop. She stopped when she was a few feet away and held up a single sheet of notebook paper like it was a royal decree, one hand gripping the top edge and the other, the bottom. "The list."

Funny, Rhys thought, because their grandfather had always said that his sister's red hair, pale complexion and middle name weren't the only similarities she shared with Elizabeth I, arguably the most intelligent and formidable queen to ever wield the crown.

Rhys swiveled in his chair, away from the drafting table where he'd been working on a new design. "Working" was a bit of an overstatement. Mostly, he'd been staring at the schematics for a radical new specialty wheelchair design and resenting the circumstances that had driven his sister to this list-making extreme. Anne ran her own public relations firm, so he couldn't discount her success when it came to reputation building; he'd just never thought he'd need to rely on her skills. He'd purposely spent his life avoiding the type of antics that would make her services necessary. Little did he know how severely that would backfire.

When Anne made no move to close the distance between them, he pointed with the pencil still gripped in his hand and asked, "Do you honestly believe that I can see what you've written on that paper from here?"

"Be patient. Before you look, I want you to be aware of a few things."

"Such as?"

"First of all, Harper helped me, as you suggested."

"Good," Rhys said with a firm nod. He trusted Harper. Harper Jansen and her boyfriend Kyle Frasier were Rhys's best friends in Pacific Cove. Okay, so they were his only friends. In the roughly two years he'd lived here, near the small Oregon Coast town, he hadn't exactly ingratiated himself into the community. The fact that he didn't allow visitors on his property, a vast historic headland fronting the Pacific Ocean, had not made him a popular guy. An occurrence that had suited him just fine, until very recently.

"I think so," she returned brightly. "Although some of the items might, um, surprise you."

His response was a noncommittal grumble. Already, he didn't like the sound of this.

"Bringing me to the second and most important point—you need to keep an open mind."

Rhys gave his head an annoyed shake. "I don't understand that term, 'open mind.' If I have an opinion about something, but it conflicts with somebody else's, or even a whole room full of somebodies, then that automatically means that my mind is the one that's closed? Why does pointing out the facts label me as judgmental? How does disagreeing with the consensus make me wrong? Maybe I'm the enlightened one."

Lifting her eyebrows, Anne dropped her chin and peered up at him through her lashes as if he'd proven her point. Which, for the record, he had not. It wasn't his fault people were so baffling and unreasonable.

"Okay, Enlightened One, let's save the philosophy discussion for another time. For now, I want you to look at this list and tell me which items appeal to you the most, and we'll get started." She stepped forward to hand over the paper but then quickly pulled it back. "No, scratch that, tell me the ones you abhor the least and that's where we'll begin."

"Just give it here," Rhys said impatiently, reaching out and snatching the list from her hand. His head was shaking before he even began reading aloud, "Charity work. You want me to do charity work when I—"

"I know, I know. The entire country knows TOFL, but because of the fact that you eschew publicity, virtually no one knows that you are TOFL." Rhys designed prosthetic limbs as well as tools and equipment for use specifically with those limbs. As a former navy SEAL, he'd seen the need for these items up close and personal. Through a consortium of fellow veterans, he'd started the charitable foundation, The Other Front Line, or TOFL, where his use of cutting-edge technology and his extensive network of military contacts got these items to wounded veterans. "If you would let me put out a press release about your work, then maybe—"

"No." Rhys cut her off. "I don't want to be recognized for TOFL. That's part of our consortium agreement—we don't generate personal publicity. I don't want anything to—"

"Take the focus away from our veterans. I know, and I get that." Expression determined, she paused for a second and then, almost like she couldn't help herself, added quickly, "Even though from a PR perspective, I don't agree.

But what about the youth center?" Privately, with a few of his consortium buddies, Rhys had proposed the construction of a youth center in Pacific Cove. A place for kids to hang out, play games and sports, study, get help with homework or just be.

"That's just money. Anyone can write a check."

Anne sighed. "But you're the driving force behind the whole concept."

"It hasn't been finalized yet. There's nothing to announce."

"Fine. Then we're back to the list. Harper and I are thinking local charity work. You know, activities where you actually show your face. Like one of those organizations that builds houses for the needy. Kyle and his brother-in-law Jay volunteer for one."

Rhys took a second to think. This was work he would enjoy that required minimal social interaction. He already knew Kyle, and he'd even met Jay Johnston and his wife, Mia, once. Jay was former Coast Guard and seemed like a good guy. "That might work."

"Keep reading."

He frowned down at the list again. "Why would I get a part-time job? I have plenty of money."

Anne rolled her eyes. "Same reason. Getting out into the community and meeting people."

"I don't have time for that kind of commitment. I have my own company to run, remember?"

"That's why I wrote, 'part-time.' The bookstore is hiring, the coffee shop needs a barista, or you could wait tables, or—"

"A barista? Yeah, no. They have to visit and be friendly all the time. In fact, that's a hard no to all part-time jobs."

"Fine," Anne shot back as if she knew she'd been reaching with that one. "Keep reading."

He did and promptly recited, "Hanging out at the coffee shop?"

"You could take your computer and work there. People do that."

"Anne, look at this setup." He gestured around the room at his complex workstation complete with drafting tables, four oversize monitors, assorted printers, robotic machinery and other pieces of specialized equipment.

"You have a point. Go on."

Rhys refocused. "Kite flying, sandcastle sculpting, going out with friends, adopting a dog." And then ticked off responses: "No, no, I have a total of two friends in this town. And I think I'd prefer a cat. Willow and I have talked about adopting a cat or two."

"Your two friends, Harper and Kyle, have already scored us a dinner invitation for tonight. Mexican food with a few of *their* friends, which is the perfect place to start. And you can't walk a cat at the dog park where you would meet other cat-loving people."

"Yet another mark in the cat column." He skimmed over a few more activities and then let out a snort. "Yoga class?"

"Harper suggested that one. She and Kyle both love yoga. Did you know that Kyle teaches a yoga class? Apparently, a lot of Coast Guard guys go."

"Yeah," he drawled flatly, sarcastically. "And I often do what everyone else does. Bowling? You think I should join a bowling team?"

"Harper says bowling is popular here in Pacific Cove. Kyle bowls on a team with Jay and Aubrey. But just getting out and going bowling would be a start."

"Who is Aubrey again?" The name sounded familiar to the point that he thought he should know her. Often it seemed that people were good with either names or faces. Rhys was terrible with both.

"Aubrey is Jay's bestie. She's the kick-butt rescue swimmer for the Coast Guard? Her husband, Eli, is a pilot."

"Right. Yes, I've met her once, too." He

doubted he'd recognize her as he recalled only a vague vision of a tall, athletic-looking blonde. The rescue-swimmer part had been what captured his attention and respect.

"Bowling would be the perfect activity for you. Very wholesome."

"Wholesome?"

"Yes, you know—upright, moral, decent, all-American. Normal. You'd meet a ton of people. Other parents with kids, probably."

Normal. Rhys hated that word. Willow's aunt, Heather, had used it, too, when she'd informed Rhys she'd hired an attorney. *Rhys, you're not normal. I cannot, in good conscience, allow Willow to live with you. You're incapable of giving her a normal life.* Completely arbitrary designation. In his case, it meant whatever the family court decided it meant. For the first time in a long time, he wished it meant him. Not because he didn't like who he was necessarily, but because it would make all of this a nonissue. Maybe Heather wouldn't be contesting his custody of their niece if he met that ambiguous societal standard that he didn't live up to.

"These are just ideas, but every single one of them has merit. Any one of these activities will get you out into the community. Meeting people. Socializing. Hopefully acquiring personal references—possibly even friends. Pick three, and I'll get them set up. I've also got a list of upcoming social events that we will be attending."

Rhys finally noticed the last item on the list. It was written below the others under the subheading "Mandatory." And it proved that his sister had officially taken things too far. "Is this last one a joke? Dance lessons are an unequivocal no."

"Nope. No, not a joke. Dance lessons are nonnegotiable. See what subheading it falls under? *Mandatory.*"

"Anne, that is the weirdest thing on this entire list. You know me—in a million years I would never, ever dance or go dancing. I avoid situations where dancing or music will be in evidence. It's the reason I don't attend wedding receptions."

Anne executed a dramatic eye roll and said dryly, "Yeah, that's the reason."

"It's one of them," he countered. One of many. Swarms of "normal" people who expected him to chat about nothing while not offending anyone were another. "That makes three things on this list that are out. Karaoke, concerts and dancing."

"Fine, but Willow's cotillion is in five weeks."

Rhys answered with an impatient, "I know that." It was the reason their niece wasn't here right now. Willow was currently in South Carolina staying with her maternal grandparents, Olivia and Les, so that she could participate in the Magnolia Junior Debutante Program, following a tradition in her family. Willow's mother Vanessa had done it, and her mother before her. Vanessa's great-grandmother had been one of the first participants. Initially, Willow hadn't been keen on taking part, but a few months ago, after Vanessa's death, she'd said it felt like something she "needed" to do. As a tribute to her mother. Rhys had eagerly agreed—anything to help her through the grieving process. He'd arranged a schedule so that he, Anne or their mother visited Willow often in South Carolina. Their mother was with her now. Rhys flew her back to Pacific Cove as often as the program's schedule allowed.

"So…?" he drawled impatiently, wanting Anne to get to the point.

"So," Anne repeated, slowly pulling one shoulder up into a shrug, "I guess Troy will do it."

Rhys tensed. He despised Troy. Troy was Heather's husband. Together, the two of them were trying to prevent Rhys from retaining legal custody of Willow. Custody that Rhys's brother, Evan, and his wife, Vanessa, Heather's sister, had wanted Rhys to have. They'd asked him to raise Willow, had even gone so far as to spell it out in their will. Rhys had sworn to them both on the day of Willow's baptism thirteen years ago, when he'd accepted the honor of being her godfather, that he'd take care of her if anything were to happen to them. Two years ago, Evan died after suffering a series of strokes. After Evan's death, Vanessa had reiterated to Rhys that she hadn't changed her mind about Willow's guardianship. Three months ago, the unthinkable had happened when Vanessa was killed in a car accident. Now, in addition to grieving for his sister-in-law, he was embroiled in a custody dispute. At least Heather had agreed to postpone the custody proceedings until after Willow's cotillion.

"Troy can do what? What are you talking about?"

"The father-daughter dance kicks off the ball. Troy can stand in as dad and dance with Willow. Mom said that Olivia said Troy dances a *lovely* waltz."

No one could hammer a point home quite as effectively as his sister. Rhys reached over and circled the words. "Dance lessons it is," he said through gritted teeth, a loud snap punctuating the declaration as the pencil cracked in two.

"CAMILE? CAMILE? EARTH to Senorita Camile."

"I'm sorry, Bobby, what?" Camile Wynn counted the fourteen tiny steps it took to shift her body around so that she could view her boss through the tiny slits in her giant-sized foam-and-plastic taco suit. For the umpteenth time, she wondered why he didn't just walk the additional three steps to face her so he could deliver his next dose of "professional advice." So far, he'd criticized her singing voice—both its pitch and volume, her Spanish accent, her inability to juggle the foil-wrapped burritos he tossed at her—she couldn't see them!—and the unsatisfactory level of her enthusiasm in general. She'd nearly quit on the spot when he suggested her dance moves lacked rhythm. Twenty-two years of studying and teaching dance in one form or another and six years of working part-time as a "product promoter" had given her unparalleled suit-dancing expertise. Bobby was treading on thin ice.

Facing him with drips of sweat running into her eyes meant he was just a blurry mass. But that was okay. Being subjected to the sight enough times already, she could easily conjure up a vision of her boss: bulbous, red-veined nose, flabby jowls, thin lips twisting with disapproval and those beady eyes looking her up and down in a way that made her skin crawl.

Sweat trickled between her shoulder blades, causing an itch so intense it was almost painful. It just had to be unseasonably warm on the weekend she'd agreed to dress up in layers of foam and plastic for the "mobile Mexican cantina's" grand opening. He'd booked her for the following five weekends, as well. Lucky for Bobby, though, because sunshine on the Oregon Coast meant tourists were scuttling around like ants at a picnic. With similarly appointed appetites. Even for bad tacos.

"What does that say?" Bobby pointed.

Camile blinked and squinted at the words stenciled on the side of the taco truck. "Uh, *the Dancing Taco*?"

"That's right, *chica*," he answered testily. "And you are *my* dancing taco."

"Bobby, I've been dancing around for five hours. I only stopped just now to get a drink of water."

"Dancing is what I'm paying you good money for, not drinkin'." This last declaration seemed to insinuate that she'd been sneaking tequila shots inside her suit or something.

Not for the first time, Camile was glad Bobby couldn't see her glaring face. She was pretty sure she would have been fired by now. She wouldn't exactly call what he was paying her "good money," but it was easy money. Normally. And she needed it. Badly.

"I appreciate your generosity. But trust me, it's important to stay hydrated. It's very hot out here, and this suit isn't well ventilated. Last weekend, I had a little episode because I didn't drink enough water." She also hadn't eaten breakfast. Or lunch. The combination had led to her passing out on the sidewalk outside a pet store while wearing a dog costume. Resulting in an astronomical hospital bill and only a partial paycheck with which to pay said bill.

"Hey, can it! Customers will hear you whining. It's hot in my *cantina*, too, babe." He hitched a thumb toward the truck. "But you know what I'm doing? I'm cooking up tacos while you're standing around out here twiddling your thumbs. Now get to shaking that pretty little caboose."

Camile liked to believe she was a tolerant individual. No, she knew she was. Her mishmash of part-time jobs proved it. She was tough, too. And resilient. Five years of working and paying her own way through college and graduate school supported that fact. Her recent thesis disaster demonstrated that she could roll with the most brutal of punches. That was putting it mildly. The thesis episode had knocked her out cold, and still, she'd managed to get up and shake it off. The phrase had become her personal theme song and mantra. But enough was enough. She wondered if it would be possible later to write off her impending reaction to heatstroke and dehydration?

"Okay, Bobby, first of all, don't call me *chica*. Or babe. And I am not *your* taco. Commenting or referencing my caboose in any manner is not appropriate. And second, how can you be making tacos when you're standing out here complaining about me every other five seconds? Is there a tortilla in your pocket? Or maybe you've got beans stashed in that ridiculous hat you're wearing?" Bobby was immensely proud of his taco-shaped hat. She should have had a clue as to how the day was going to proceed when she'd first shown up, and he'd referred to himself as "Chief Taco-Head."

Bobby's edges might be blurred, but she could see well enough to make out the deep red shade of his cheeks, now a close match to the color of the "spicy *fuego* sauce" he proudly served on the side of every take-out order. She knew for a fact it was nothing but ketchup and cayenne pepper.

His tone dipped low and venomous. "What did you say to me?"

"You heard me, you lazy, ignorant, sexist windbag. From where I'm standing, it looks like Howard is doing the taco making." Camile gestured at the truck where the teenage Howard had been sweating over the grill all day while being subjected to both Bobby's ugly reproach and his smelly proximity. In many ways, the taco suit was probably preferable. She drew her arms inside the suit's narrow armholes and set about extricating herself from the confines of her fiery inferno. "But just in case, I'll increase the volume and the clarity in the way you coached me to do earlier." Camile shouted, "You're mean, Bobby. And disrespectful and unfair and vile, and your tacos taste like something the ocean vomited up at high tide. No offense, Howard. I know this is just a crap job to you, too."

"Uh, none taken," she heard a cheerful-sounding Howard reply. "I hear ya. I told him not to mix these weird oats and stuff in with the meat."

Grateful for her small frame and the strength and flexibility that years of dance had instilled, she shimmied the suit upward until it hovered above her head. The taco slowly tipped sideways. Camile gave a little shove, and it hit the sidewalk with a surprisingly loud thwack, frightening a curious dog who let out a bark and scuttled sideways. Camile went to comfort the little guy, and that was when she realized they'd attracted an audience. A fairly good-sized one, too. With her limited visibility and furious, intent focus on Bobby, she hadn't noticed.

"Shut your stupid piehole, Howard!" Bobby bellowed.

Camile whirled around and pointed at him. "Don't talk to him like that! Bobby, you're just proving my assertion, can you not see that?"

"Yeah? Well, you're fired."

"Dang," she retorted sarcastically. "Are you sure? Because I was desperately hoping for a reference. Taco dancing is just the thing I've been hoping for to round out my résumé. I was counting on The Royal Ballet hiring me upon your recommendation."

Bobby was apparently even dumber than she realized. "Ha," he sputtered. "Not a chance."

Camile looked toward the truck, where a wide-eyed and red-faced Howard appeared to be desperately trying to stifle a laugh. "Howard, I know for a fact Nina Marie's Berries & Cream is hiring. You know, the old Quinley berry farm?" At Howard's enthusiastic nod, she went on, "Three dollars an hour above minimum wage, more if you get cleared to make deliveries. Head out there now and tell the owner that I sent you. Her name is Nina." Camile knew this because Nina was her oldest sister. She'd offered Camile the job again that morning, but Camile didn't want to work for her big sister for reasons that Howard wouldn't have to grapple with.

"Seriously? Awesome! Thanks so much, Camile. Hey, Bobby, I quit." Howard's apron sailed through the order window on the broad side of the truck and landed in a heap at Bobby's feet.

Camile shot Bobby a satisfied grin, pivoted gracefully and took off down the boardwalk. "*Adios*, Chief Taco-Head," she called with a wave over her shoulder. Cheers and loud applause followed in her wake. Checking her watch, she saw that she now had plenty of time to go home, rehydrate and shower away the caked-on layers of taco-scented sweat before she met her sisters and some friends for dinner. She briefly considered a nap, except she knew that if she lay down, she wouldn't want to get up again until morning.

Once inside her ancient, air conditioner–less, semireliable car, she rolled the windows down, guzzled the contents of her insulated water bottle and dug her phone out of her bag. She texted Nina about Howard. There was a message from her other sister Aubrey, which she'd been expecting, with details of the evening's dinner outing. Camile opened the message. A combination of amusement and disbelief stirred inside her as she stared at the words: 7:00 p.m. at La Playa Bonita. It's that new Mexican place in Remington! It's taco night! Fun, right? I can pick you up if you want?

"Tacos, seriously?" she whispered. So much for washing her latest bad job experience down the drain. Letting her head fall to the steering wheel, Camile had to laugh. She had to. It was either that or cry.

CHAPTER TWO

"Oh, LOOK! There's Harper and Kyle," Anne chirped brightly, pointing across the restaurant. "This is going to be super fun. I hope the salsa is good. You know how salsa can make or break the entire Mexican food experience for me." Hooking an arm around Rhys's elbow, she urged him forward.

Rhys didn't budge. Anne's overly enthusiastic tone was chiming in his brain like a warning bell. Yet another sound to synthesize with the already-grating restaurant noises scraping against the inside of his skull. *Excessive* was the word that came to mind as he surveyed La Playa Bonita's interior. The wall to his left sported a mural of jungle animals scattered among a canopy of foliage. Cheeky monkeys swung from vines and a snake coiled around a tree limb. A toucan-shaped piñata hung from the ceiling above. Along the far wall, fish and sea creatures frolicked against a background of bright blue. It was there, amid the equally eye-catchingly bright ocean, that Rhys spotted

Kyle and Harper seated at a large table. Several tables, technically, pushed together end to end. Enough to seat the—Rhys quickly counted—eight other people congregated there. There were still empty seats, as well.

Allowing himself a moment to process the situation, he attempted to adjust to the uncomfortable acceleration of his pulse and accompanying pressure building smack-dab in the center of his chest. Despite his distress, he kept his tone level. "I thought you said we were having dinner with Kyle and Harper and a few of their friends."

"We are," Anne said, only a little less brightly.

"Eight is not a few."

"Close enough."

"Hardly. In this context, eight is much closer to numerous, several, or even a bunch than a few."

Anne muttered something under her breath while reaching out with one hand to grip his wrist lightly. "Come here," she said, pulling him sideways behind a large, square pillar. In a low voice, she added, "See what you did right there? Don't do that at dinner, okay? We're trying to get people to like you."

"Don't do what?"

"Don't be…argumentative."

Rhys stared at her, perplexed. "I'm never argumentative."

"Yes. You are. I said there were a few other people and you corrected me."

"Well, you were wrong."

"Rhys!" she hissed. "You're arguing with me right now."

"No, I'm not. I'm simply pointing out an indisputable fact."

Anne scowled up at him. "It comes across as disagreeable. I know that you know what I'm talking about."

He did. It was not the first time she'd pointed out this tendency of his. Nor was she the first person to do so. But it was also inaccurate. "Correcting misinformation is not arguing."

"Rhys, this desire you have to be right all the time is annoying. It rubs people the wrong way."

It wasn't that he *wanted* to be right all the time. Not at all. He simply couldn't abide anything other than accuracy. And the truth. He shrugged a shoulder. "People should get their facts straight before they speak."

Expression earnest, her eyes searched his for a few seconds before she gave her head a little shake. "Sometimes I think you truly do not care what people think about you."

Rhys managed a small smile at that. "Then sometimes you would be correct."

CAMILE SAT WITH her back toward the wall, her position allowing her a view of a large section of the restaurant. She predicted good things for the eatery's future based on the atmosphere the owners had created. The decor was jungle-tropical themed—fun and festive and inviting. The upbeat Latin pop music wasn't too loud and called to mind soft sand and warm beaches. She'd just dipped another chip into the excellent salsa which, in her opinion, was another huge indicator of the establishment's potential success, when she noticed a striking couple standing across the room.

Specifically, what she noticed first was the woman's gorgeous red hair. A quick assessment revealed that the rest of her was equally as pretty. Her attention shifted to the man standing by her side. Causing her heart to slam sideways against her rib cage. Hard.

No… It couldn't be, could it?

Morbid curiosity overrode her latent humiliation and had her squinting for a better look. The chip in her hand remained suspended in midair between the salsa bowl and her mouth, as she realized that his hair drew attention, too. Was that irony? She imagined it like a slapstick skit, two beautiful, stunning-haired people triggering double takes wherever they went. Unfortunately, it wasn't funny in this case. Not at all. Because it helped confirm his identity.

Rhys McGrath's hair wasn't red, but it was the most striking shade of blond. About a hundred different sun-kissed shades all woven together and falling nearly to his shoulders in thick golden waves. She'd recognize that hair anywhere because when she'd first laid eyes on it, on him, she'd been struck with a series of thoughts. The first was that he looked like a surfer, which was silly because she'd never actually known any surfers. But she was pretty sure they would look like him. If he'd been wearing board shorts instead of an expensive suit. The second had been less of a thought and more of a desire. Her fingers had tingled from wanting to run them through those loose, luxurious curls. She just knew they would feel all velvety soft. The third was that a guy who'd not only been blessed with such beautiful hair but also wore it in that laid-back, hip kind of style would probably have a personality to match.

Exhilaration had left her almost giddy as she'd slid into the seat across from him in the swanky downtown Portland restaurant for what felt like a truly promising blind date with a brilliant engineer. And for a brief moment, she'd believed that Rhys McGrath was exactly the kind of beach-bum-meets-handsome-professor she'd pegged him for.

How wrong she'd been.

That was when the right-here-right-now Rhys McGrath turned and looked in her direction. A rush of adrenaline surged through her bloodstream, prickling her skin and scattering her thoughts. Did he recognize her? What should she do? Pretend not to recognize him? Hide? One thing she would not do was give him the satisfaction of knowing how badly he'd humiliated her. That meant hiding was out. She didn't like that option anyway; Camile was not a hider by nature. She could throw her margarita in his face. Tempting. But a bit too clichéd for her, and too overt. Drink tossing would suggest anger on her part. Was she angry? Yes, of course, she was. No one deserved to be treated the way he'd treated her. Many times, she'd fantasized about tracking him down and giving him a piece of her mind. And yet, she hadn't wanted to humiliate herself further. Just like she didn't want to do so now. It had happened a long time ago. She was over it. Ideally, she'd want him to think that it hadn't bothered her in the first place. So her approach should probably reside somewhere in the middle of the two extremes. More of a cold-shouldered recognition.

Bracing herself, she prepared to meet the intensity of those blue eyes. Yep, she remembered those, too. Because for the brief time they'd been focused on her—over the appetizer he'd ordered and left untouched—she'd felt interesting and listened to and attractive and... And then he'd bolted like a cowardly jackal. Why did this still bother her?

He shifted back toward his companion, and Camile realized that maybe he hadn't been looking at her, per se, but just gazing in her general direction. From the look of their heated conversation, he had other things on his mind. Camile exhaled the breath she'd been holding and forced fresh air into her lungs. No reason to think that he'd even noticed her, let alone recognized her. The date had been a long-ago occurrence that was short in duration; two years ago and twenty-three minutes long, respectively. She'd grown her hair out since then, changed the color as she tended to do. On the date, she'd worn it down and curled. There'd been makeup, a fancy dress and no glasses. Pretty much the opposite of how she looked this evening.

"Camile?" Her sister Nina's voice broke through her reverie. "Sweetie, are you okay?"

"What?" she answered, slow-blinking in Nina's general vicinity.

"Are you all right? I lost you there for a minute. You're a little pale. Is something wrong with the salsa?"

Camile glanced down at the chip still held rigidly in her fingers. Her mouth was way too dry to eat it now. With her other hand, she reached for her margarita and took a sip. She ate the chip, washing it down with another sip. Which she then chased with a nice healthy gulp.

"Yes. No. Sorry. Salsa is yummy. I'm fine. Just a little tired. Long day."

Nina shifted her tone to an exaggeratedly loud whisper. "You're not going to pass out again, are you?"

Camile gaped at her eldest sister before letting out a groan of frustration. Middle sister, Aubrey, who was seated on the opposite side of the table and had been engaging in conversation with her friend and former Coast Guard teammate Jay, swiveled toward them.

Like a lighthouse beacon, Aubrey homed in on Nina. "Passed out? And what do you mean, *again*?" She peered at Nina and then Camile before demanding, "What is she talking about, Camile? When did you pass out?"

Sighing, Camile gave her head a little shake. She frowned at Nina. "I thought we agreed we weren't going to say anything. How is this *not* telling Aubrey?"

"I didn't tell her. She eavesdropped." Nina added an innocent shrug as if this were a valid explanation for her obvious intent to let Aubrey know about the episode.

"*Why* would we not tell Aubrey?" Aubrey asked, their statements overlapping. "What happened?"

"A minor bout of heatstroke. It was nothing. I'm fine."

"If you consider dehydration nothing," Nina added. "Then sure, yeah, it was nothing."

"Nina," Camile groaned, "why are you doing this to me?"

"You were dehydrated?" Aubrey scowled. "When did this happen?"

"Last weekend, at that pet store opening. I worked a double because Becca got sick. The owner offered me double time. It was very good money." Or it would have been if she'd been able to finish the job.

"Camile, we've talked about this—"

Camile scooped up another chip and pointed it at Aubrey. "Exactly! Which is why I didn't mention it." When working in costume, Camile limited her fluid consumption to minimize bathroom breaks. It was a pain to get the suits off and on. Aubrey knew this. She disliked it and had warned Camile that something "serious" might happen. Her sister could be so annoying when she was right, and she was right an annoying amount of the time. Precisely why Camile hadn't wanted her to know. Aubrey had it all together, had always had it all together, and as such, enjoyed favored status with their parents, especially their father. Nina's recent berry farm success had elevated her up the ladder, as well. Unlike Camile, whose life seemed to be unraveling faster and faster every day.

But apart from the taco fiasco, the pet store job had been great. Mostly great. Exhausting yes, but she'd enjoyed mingling with the dogs and their owners. Sure, the suit was old, making it hotter and stuffier than newer styles. And yes, she'd been, um, mistaken for a fire hydrant. Twice. But all in all, it was worth it. Until she'd accidentally turned off the "water alarm" on her phone, which resulted in a couple of missed hydration breaks. That, and skipping breakfast, and then lunch, had resulted in her passing out in a heap of fur-covered humiliation. She couldn't think of much that was more embarrassing than being rushed to the hospital while wearing a giant foam dog suit. Except for maybe being abandoned at a table for two during the first act of a first date.

Her gaze strayed back to where she'd last seen Rhys… Gone. She exhaled a loud sigh of relief.

Nina answered Camile's question. "Because you work too hard. And too much. Both. And if you'd just take the job on my farm, then you would never end up in the hospital hooked up to IV fluids."

"The hospital? My baby sister was in the hospital, and I didn't know about it?" Aubrey asked the questions in a voice as smooth and sweet as chilled cream, effectively telling Camile that she was fuming. Not that she needed confirmation on that score. Aubrey did not like being out of the loop. "Do Mom and Dad know?"

"Of course not!" Camile exclaimed, horrified by the notion.

The three sisters were quiet for a beat. They all knew there was no way their parents, Brian and Susannah, would ever keep a major family incident like that from Aubrey. A rescue swimmer for the Coast Guard, Aubrey was like the self-appointed captain of the Wynn family safety squad. And as Aubrey was practically a clone of their father, a retired Coast Guard captain, father and daughter's type-A personalities united to form an overwhelmingly bossy benevolence that, while well-meaning, could also feel smothering. Resulting in Camile's tendency to sometimes be less than completely forthcoming. She counted on Nina to be her ally in this. Or at least, she used to.

"Aubrey, please, don't tell them. It was nothing." Thankfully, their retired parents were spending the summer touring the country's national parks in their RV.

"I won't."

"Thank you."

"If you promise to cut back on your schedule."

She barely managed to stifle a scoff. *How in the world am I supposed to do that and pay my bills?* The question burned hotter than salsa on the tip of her tongue, but she swallowed it down. Because saying it would only result in unwanted and unneeded help and advice. "Done," she said instead.

"Really?"

"Sure." Camile added an easy shrug. "I was fired from the taco-truck job today, so I have an entire day off tomorrow." She also had the following five weekends free, but she wasn't going to mention those. The hours would easily be filled with one of her other part-time jobs. Hal had already asked her if she could squeeze in more time at the bowling alley.

"Camile, that's not what I meant."

She sighed. "Aubrey, I appreciate your concern. I do. But I am fine. And I can't just—"

Before Camile could finish her thought, she was interrupted with a cheerful, "Hey, guys!"

"Harper, hi!" Nina greeted the smiling woman who approached them.

"Sorry to interrupt, but I want to introduce you ladies to my friends."

Professional photographer Harper Jansen and her fiancé Kyle Frasier were recent additions to their social group. Kyle was former military and Jay's brother-in-law, so he was already an acquaintance. But Camile and Harper had recently struck up their own friendship when Camile had been hired to teach ballroom dance classes at the local studio along with Harper, who taught ballet.

The two women had hit it off immediately, and normally Camile would be thrilled to meet her friends. But not now. Because Harper's friends were none other than Rhys McGrath and his red-haired companion who, Camile couldn't help but notice, was even prettier up close. A perfect match to his own dazzling good looks. Camile hated that she'd wondered if it was the way she looked that had been so off-putting to him. Even though no woman in her right mind would want a man who would judge a woman based on that alone. Right? Ugh, why was that so much easier to say than to believe?

Harper gestured toward the couple and began introductions. "This is Anne McGrath and her brother, Rhys." Then she swung an arm toward the table. "These are the Wynn sisters. Nina, she owns the organic berry farm I was telling you about. She makes the best marionberry pies in the world and also has the best dog in the world, a border collie—also named Marion. Adorable, right?"

Placing a hand on the back of Aubrey's chair, she said, "This is Aubrey, who I think you've met before, Rhys? Aubrey's married name is Pelletier, but I think it's fun to introduce them as the Wynn sisters. You just met her husband, Eli, the helicopter pilot. Aubrey is a rescue swimmer for the Coast Guard. Like Kyle, Rhys is also a former navy SEAL, so that gives you military people all kinds of things to talk about…"

More chatty details followed. Camile vaguely registered the greetings exchanged—"Wonderful to meet you," "So glad you could join us," "How's the salsa?"—while furtively watching for some hint that Rhys recognized her. Examining the siblings, she realized that the resemblance between them was glaring. The reason she hadn't immediately spotted it was the difference in their coloring; Anne had a creamy pale complexion while Rhys sported golden skin tones, the kind that would tan easily in the sun. Like a surfer, she noted acerbically. Genetics had been kind with their matching features: the same defined cheekbones, squared jaws with cleft chins and astonishingly blue eyes. But where Rhys's expression was flat and cold, Anne's was animated and warm.

"And this is Camile. We work at the same dance studio, which is beyond awesome for me. She's just finishing up her graduate degree and shares my passions for yoga, cats, muffins and salsa."

"Me, too!" Anne gushed. "About the salsa, anyway. And Rhys is thinking about adopting a cat." After a chuckle and a quick glance in his direction, she added, "I was just mentioning the salsa thing to Rhys. It's a deal breaker for me. I will literally choose which Mexican restaurant I eat at according to the salsa."

Camile hung on to a tight smile and mumbled something favorable about the salsa. Harper, bless her and her endless supply of trivia, began a conversation about the health benefits of capsaicin and the varying amounts found in different varieties of peppers.

Camile snuck another glance at Rhys. Nothing even remotely close to embarrassment, regret, horror or recognition registered on his face. There was nothing much there at all other than cool reserve and chiseled beauty. Now that her initial shock had run its course, she wasn't sure if that was better or worse. She thought it might be worse, because *that* was how forgettable she was.

A waitress appeared at the other end of the table.

"Hey," Kyle called from where he was already seated and chatting with Eli. "You guys know what you want to drink?"

The trio migrated toward Kyle and settled in some empty seats. For a moment, Camile was relieved. Aubrey seemed to be sidetracked from their previous conversation regarding Camile's propensity to work too hard. (Ironic, considering Aubrey's profession as a Coast Guard rescue swimmer who also ran an extensive swimming program for kids in her spare time.)

Drinks were served. Another member of the waitstaff replenished the chips and salsa.

Camile's relief soon began to crumble as the situation played out like some sort of tragicomedy. Because while Rhys had settled a couple spots away, his seat faced hers, and she couldn't converse with anyone at that end of the table without looking *toward* him, which somehow kept ending up being *at* him. And that was where Harper was, across the table from Camile and next to Rhys, and she kept chatting with Camile about the dance studio. They both loved dancing and talking about dancing, and Camile kept getting caught up and inadvertently prolonging the discussion.

Rhys barely spoke at all, to anyone. She kept *feeling* his eyes on her, though, and at one point, her gaze collided with his. He smiled. It appeared forced and stilted. She returned it, albeit tentatively, and thought she saw a spark of awareness that might have been recognition. But it was so fleeting and followed by more nothing that she finally decided she must have imagined it. She did her level best to ignore him and eke out what enjoyment she could from the rest of the evening.

Rhys checked the time on his watch. They'd been here nearly two hours. He wondered how much longer Anne would insist they stay. Their plates had been cleared ages ago. He was out of small talk, not that he'd had much to begin with. Chitchatting was not in his wheelhouse. To make matters worse, one of the Wynns he'd met earlier kept distracting him. The pretty one.

He couldn't remember her name, but he did recall from Harper's introductory bio that she was the youngest sister, and newly graduated from college. A simple calculation suggested, if she'd attended straight through, that she was in her early twenties. Probably too young for his thirty-two. Not that he was interested. In fact, he was trying not to look at her for fear he'd give her that impression. But he knew he was failing miserably. Seated where he was, he couldn't help but overhear the conversation between her and Harper. And like Harper, she was bright and witty and sociable to a point that he found attractive and intriguing and enviable and exhausting all at the same time.

At the other end of the restaurant, in the bar, a band began to play. It sounded similar to the upbeat Latin music that had been previously playing in the background, except even louder. A man's voice announced that it was time to *"Bailamos!"* Rhys nudged Anne, hoping they could *vámanos.*

"Oh, that reminds me!" Anne said to Harper. "I need to ask a favor."

"Sure, what's up?"

"Can you teach Rhys how to dance?"

Harper's eyebrows inched upward as she grinned at Rhys. "You want to learn ballet?"

Rhys felt his gut twist at the mention of the dancing. He knew he needed to do this, but just the thought of it left him vaguely nauseated. But Harper was so engaging and completely nonjudgmental; he knew that if anyone could help mitigate this dancing fiasco, it would be her.

"No, he has an event coming up, and he needs to learn how to waltz. He wants private lessons."

"Oh…" Harper drawled. "Like ballroom stuff. Well, you don't want me. You need—"

At that moment, the pretty one stood. Rhys watched her, noting that she was roughly a foot shorter than his six-foot-three-inch height. She was petite but curvy and fit. He admired the cut of her arm muscles in her sleeveless dress.

"Wait, Camile, you're not leaving yet, are you?" Harper asked.

Camile. How could he forget such a lovely name? It made him think of cobblestoned streets and vintage Paris, and it suited her perfectly.

Camile stepped around the table and came closer until she was standing by Harper's chair. Rhys turned and enjoyed a better view of all of her. She was *very* pretty, and in a unique way that he liked.

"I am. I've had more than enough of tacos for one day if you get my meaning." She added a wink, and she and Harper shared a laugh, clearly enjoying a private joke.

Camile removed her glasses and tucked them into her bag. Then, smile in place, she leveled her gaze right on him. And for a moment, Rhys couldn't move. The color of her eyes was such a pure green that it made it difficult to label them. But it was the way she looked at him that held him spellbound. With this challenging glint. What was that about? His eyes traveled over her face and lingered on her mouth where he encountered…*that smile.* Confident and bold with a little mischief thrown in, her smile trained on him was the best thing Rhys had ever seen, and it felt both fiery and cryptic. He knew that whatever mystery it conveyed wasn't for him, not really, because she didn't know him. But at that moment, he wanted it to be; private jokes and secret smiles with lovely Camile—his new fantasy.

Harper placed a hand on her elbow. "Can I ask you something?"

"Of course," Camile said, putting an end to their eye contact. Rhys wanted to protest. Like when the power unexpectedly goes out, stealing all the light, and makes you resent the dark in a whole new way.

"Are you still looking for extra work?"

What! Rhys thought fast as he finally understood where this was headed. He knew from their dinner conversation that she was a dancer, too. Harper was going to ask Camile to give him lessons. No. That could not happen. He'd thought, hoped, that Harper would agree to teach him. And if not her, then maybe an elderly woman with a sweet nature and a husband she adored. Someone without a paralyzing smile he wasn't attracted to and who wasn't attracted to him for the wrong reasons. Someone who wouldn't get to know him and quickly tire of him. For the second time in one day, he desperately wished he was normal in a way that he hadn't in years.

"Always, Harper, you know that. In fact, I have a gaping hole in my schedule right now. Maybe Gia will add that swing class to the schedule. It would be so fun to teach it together."

"That would be super fun. I'm working on her. But I may have a related job for you. Rhys here happens to be in need of a private dance instructor."

And just like that, the smile vanished. Technically, it was still there in the curve of her mouth, but Rhys saw the light dim in her electric green eyes. She was not pleased with this idea. He wasn't sure what to make of that based on what had transpired between them a moment ago. Sure, it had only been a look, but he'd felt *something*. He'd assumed... The truth was, it wasn't uncommon for women to be physically attracted to him, and he'd believed that was the case. Apparently not. That revelation should have been a relief. It was not.

Still, he wasn't keen on the idea of paying her to watch his dancing-induced humiliation. Although, if Harper thought she was the best person to teach him, she undoubtedly was.

Anne explained, "Rhys needs to learn how to dance."

"What kind of dancing?" Camile asked.

"Simple ballroom stuff. The waltz, for sure, and maybe a fox-trot?" She looked to a nodding Anne for confirmation.

Rhys wanted to protest, to let them both off the hook. But then he looked at Camile again and felt that same pull—and that same resistance on her part. Why, if she needed the work, did she not want the job? Instead of putting him off, it made him curious. And determined.

CHAPTER THREE

CAMILE FELT LIKE a fox caught in a trap. How was she going to get out of this? She wouldn't wish Rhys McGrath on her worst enemy, much less herself. Like ripping off a bandage, she'd attempted one final push to jog his memory and dispel the awkwardness. Removing her glasses, she'd looked him right in the eye and had all but dared him to remember her. And she'd gotten nothing from him but what appeared to be mild curiosity. Or maybe it was indigestion. Who could tell?

Harper knew she enjoyed this kind of work. It was popular in wedding parties these days for the participants to take a few lessons before the big day, upping the fun level at the reception. Brides and grooms were wowing their guests with everything from the waltz and the tango to the samba and country line dance. And it wasn't just the happy couple caught up in the craze. Bridesmaids, groomsmen, family members, you name it, people wanted to learn the moves and get their groove on. Camile had given lessons to them all. She'd choreographed group routines for entire wedding parties.

But there was no possible way she was going to extend her expertise to Rhys McGrath and his bride-to-be if, in fact, his upcoming nuptials was the event in question.

"When is the big day?" she asked, trying to stall. She knew a couple of people she could pass this job to, but they both lived in the Portland area.

"Five weeks," Anne answered, confirming her assumption.

"How fun!" she exclaimed, unable to wrap her tongue around a more suitable phrase of congratulations.

But then Rhys made a little noise, like an unconscious groan of protest. Camile watched Anne jab him with an elbow. It didn't seem to faze him. He plucked a napkin from the table-top dispenser. Why did it not surprise her that he was learning to dance under duress? Maybe his bride-to-be was demanding and difficult. Wouldn't that be karma at its finest? Weddings could be extremely stressful. She conjured a satisfying vision of him and his equally as attractive yet horrifyingly bridezilla-esque partner arguing on the dance floor. She immediately chided herself for being spiteful. Just because he'd ditched her on a date and didn't even have the decency to remember her didn't mean he deserved lifelong unhappiness. And certainly, his future wife hadn't had a hand in his bad behavior. Camile knew she should feel grateful for having dodged the bullet that was Rhys McGrath. Still, what kind of person did that? Not someone she wanted to associate with on any level, certainly not on the dance floor, not even as his teacher.

Surprising that he was friends with Harper. Although, Harper was one of the sweetest people she'd ever met and Camile imagined her overlooking monstrous faults in even the most unpleasant of people.

Nina appeared by Harper's side. With unmistakable eagerness, Anne suggested, "How about if we meet tomorrow to discuss it? Would that work? Rhys needs to start these lessons as soon as possible."

Head bowed, now furiously doodling on the napkin, Rhys appeared to have lost interest in the conversation.

"Um…"

"How perfect!" Nina cried, throwing an arm across her shoulders. Right before throwing her under the bus. Again. "You have the entire day off tomorrow."

"Or," Rhys said, finally looking up again, "we could skip the meet and greet and start the lessons tomorrow. You're obviously highly qualified, or Harper wouldn't have recommended you. Here." He held out the napkin.

Reflexively, Camile took it but didn't look at it. She was too busy watching him and realizing that he hadn't been as removed from the conversation as she'd presumed.

He added, "That's my offer for five weeks of lessons. I'm sure it will suffice."

Anne frowned at her brother before addressing Camile again, "I'll text you tomorrow. We can discuss it then."

"'I'M SURE IT will suffice,'" Camile muttered in the parking lot as she unlocked her car. "Unbelievable, this guy." She got in, stuffing the unread napkin offer along with her phone inside her bag. The only thing that had kept her from handing the napkin back to him and declining on the spot was her inability to come up with a believable reason that didn't involve airing her date humiliation to her friends and family.

On the drive to her apartment, she tried out various excuses: she was too busy, she needed to concentrate on her thesis, she didn't give private lessons. That last one was a lie, and Harper knew it. They all sounded lame, even to her.

Since it was Saturday night, she parked her

car on the curb in front of the building that housed her downtown apartment. Most of the time, she left street parking open for dance studio clients and Blue Carafe patrons. Blue Carafe was the coffee shop across the street where she worked another of her several part-time jobs. When Camile had secured the dance instructor job with Pacific Dance, she'd been thrilled to learn that the small apartment above the studio was available for rent. The studio comprised the entire bottom floor of the building, one of the oldest in town. The two-story brick structure was massive by Pacific Cove standards and teeming with history and character.

The building's owner, Gia Montoya, had a difficult time finding tenants due to the noise from the studio below. Camile didn't mind, especially for the bargain price of the rent. For the most part, she enjoyed the chaos that drifted up from below: music, the commands of the instructors, kids' laughter, the patter of feet, and all the accompanying sounds of dancers hard at work. The dance environment was one place where she felt confident and in control. Tap class could be a little much, but when she needed quiet, it was nothing that her set of expensive noise-canceling headphones couldn't handle. Camile adored those headphones, a thoughtful and generous gift from her college friend Laura. Laura had given them to her the day after Camile had learned that she'd bombed her thesis defense. An added bonus for her was Gia's agreement to let her rent the space month by month since Camile wasn't sure what her future held at this point. Right now, she didn't want to think about it.

Access to her apartment was through the building's front and very grand main entrance. Double-leaded glass doors opened into a mosaic-tiled foyer where a crystal chandelier hung high above. Camile loved the vintage feel of the building and the fact that so many of the structure's original fixtures remained: hardwood floors in the studio classrooms, intricately carved wainscoting, elaborate chandeliers and metal-scrolled sconces. Tonight, she extra loved the heavy cast-iron tub in her apartment's bathroom, where she planned on taking a long soak before bed. A narrow flight of stairs led to a landing where there were three heavy, six-paneled oak doors complete with antique glass doorknobs.

Her apartment was on the left, the studio's office space on the right, and a large storage room straight ahead. Once inside her one-bedroom studio, she blew out a sigh of relief. Now that she was home, the floodgates of exhaustion broke through with full force. Yawning, she reached inside her bag and retrieved her phone.

And the napkin.

Before she could think about it, her gaze was drawn admiringly to Rhys McGrath's exceptionally neat handwriting. Her brain, however, could not compute the numbers he'd written upon it, or the final figure he'd circled. She was even more tired than she thought. That couldn't be right, could it? A rush of adrenaline revived her, scattering her pulse, and she tried to think past the loud whooshing sound in her ears. He was offering to pay her five hundred dollars per lesson and asking her to commit to four lessons a week for five weeks? Ten thousand dollars? That was outrageous. She charged fifty dollars per lesson in Portland. No wonder he'd assumed the amount "would suffice."

Anger coursed through her, irrational as it was. Because the fact that he'd offered such an excessive amount meant her mind was already sorting through the possibilities and the problems that kind of money could solve for her. She could quit her job at the car wash and cut back on her total work hours, possibly eliminate product promoting altogether, especially if she picked up some weekend shifts at the bowling alley. Living in Pacific Cove for the summer meant driving to the city for most of those jobs anyway, a journey that did not pay travel expenses, not to mention her poor car was on its last legs. She wouldn't have to wear another smelly suit all summer long, taco or otherwise. She would keep her hours at Blue Carafe, both because she enjoyed working there and because of its convenient location. She'd stay on at Tabbie's, too, because she liked waitressing and the tips were generous. And of course, she'd keep teaching her other dance lessons. With this kind of money, she could devote real time to her thesis, figure out what went wrong, fix it and then decide what she was going to do next. Camile still couldn't fathom exactly how she'd messed up her sources so badly. Working forty-plus hours a week while writing it was her only excuse. Maybe she could even catch up on her sleep. Yearning coursed through her so fiercely it brought tears to her eyes. Making her curse Rhys McGrath all over again.

Who was this guy? How could he do this to her? Tempt her like this? It was inexcusable. Her indignation rapidly gave way to disappointment, followed by bone-deep sadness for the mess her life had become. Saying no to his offer would be one of the hardest things she'd ever done.

"RHYS, I DON'T think Camile Wynn is the type of woman you can strong-arm into giving you dance lessons. Could you really not see her hesitation?" Anne wheeled the heavy sander in Rhys's wood shop against the wall as he'd instructed. "And why do we have to do this right now? She hasn't said yes, and I haven't had coffee."

He'd seen it. But he'd wanted her to agree.

"I assumed her hesitation was due to the fact that she needs the work but was afraid it wouldn't pay enough to be worth her time." He hoped so, anyway. What else could it be? There hadn't been time for her to get to know him well enough to dislike him, had there? People often disliked him in short order but usually there was more interaction involved. "So I made it worth her time." He'd then gotten up extra early to transform his wood shop into a makeshift dance studio. He'd also baked muffins. "And we have to do this now in case she agrees to start the lessons today."

Anne crossed the workshop, unlocked the casters on a radial arm saw and moved it toward the wall. "Why in the world would you assume that?"

Rhys unplugged his table saw and lowered the blade. "Money talks, Anne, you know that."

"Yes, but it does not say *everything*. Good

grief, Rhys, I continue to marvel at how you can be so incredibly smart and so unfairly good at so many things, and yet be so utterly abysmal at interpersonal communication."

"Thank you."

"It wasn't a compliment."

"Are you sure? It gave me warm fuzzies right here." He patted his chest around the vicinity of his heart.

"Rhys, you need to take this seriously."

"I am trying, Anne." At her dubious frown, he added more sincerely, "I am. Evidence the creation of a dance floor in my wood shop."

"What if she says no?"

"Then we'll find someone else, and you can continue lecturing me about my people skills." But Rhys didn't want Camile to say no. He couldn't explain how his imminent humiliation now paled in importance when compared to the notion of her declining. Of not seeing her again. "What time will she be here?"

"Fine, but I don't think she likes you. Don't be surprised when she turns you down. An hour or so."

"She doesn't have to *like* me, Anne. We're going to dance, not date."

"WAIT A MINUTE!" Nina's shout ricocheted through Camile's earpiece as she drove toward

Rhys McGrath's house. The day was shaping up to be a stunner with both the morning sky and the ocean displaying their most highly prized shades of blue. Wispy white clouds floated high above like shreds of gauzy lace. The calm water of the horizon shimmered like a blanket of connected sapphires. It was only 8:00 a.m., but the narrow, two-lane highway that followed Oregon's coastline was already bustling with summer traffic.

It was the first morning she'd had off in ages. Granted, it wasn't the result of the most positive circumstances, but still, she should be sleeping, or at least lounging around with a book and a cup of coffee. She'd intended to give McGrath her decision over the phone, but Anne had been the one to call her first. And when she'd asked if Camile would like to come out for coffee and muffins, she'd found herself acquiescing both because Anne seemed so nice and because she couldn't immediately think of an excuse not to. Nina had essentially announced to the entire restaurant that she was free for the day. So here she was, Bluetooth in place, driving to Rhys's house and relaying to Nina the contents of the napkin note.

Her sister continued in a slightly more subdued tone, "You are telling me this guy offered you ten thousand dollars to teach him how to waltz? And you're going to say no? Why?"

"I don't like him."

"You don't even know him."

Camile was irritated at her sister for ratting her out to Aubrey, but Nina was the person she most often confided in. Harper was rapidly reaching bestie status, but she couldn't talk to her about Rhys, not when they were friends, too. At least, not about this. And she had to talk about *this* to someone.

"I know him better than you think."

"Cagey," Nina accused flatly. "You know I hate that. What does that even mean?"

"Do you remember a couple of years ago when I had that horrific blind date in Portland?"

"You mean the guy who stood up suddenly, without even taking a sip of his top-shelf gin and tonic or a bite of the forty-dollar crab cakes he ordered, left the table, and never came back?"

"That would be the one."

"No *waaayy*!"

"Yep. It's him. Rhys McGrath. And apparently, he doesn't even remember it or me. And I had to pay for those crab cakes and drink that I couldn't afford."

"Camile. Wow. That's why you were quiet last night at dinner."

"Was I quiet? I tried so hard to act normal, but I think I was in shock. I kept waiting for him to say something, to give me some hint that he remembered. But then, when he passed me the golden napkin, I realized that not only was he not going to *mention* it, he doesn't even *remember* it. Or me."

"Golden napkin!" Nina belted out on a laugh. "That's funny. You know what you should do? You should take the job and teach him all wrong. Make him look like a fool. Convince him that this unique style of square dancing is trending at weddings these days." She started singing a playground version of a hoedown, "Swing your partner round and round, kick her in the shin and knock her down."

Camile laughed. "I love you—you know that, right? I just wanted someone to confirm for me that turning down this kind of crazy money is okay."

"Of course it's okay! Although…" Nina drew out the word and left it hanging in silence for a few dramatic seconds. "It would also be okay to take it. That's a lot of money, Camile, for doing something you truly enjoy. You could do like Aubrey suggested and cut back on your schedule. Then you'd have time to fix your thesis." Camile cringed as Nina echoed her thoughts from the evening before. "Then again, if you would accept the job I offered you, you'd also have time for your thesis."

Which was exactly why Camile didn't take the job her sister offered. She knew it was Nina's way of helping her out. But she couldn't—she wouldn't—accept it. Since "the disagreement" with her father five years ago, she hadn't accepted help from anyone. At the end of her junior year of college, she'd decided to change her major from premed to psychology. She'd known her father would be disappointed, but she hadn't anticipated the depth of his disapproval, or his threat to cut off all financial support. She'd called his bluff and vowed to get her degree—the degree she wanted—without any help from her family. That included her sisters. At least they'd been supportive of her choice. Stomach twisting with anxiety, she reminded herself not to think about the fact that her inability to succeed in this ambitious undertaking was the reason she was still dancing around in taco suits and working endless hours at multiple part-time jobs to pay her bills. Not to mention the blow to her self-esteem. Which had also taken a hit from the man she was on her way to see.

"That reminds me, I forgot to ask you last night, did Howard come and see you?"

"Oh, Howard! He did. Seems like a great kid. Thank you. He starts today."

"Awesome. Okay, I'm getting close to McGrath's house, and I need to pay attention to the directions Anne gave me. I guess there's a private drive with a gate, and I need to buzz in or something."

"Camile, you don't know who this guy is, do you? Beyond your own date experience, I mean?"

"What do you mean?"

"I guess it makes sense that you wouldn't know since you've been away at college and didn't come home last summer. Let's just say that Rhys McGrath is probably the most mysterious and enigmatic resident that Pacific Cove has ever seen."

Camile pulled onto the private lane and stopped her car. "Nina, what are you talking about?"

"He'd be the most eligible bachelor in town except he's not exactly well liked. *Rude* is one of the nicer terms I've heard. I've never seen that side of him myself, but he's definitely not a social guy. And you're about to go where very few people have gone. He won't let anyone on his property. As far as I know, Harper is the only person to photograph it in the last fifty years or so. In fact, Harper and Kyle are the only people I know who've ever seen the inside of his house." Nina quickly filled her in on what she knew about Rhys McGrath and the acres of oceanfront property he painstakingly guarded. As well as a few of the rumors she'd heard, most of them completely outrageous.

"Wow."

"Yeah, to say he's private is the understatement of the century. We're all still reeling from the fact that he came to dinner. The man does not socialize."

"Huh."

"I know. You need to call me later and tell me everything."

"I will."

"But first, you're going to tell him off and explain why you're not taking the job, right?"

Camile had lain awake the night before pondering this very question, fantasizing about how good it would feel to give the guy a piece of her mind. But then she'd realized something. "I don't think so. He didn't tell me why he rejected me. Why should I give him the same courtesy?"

MINUTES LATER, Camile was gawking at the gorgeous house before her. *Well, clearly, he can afford the money he offered me.* She chided herself for the thought; this wasn't about money. Opening the car door, she climbed out and took in the scene, the simple beauty of the home's design, the spacious grounds, the panoramic view of the ocean. Closer to the edge of the bluff, the old lighthouse stood tall and regal, its white-painted finish reflecting the soft orange shades of the morning sun. A quaint shingle-roofed cottage was next to that. Trees skirted the perimeter. Farther in, flowers and bushes were in colorful bloom. Except for the neatly mowed lawn, the vegetation appeared to be mostly native and left to its own devices—an appealing dichotomy of both welcoming and wild.

A cheerful Anne opened the door before Camile could lift a hand to knock, not surprising since she'd had to check in at the gigantic wrought-iron gate to access the driveway that led here.

"Camile! Good morning. Thank you so much for coming out."

"Good morning. My pleasure. It's a lovely day for a drive."

"A drive?" Anne repeated as her face fell, her cheerfulness sliding away along with it. "I knew it. You're turning down Rhys's offer, aren't you?"

What? How could she possibly know that? "Yes."

Raising one hand, Anne pressed it flat to her forehead for a second and muttered soft words that Camile couldn't quite decipher. After a quick glance behind her, she seemed to pull herself together and, with a narrow-eyed look of consideration, lowered her voice and asked, "Can I ask why?"

Camile hesitated. She hadn't prepared for this. She'd been all set to gracefully yet firmly reject Rhys's offer without an explanation, to leave him wondering. Perplexed and maybe even a little irritated would be a bonus. But how did she tell his sister that it was because he was a date-dodging jerk?

"Is it because you don't like my brother?" she asked, and Camile wondered if her feelings were that transparent.

"I don't really know him," she hedged.

Anne sighed. "I know, but I mean your first impression wasn't great, was it?"

Nope, and neither was the second, Camile wanted to say. A bubble of irony-laced laughter swelled inside her as she tried to think of how to best respond .

Thankfully, Anne went on, "I told him it was a mistake to offer you that kind of money." The surprise must have been evident on her face because she quickly qualified the statement. "Not that *you're* not worth it. I just meant that it was so high-handed and alphalike, assuming it was an offer you wouldn't refuse."

Camile couldn't help but chuckle at that. "Basically."

"Ha." Anne delivered a satisfied chortle. "Secretly, I was glad you didn't look at that stupid napkin right then because if it were me, I would have taken one look and handed it right back to him. On a napkin? With the—" deepening her voice, she managed a solid impersonation of her brother "'—I'm sure it will suffice.' I mean, come on! So off-putting, right?" Before Camile could confirm, Anne began walking backward, waving Camile forward. "Rhys is skyping with Willow. He'll be out in a few minutes. Come in and have coffee with me?"

As tempting as it was to bolt and have Anne give Rhys the news, Camile found herself acquiescing. Like walking into the pages of a storybook, she seemed compelled to move forward while the moment spun out of her control. Part of her knew she should turn back, and yet she continued on, rationalizing her actions as she went: she liked this woman; Anne was Harper's friend, and she was Harper's friend; Harper had brought the McGraths to dinner, so chances were high that Camile would be running into them again. The last thing she wanted was for Anne, or Harper, to think she was rude.

Or, she realized in a flash of honesty, for Rhys McGrath to think she was a coward.

CHAPTER FOUR

STANDING IN THE KITCHEN, Camile studied the impressive timber-frame construction of the home. Huge recycled wooden beams, posts and rafters were highlighted with light-colored arches and purlins throughout. The open floor plan made it possible to see the vast living room, dining area, kitchen and entryway all at once.

The color scheme was a harmonious mix of muted grays, greens and blues. The decor was an appealing and interesting montage of antique furniture, vintage woodworking tools, pottery, funky metal sculptures and assorted knickknacks. Photographs hung in artistic groupings on the walls. Everything came together in a cool, artsy way that made her want to walk around and examine it all. But the effect paled in comparison to the spectacular views beckoning from the tall windows that fronted the home on the ocean side.

Anne poured coffee into two blue and purple glazed ceramic mugs and pointed to an assortment of add-ins in tiny matching pots and pitchers: heavy cream, almond milk, sugar, artificial sweetener. Camile added cream and sugar.

"Muffin?" Anne gestured at the platter sitting on the counter nearby. "Fresh-baked. They're triple berry—blueberry, blackberry, raspberry. The berries are from your sister's farm."

As usual, she'd skipped breakfast, and the smell was reminding her stomach. "Absolutely. They look delicious."

Anne handed her a small plate and took one for herself. They both dished up muffins and then settled at a rectangular-shaped dining table constructed from three thick wooden planks. They were a dark golden-blond color, and the curling, intricate grain patterns of the wood stood out beneath a light, clear finish. The edges of the slabs had been left close to their natural state, the bark peeled away to reveal the texture beneath.

"This table is incredible."

"Rhys made it."

"He *made* it?" Camile repeated, hating that she felt as impressed as she sounded.

"This gigantic old maple tree blew down on the property last winter, and he made this table out of it. Cuz that's what people do when a tree falls over, right? They craft something out of it." She added a little shake of her head but there was pride in her smile. "He built this house, too. He's much better with tools and machinery and…things than he is with people."

Camile didn't know what to say that didn't sound fawning and gushy. And she didn't want to fawn or gush or be impressed with Rhys McGrath's skills in any way. She recognized that Anne was trying to make excuses for his atrocious personality. That she could definitely comment on, but not without revealing information—namely about their date, also a subject she didn't want to raise. Instead, she filled her mouth with a chunk of muffin, which was hands down the most delicious thing she'd eaten in months. Possibly forever.

"Wow," she said after savoring another bite. "This is to die for. Seriously, this might be the best muffin I've ever eaten. Please don't repeat that in the vicinity of Bakery-by-the-Sea. I'm one of their best customers."

Anne laughed. "Rhys made them."

"Are you kidding me?"

"I know. He bakes, too." Again, there was a mix of bafflement and respect in her tone. And then a hint of sadness when she added, "My brother spends a lot of time alone. Too much. Or at least, I think so."

"So do you live here with him?" Camile

asked, avoiding another leading statement by asking a question of her own. Because admittedly, she was curious about the McGraths. Anne, mostly. Not Rhys. Okay, a little bit Rhys, but she only wanted to hear the bad stuff where he was concerned. She did not want to hear about the talented-woodworker-builder-world-class-baker guy.

"Part-time. I have my own place in Portland. My business is based there, but I'm hoping to be here full-time when Willow officially moves in. I'll have to travel more, but it will be worth it." Camile also did not want to hear about the fiancée, the woman who she could safely assume Rhys had not walked out on during their first date.

"What kind of business?"

"A PR firm."

"That sounds interesting."

"It is. Very. Under normal circumstances, I would use my skills to convince you to take my brother on as your dance student. But these are not normal circumstances."

Uh-oh. Camile should have known that Anne had taken her refusal too well. She was suddenly struck with the feeling that this had all been designed to convince her. Suspiciously, she wondered about the muffins. She and Harper had this weakness in common, and she remembered Harper mentioning it at the restaurant. Had Anne asked Harper which flavor Camile liked?

"Anne—"

Anne cringed a little and held out an interrupting hand. "I know what you're thinking. I am very good at my job. Reading people is my special gift, and I can see that you're not going to budge at my not-so-subtle attempts to change your mind about Rhys. So, instead of giving you a pitch, I'm going to try the truth. My brother has a huge heart. It's just buried under these layers of…"

Rudeness? Arrogance? Narcissism? Camile was tempted to tell her about the date. But she knew very well that Anne would relay it to Rhys. And Camile was growing secure in the knowledge that Rhys didn't remember her. Now that she'd accepted that, and because they were likely going to be acquaintances going forward, it seemed better not to have to relive that initial encounter.

Anne went on, "I wouldn't ask if this dancing thing wasn't very, *very* important. Despite the way Rhys presented it, his learning to dance is personal. Willow is so special. She deserves this. She deserves…" Tears pooled in her eyes, and Camile knew instinctively that they were genuine. Apparently, the two women were close, which would be a nice thing for sisters-in-law. Blinking rapidly, Anne inhaled a deep breath and continued, "I realize that none of this matters to you—you don't know us. But Willow has been through so much. Her dad passed away two years ago. And then, three months ago, her mom died in a car accident. She lost both of her parents within two years. I'm sure you can imagine how difficult that's been for her, for all of us. If you knew my brother better, you'd understand that the fact that Rhys is even willing to do this speaks to his love for her. I mean, we're talking about a guy who didn't even go to his own prom. I'm asking you to give Rhys another chance."

Camile felt a surprising and inexplicable softening of her heart. Not her resolve, though. Not enough to be his teacher. There were plenty of qualified dance instructors out there. Camile was about to recommend a couple when Anne went on, "I'd like to propose a trial basis. Commit to…say, two or three lessons, and see how it goes. I promise you that what Rhys lacks in natural talent he will make up for in hard work. If nothing else, he's an excellent student."

Two lessons would be a thousand dollars. Camile had to admit it was tempting. Could she handle being with Rhys McGrath for even two hours, though?

At the other end of the spacious living room, a door opened, and Rhys strode into the room. "Are you talking about me?"

"Rhys, we have much better things to discuss than your boring self," Anne teased, and winked at Camile.

Rhys approached the table. With a tentative smile trained on Camile, he looked into her eyes and she found herself reluctantly captivated by their blue depths and his earnest expression. He almost seemed nervous. He said, "I'm late, and I apologize…" For a split second, she thought he'd forgotten her name again, but that wasn't the case. And the way he said it, "Camile," in this low and silky tone like it was its own sentence sent her stomach responding with a nice, albeit annoying, flutter. "I'm sure Anne told you I was skyping with Willow. She's in South Carolina with her grandparents right now. I confess that when she calls, I pretty much drop everything. Yesterday, I basically hung up on a United States senator to take her call."

Camile stared up at him and hoped she did a passable job of stifling her surprise. So he had a sweet side, so what? As Anne stated, this had nothing to do with her. How did that saying go—*poor planning on the part of a jerk like you does not constitute an emergency on mine?* Close enough. But it also raised a question. "So she won't be joining you for the dance lessons?"

"Nope. She's getting lessons there."

Anne grinned up at Rhys. "I cannot wait to see her face when she finds out you've done this for her. She will be over the moon." Then she explained to Camile, "It's a surprise. The girl knows Rhys very well. She knows he hates dancing, and she'd never dream of asking him to learn for her."

Oh, perfect, Camile thought, *this just keeps getting better and better.* A surprise gift of dance for the sweet and selfless fiancée. Who happened to be grieving the loss of both parents. How completely thoughtful and romantic, and wasn't she about to be the evil queen of killjoys here?

Heaving out a sigh, Rhys slid one hand around his neck and held it there for a few seconds. "Let's just hope I can do it." Eyebrows at half-mast, he said to Camile, "You've got your work cut out for you, I'm afraid."

Rhys and Anne exchanged another meaningful glance. Camile saw what looked like uncertainty and vulnerability in his. Anne reached over and squeezed his hand. He smiled, but it wasn't truly a smile. The lips were curled upward in the right places, but the gesture conveyed only sadness. Like genuine, soul-deep sorrow. The moment passed quickly but, like Anne, Camile was good at reading people. And she felt it, the emotion, almost as strongly as if it was her own. Because Camile knew what it was like to suddenly realize you were out of your element. She knew what it was like to fail. And to then absolutely not know what to do about it. At that moment, she *felt* how much it meant to him to succeed at this, and she also knew she could help him. Dancing, teaching him, she *could* do.

His expression had shifted back to that inscrutable confidence when he asked her, "Are you ready to see my wood shop turned dance studio? The place where I'm ready to make a fool of myself for the girl I adore."

And apparently, that was what it took to strip away the last of her resolve, to convince her to agree to teach Rhys McGrath, the man who'd so cruelly rejected her, how to dance. With a resigned smile at Anne, she gave in. "Sure. Let's do this."

Two days. Two lessons. A thousand dollars in her pocket. Two hours in the company of Rhys McGrath and then she'd find him another teacher.

CAMILE HAD BARELY made it back to her apartment when she received a text from Harper. Assuming she'd already spoken to Anne or Rhys, Camile shook her head at the speed of the Pacific Cove grapevine. But concern flooded in as she read the message: Call me as soon as you can. Do not delay! Important!

Before she could even tap the screen to call her, another text came in: Everyone is fine, btw.

A text from Nina followed that: Call me ASAP!

No doubt her sister wanted to know how her meeting had gone, too. She called Harper first, who picked up immediately. "Camile! Thank goodness I caught you."

"Harper, what is it? You sound pretty frantic for everyone being okay. What's wrong?"

"Since you don't seem to know already, I assume you haven't been on social media this morning?"

"No. I've been out at Rhys McGrath's house."

"Oh, right. That's good. But Camile, you... You're all over the internet."

"What do you mean?" Panic rushed through her for absolutely no reason that she could think of. A quick mental sweep of her life didn't reveal anything untoward or even particularly embarrassing, thesis defense aside. She pretty much walked the straight and narrow. Had done so her entire life. Even in high school. Of course, with a Coast Guard officer as a dad, to attempt any other path would have been pointless. No drugs, no drinking to excess, no late-night shenanigans. Not only was her closet skeleton-free, it was clean and neatly organized.

"The speech that you gave Bobby yesterday when you quit the taco truck?" Harper paused to snicker. "You didn't mention that you told him his tacos tasted like sea vomit, by the way."

Uh-oh. "Someone recorded it?"

"Yep. You've gone viral."

Panic receding slightly, she said, "Oh boy."

Masculine laughter boomed through the line a second before Kyle's voice came through. "Camile, you were pure brilliance. Everyone is talking about it. They love it. My personal favorite is when you asked him if he had a tortilla in his pocket." He guffawed and then added, "That guy is a jerk. Chief Taco-Head…" His voice disintegrated into laughter.

Harper came back on. "Sorry, he insisted. You're his new hero."

Camile sighed. She did not want internet fame. "Well, it's nice to be someone's hero, I guess. He is a jerk. Bobby, obviously. Not Kyle."

"I knew who you meant. And Kyle is right.

You've got a ton of community support. That, I think, is sort of the problem."

Camile felt a prickle of concern skitter up the back of her spine. "What do you mean?"

"People are boycotting his taco truck. His business has dwindled to nothing. He's blaming you."

"He's the only one to blame. Among other things, he puts fillers in his carne asada."

"Camile, he doesn't see it that way. The jerk says he's going to sue you."

EVERYONE CAN DANCE. Camile firmly believed this. Tone-deaf, uncoordinated, unenthusiastic, uptight, it didn't matter—she prided herself on being able to teach even the most difficult of students how to dance. She'd once taught a woman who was clinically beat-deaf how to jitterbug and she'd gone on to win second place in a local talent contest. It was simply a matter of discovering the underlying issue inhibiting their ability and then fixing it or working around it. Judging from the pained look on his face, Rhys fell into at least two of these categories.

She couldn't help but feel a little sorry for him. Which was okay, she reassured herself. Even though she was a professional, it was normal for her to empathize with her students. Connecting with people was one of her strengths. She firmly believed it made her a better teacher. It didn't mean she had to like the guy.

The day before, when Rhys had said "wood shop," she'd expected a drafty metal building with a concrete floor, heavy machinery sitting about, and no windows. She should have known better than to assume anything where he was concerned. Rhys had led the way through the kitchen to a door that entered an enclosed hallway leading to another building, like a wing to the house that wasn't visible when you pulled up outside. Rhys explained that one end contained his office and lab and the other, his workshop. When they'd stepped inside, Camile had been surprised to find the same stunning ocean views and a space that could easily function as a small dance studio. All the tools, machinery, metal and wood had been moved to one end of the room. He'd asked what she thought. Offhandedly, she'd replied that the only thing missing were mirrors. Then, still reeling from the commitment she'd made, she'd announced the lessons would start the next day.

She'd needed some time both to come to terms with what she'd agreed to and to develop a strategy. At the time she hadn't known that she'd also need to find legal counsel. Even though Bobby hadn't made an official move yet, Harper felt certain he would. When Camile had told Nina, who'd texted because she too had seen the video, about Bobby's alleged intentions, Nina had insisted that Camile consult with her attorney. One long phone call with the esteemed and friendly Bailey Leeds and Bailey had assured Camile that she could consider herself represented, when and if the need should arise. Feeling both relieved and depressed, Camile had hung up and mentally added another bill to the pile that seemed to be growing despite her best efforts otherwise.

Turned out that even the threat of a lawsuit didn't leave much brain time left for dance strategizing. But she had managed to polish off a pint of ice cream while assuring herself that she was taking the high road by helping Rhys out. It felt good to remind herself that, by her standards anyway, said road was also paved in gold. The thousand dollars she'd been counting on would now go to pay her attorney. Stupid, smelly Bobby.

Now, here she was, the very next afternoon, standing side by side with Rhys McGrath before a wall of mirrors and gearing up to start their first lesson. Yep, that was right: tall mirrors now covered most of one wall. Camile didn't ask how he'd managed it. He'd probably made them, too, she thought wryly.

"So," she said to his reflection, "the waltz is just a simple box step."

"Simple?" Rhys repeated skeptically.

"Yes. With a rhythmic one-two-three count."

His answering frown was part uncertainty, part confusion.

"In my experience, people who think they can't dance don't understand how it can be broken down into numbers." This was true. She'd taught plenty of left-brain-dominant, type-A engineer types like she'd pegged Rhys to be. Sure, they might not ever add head-turning pizzazz to their dance repertoires that her more rhythmically inclined students managed, but a surprising number of them did. The upside was that she'd discovered that the competitive drive this personality type possessed could overcome just about any mental shortcoming. "I'm guessing you like numbers?"

"I do."

"Great! As I was saying, the box step forms the basis of the waltz. You essentially make a box shape on the floor with your feet." With one hand, she traced the shape of a square. "You'll start with your left foot. Like this." Camile held her arms up as if embracing an imaginary partner and took a step forward. "The right foot follows diagonally to the right, and then the left joins it there. Then the reverse, to close the box." Performing the steps, she narrated the motion, "Right goes back, then left diagonally, and close the box." She repeated the sequence a couple more times, counting out loud, "*One*, two, three. *One*, two, three. Six simple steps and you're waltzing." She offered him an encouraging smile. "See? Easy-peasy. Now your turn."

He nodded, managing to appear both gravely serious and completely unconvinced. Scratching his chin, he tilted his head down. "But what are you doing with your feet? They're sort of gliding above the floor. Like a hovercraft."

Camile couldn't help a chuckle. "It is sort of like that. But don't worry about technique right now. Just do the steps. I'll teach you the hovercraft glide later. Go ahead."

"I'm sorry. Can you demonstrate again?"

"Don't be sorry. That's what you're paying me for." Counting, she began repeating the count along with the steps.

"One, two, three," he joined in softly, almost as if he was doing it unconsciously while he studied her movements. "Okay, I think I got it."

"And go…" Camile said.

He did, completing a single box. Camile felt

herself thaw a bit at the furrow-browed look of pure concentration on his face. Normally, she'd talk to or tease a student to get them to relax. She resisted the urge here. She was determined not to establish any kind of rapport. Two lessons, one dance, she reminded herself. Get in, get out, done.

"Good! You got this. Again."

He repeated the movement.

"Now, this time, don't stop. Just keep box stepping, and I'll do it with you." They performed the movements together with Camile counting and snapping her fingers.

Still moving, she danced around in a half circle until she was facing him, mirroring his steps. "Excellent. And there you have it. Now you're going to try it with me."

He stopped in his tracks, brow lines back in full force.

Facing him, Camile patted her left shoulder and instructed, "Right hand here." He complied, and she ignored how nice the heat of his hand felt as it seeped through the thin fabric of her tank top. "Left arm up." He obeyed. Silently, she admitted there was something vaguely satisfying about barking orders at him. But this action, the press of his palm against hers, the feel of the work-roughened texture of his skin, her hand enfolded in his, was slightly more difficult to ignore. She told herself it was just the shock of it all, being here with him. Dancing.

"Ah," he said, tilting his chin toward the floor again. "Now I see why you're wearing heels."

"Is that your way of insulting my height?" she joked, breaking her own rule before she could stop herself.

He brought his gaze back up and locked it on to hers, and Camile was a little taken aback by the intensity she saw there. "No. Absolutely not. Why would that be insulting? I'm sorry if you took it that way."

"Um, it's—it's fine," she stammered. "I was joking. I know I'm short. It would be difficult to forget as the only short person in a family of very tall people. You know, recessive genes or whatever."

"That would not be the case," he said. "Height is polygenic. And there are other variables. It's more quantitative than that. So the term *recessive* doesn't apply when it comes to height."

Camile squinted up at him, trying to decide if he was serious. When he didn't blink, she said, "I know. At least three genes are involved and like six alleles, right?" Genetics had been one of her favorite premed courses. "Plus, there are nutritional and environmental factors. I wasn't being literal. I was exaggerating for effect. Making fun of the fact that I drew the *short* straw in my family." She added a wink.

Gaze narrowed in on her, he shook his head a couple of times very slowly as if thinking carefully about how to respond.

Embarrassed by her lame joke, she clarified, "That was a bad pun. Sorry."

When he spoke, his eyes traveled over her while his mouth hinted at a smile. "No, you're wrong. It was not a bad pun. It was a very good pun. But there's nothing inferior about your genetic fate. Quite the contrary. Height is also a very subjective preference as far as attractiveness goes. Studies have shown that shorter women with discernible curves are the most symmetrically pleasing. I happen to agree with the consensus."

Camile stared into his earnest blue eyes and felt her lips part. What the…? Her neck went hot as she tried to wrap her brain around this moment. Obviously, the man was brilliant in a way that resulted in a unique perspective. But the part that had her speechless was the fact that he'd just given her a really lovely compliment. Like, spellbindingly good. And he seemed sincere. Granted, the delivery wasn't the smoothest, but the meaning was there. It also caught her off guard and made her feel warm in even more surprising ways. Ways she shouldn't feel. Not with Rhys McGrath, date absconder, social snob and possibly worse, if any of the rumors were true. Not to mention that the guy was learning how to dance for another woman, his troubled and special and cherished fiancée.

All of this added up to the conclusion that she didn't know what to do with it. So she ignored it and concentrated on what she was here to do.

She said, "Women of all heights generally wear heels when ballroom dancing." Granting him a small smile, she gave his shoulder a reassuring, platonic-style pat that may have come across nearly as awkward as his compliment. "Now just pretend I'm not here and do the same thing you were doing before."

CHAPTER FIVE

RHYS WOULD HAVE laughed, except this situation was anything but funny. He could no more pretend that he wasn't holding her in his arms than he could walk out the door, jump off the bluff and soar over the Pacific Ocean. And how could she think he'd insult her height? She was petite, yes, but so what? People came in all shapes and sizes. She wore a tank top and leggings with a short flowy skirt that complemented the shapely, sinewy muscles of her legs honed from years of dance.

He was completely distracted by everything about her. Maybe he shouldn't have complimented her like that. But he'd meant it, so he'd said it, because that was what he did. Usually to his detriment. But she'd seemed to like it. Initially, anyway. The shoulder pat sort of distorted the message. She probably thought he was weird. Anne was right that he wasn't great at reading people. Especially women. He should have listened to his instincts and not agreed to let a woman he was attracted to teach him how to dance. Although, ironically, the fact that she didn't seem to return the sentiment made things worse instead of better. And reminded him that this was not a good idea on so many levels. Mainly the level where he ended up looking and feeling foolish. He needed to push his feelings aside and stay focused on the task at hand. He needed to remember that a little foolish would be more than worth it in exchange for Willow's happiness. He would learn to waltz for Willow even if Heather wasn't waging this custody battle.

Camile shifted in his arms, treating him to an enticing draft of her flowery scent. Lilac, he'd already noted. But not the strong odor you get when you put your face right up to a flower. More like the subtle trail that floats in on a breeze through an open window. He wanted to tuck his face into the curve of her neck, nuzzle the slim column of her throat and analyze it some more. *Yeah, good idea, Rhys, sniff her like a creeper. That'll score points for sure.*

"Rhys?"

He blinked a few times, trying to recover as he realized he was staring at her collarbone, at the place where it joined her neck. He liked that spot. "What?"

"Are you ready?"

"Um, sure."

"I could play some music if you like. Or would you rather I just count?"

Shaking his head, he answered absently, "I don't like music."

She laughed in obvious disbelief. He didn't correct her. He didn't want to answer the questions she'd undoubtedly have about that. He didn't need to hand over more evidence of his eccentricity.

She said, "Then I'll just count for now."

"Okay." He stayed still, trying to decide how to proceed.

A few more seconds went by until she said, "You lead, remember?"

He remembered. That was not the problem. "Yes, but how do I let you know that I'm about to dance with you? Shouldn't I warn you somehow? Count down or something?"

"Normally, the music will sort of guide you. But for now, just start, and I'll follow." She added an encouraging nod.

"What if I step on you?"

"These are special steel-toed heels. I won't feel a thing."

He dropped his chin to study her feet. "Are they really?"

"No. I was joking."

His head came back up to find her grinning. He smiled, too, because he couldn't help it. Even though he felt a little silly falling for her bit.

"I'll be fine. Trust me, I've been stepped on plenty. But I'm also very good at dodging giant man feet."

Quirking a brow, he asked, "Is that your way of insulting the size of my feet?"

A chuckle rippled through her body. "Good one," she said after a moment, her lips still curled with amusement. "I totally deserved that."

Rhys decided dancing lessons might not be so bad if he could just hold her like this, smelling her and making her laugh, and not actually having to dance.

"Are you ready?" she asked again after she gathered herself.

He sighed. "I suppose if I have to be."

"I'll prompt you with a *ready, and, one*, okay?"

Shaking his head, he said, "Not okay."

"Why not?"

He confessed, "I have no idea what that means."

"Seriously?"

"Why would I joke about that when I'm paying you five hundred dollars an hour?"

"The same reason you were just joking about the size of your feet. It's not easy to tell with you. But it means you step forward with your left foot when I say *one*."

"But then one is actually three, isn't it? And it seems illogical to start on three."

A crease formed between her eyebrows, and Rhys realized he might be doing the thing that Anne specifically told him not to do. The arguing. Except that he wasn't, really, or at least he didn't mean to. But maybe Anne was right that his precision annoyed people. He found that he didn't want to annoy Camile. Interesting. Because normally his desire to clear up these types of logistical misunderstandings overrode most everything else. Including feelings.

Not the case here.

He was forming an apology when she tipped her head to the side, and said, "Maybe. I think I see what you mean."

"You do?" he answered skeptically.

"Yeah." Nodding, she said. "Let's go after two full three-counts. On the third one, you start dancing. On the *one*. Will that work?"

Carried along on a sigh of relief, he answered, "Yes."

RHYS WAS STRUGGLING. Trapped in a conversation that seemingly had no end. With a well-dressed woman who kept trying to touch him. Did she think squeezing his elbow was going to help her cause? He wished that she'd just get on with it. He knew what she wanted. What *he* wanted was for her to ask the question so that he could say no and then they could be done talking in this endless, pointless circle.

Jabbing a long, painted fingernail in his direction, she said, "You might be surprised to learn that there aren't as many wedding venues along the coast as you'd think."

"You might be surprised to hear that I've never thought about coastal wedding venues at all. Therefore, it's a number I've never attempted to calculate."

She laughed like he'd told the funniest joke she'd ever heard. Then, faster than a photon beam, she was all business again. "My daughter Bethany and I have checked out twenty-three different venues." Leaning close, she repeated each number, enunciating dramatically, "Twenty. Three. Not one of them has left her inspired, poor thing."

Isn't it the marriage that should leave you inspired? Trying desperately to heed Anne's advice, Rhys managed to swallow the question, but only barely.

The woman had introduced herself back at the beginning of the conversation not long after he and Anne had arrived at the party where the sprawling oceanfront home provided a spectacular setting in its own right. But that was approximately a hundred years ago now, and for the life of him, he couldn't remember her name. Sheila, maybe? Or Shelly? Possibly Shayla. Or not. He was pretty sure it started with a "sh" sound, although that did him no good when trying to find a way to interrupt her. Or maybe it would. A loud "shh" might get her to stop talking long enough for him to slip away. He grinned a little at the thought, and too late he realized he'd encouraged her.

"That's why it's so great that I met you here today. Bethany wants to get married at *your* lighthouse. Can you believe that? Isn't that amazing?" As if she were granting Rhys some sort of special gift.

"Does she?"

Shh-Lady sidled closer, way too close, and confided, "She says it's her dream wedding venue. She says it's perfect, the most incredible piece of property she's ever seen. Isn't that sweet?"

Rhys took a small step backward. "Uh…" Sweet? Was that somehow a compliment? Like he deserved the credit for her daughter's unfounded opinion, the formation of which was literally impossible. He couldn't let that comment pass. "But your daughter has never seen my property," he countered.

"Oh, but she's taken a good, long look-see on Google Earth. And Bethany has decided that it's the place she and Richard Junior should begin their wedded life together. Isn't that romantic?"

Rhys knew very well that romance had nothing to do with Bethany's desire to get married on his property. He'd learned that keeping his two-hundred-plus acres of headland and accompanying coastline closed to the public ignited both speculation and covetousness. People craved what they could not have. In this case, exclusivity. They wanted to be the ones to get married, have a party, a reunion, a celebration of whatever important life event on the property belonging to the recluse who denied access equally.

There were myriad locations up and down the coast where people could engage in any of these activities, and with views that were just as nice as his and with plenty of parking and amenities suitable to such an occasion. Coastal venues abounded for this express purpose. His property was not one of those. But this did not stop people from trying. Up until this point, his secluded lifestyle meant he rarely had to contend with their pitches face-to-face. Mostly they contacted him via his website's email. He'd been shocked at how demanding, rude even, people could be. Rhys found it odd that just because a place had once served a purpose to the public, it somehow meant that it could never be private.

In the time he'd lived there he'd allowed exactly one person to tour and photograph his property, and that was Harper. Two if you counted Kyle. But Kyle didn't care about the property or photographing anything; he'd just wanted to impress Harper. *That* was romantic. Kyle had contacted Rhys and explained the situation. It was Kyle's honesty that had swayed Rhys. They'd both been navy SEALs, and that had provided a foundation for their friendship.

Rhys had managed to remain silent on the romantic angle, and for a moment he thought she'd given up. No such luck.

Regrouping, she tried a different tack. "The history of your property is so fascinating. I read that your great-great-grandfather was the lighthouse keeper there. And he fell in love with a pirate's daughter, right? She fell off a ship, and he rescued her when she washed up on the rocks."

"No. On all counts." Rhys had inherited the property from his grandfather, but the land had been in his family for generations. The government had long ago leased a portion of the headland for purposes of the lighthouse, which was designed and built by the Army Corps of Engineers. When the lighthouse was decommissioned, the lease was jointly terminated, with ownership staying with his family. When Rhys built his home there, he became the first of his family to ever live on the property. This was all a matter of public record. Where did people come up with these ridiculous tales?

The woman reached for him again. Rhys took another step backward. Any farther and he was going to fall over the deck's railing and into the water below. Now that he thought about it, that might not be so bad. It couldn't be more than fifteen feet. Nothing that he hadn't done many times as a SEAL, and in this situation, there would be no one shooting at him.

All business now, she zeroed back in on Rhys. "My husband and I will give you ten thousand dollars if you allow our daughter to get married on your property. We'd like to have the reception on the grounds, too, including access to the lighthouse."

"No," Rhys said politely.

"Twelve thousand."

"The property is not for rent." Rhys glanced over his shoulder and down where blessed silence now beckoned from the water below.

"Fifteen thousand. That's almost half of the wedding budget."

"Thirty thousand dollars," Rhys muttered, "on a wedding? You do realize there's no return, right? It's not an investment. Have you thought about hiring a financial advisor?" Again, she wailed with laughter at his nonjoke. Did weddings cost that much? Willow's wedding would be his responsibility, wouldn't it? He should probably start budgeting for that now.

Rhys tuned back in to realize he'd missed another share of the one-sided negotiation. "…seventeen thousand dollars is nothing to sneeze at."

"No, it certainly is not."

"But it's our little girl. There's nothing we wouldn't do for our kids, right?"

That was certainly true. He was learning to dance for Willow. Which made him think about Camile. Thinking about Camile was so much better than listening to this woman. Even dancing with her was better than this. Harper had been right—Camile was the best person for the job. He was hopelessly without rhythm and yet she'd given him hope. And something to look forward to. Even if his feelings were not reciprocated.

"Yes," he said, and only realized he'd said it out loud when, right before his eyes, the woman's determined grimace transformed into a smile of unfettered delight.

"Wait!" she cried. "So that's a yes? Thomas!" she shouted. "He said yes to seventeen."

"No, I did not. I did not say yes to seventeen." Grimacing, he pointed a finger in her general direction. "Charlotte? Sherry? Shana?"

"What? Who?" Face scrunched with confusion, she spun a half circle before whirling back around to tackle Rhys again. "Did Charlotte Galloway get to you first about her daughter Lyndsay's wedding?" Her tone was venomous now. "She's only a waitress, you know? She can't afford what I'm offering. Lyndsay is wearing a secondhand dress she bought from a consignment shop. I told her I was going to—"

"Is it Shiloh?"

"Is what who? Who are you talking to?"

"You," Rhys said tiredly, and then smoothed a hand across his brow. "I'm talking to you. I'm sorry, I'm afraid I can't remember your name."

Tight-lipped now, she said, "It's Keisha. Keisha Williams. My husband and I own Pacific Cove Real Estate?" She gestured behind them. Rhys turned and looked. The smiling faces of Keisha and a man he presumed to be Thomas decorated the gigantic banner hanging on the side of the building. He suddenly recalled Anne mentioning the party was being hosted by a local "power couple," a husband-and-wife realty team.

"Yes!" Rhys added a finger snap. "Keisha, that's right. I apologize. I'm terrible with names, and I've met a lot of people today. Look, Keisha, I appreciate the generous offer." He didn't, but he thought Anne would be proud of his diplomacy. It took effort. "But my property is not for rent at any price. It's not about the money."

"I see," a deflated Keisha said, and then made a puffing sound through her nose. Indicating that she clearly did not "see."

"I'm glad," Rhys said, because he was glad the conversation was over. He scanned the crowd. He needed to find Anne and get out of here. This was exhausting.

"What's it about, then?" Keisha demanded, all the syrup now conspicuously absent from her tone.

"I'm sorry?"

"A woman who works in our office said that you're a bigamist and you keep a bunch of wives there that you don't want people to know about." She ground out a bitter laugh as if to prove it was a harmless joke designed to show there were no hard feelings. "Is that it?"

That *was* it. Not the reason, of course, but it was the end of his proverbial rope. He had to defend himself. Surely Anne would understand?

"Keisha, it's none of your business why I choose to keep my private property private. Or my private life private, for that matter. But even if I did allow people there, for any reason, you would never in a million years be one of them."

"I'VE HEARD HE'S a drug dealer," Katie, the shorter, blonder woman said to her friend Emma.

"How can he be selling drugs? Who's he selling them to?" Emma countered. Emma had a workout-perfect figure and a cute, upturned nose. "No one ever sees him. Except, apparently, yesterday."

Camile couldn't help hearing the conversation between the two women. A morning shift at Blue Carafe meant she'd been preparing drink orders since 5:00 a.m. Katie and Emma, she'd learned, were here meeting for coffee after their sunrise power walk on the beach.

Katie shook her head and tucked a loose tendril from her messy bun behind one ear. "Benny Mathis says boats come in from the ocean and anchor close to the cliff in front of his house. Then different boats come, and he loads them with the drugs. Probably stores the stuff in the lighthouse. Keisha said he got *real* prickly when she mentioned using the lighthouse for Bethany's reception. Makes sense if you think about it."

"It's brilliant, for sure. But someone that hot should not be dealing drugs. He should be in the movies. Or modeling underwear." Emma giggled. "I tried flirting with him once at the grocery store, and he barely even looked at me. He's strange, for sure."

Rhys. They were talking about Rhys. Camile would have laughed except she knew all too well how fast small-town gossip could spread. She was currently experiencing the double effect that was social media. Rumors of drug dealing were not funny. Nina had told her that Rhys had been the subject of speculation since he'd moved to the area, but this was outrageous.

"He's rude!" Katie said. "I was waiting for a take-out order one time at Salmon Crackers, and he came in. I introduced myself. I said, 'Hi, I'm Katie. I'm a Realtor here in town, and I heard you built a new home out by the old lighthouse?' He let out this painful sigh and said, 'Yes.'" Katie paused for effect. "That's it, just a 'yes,' and then he walked across the room, turned his back to me and stared out the window. It was totally obvious he did it so I wouldn't talk to him anymore. Rude," she repeated the word firmly.

"That is kind of rude," Emma agreed. "But maybe he was having a bad day. I mean, drug dealing sounds a little far-fetched…" She trailed off as she squinted at Camile. "Hey, you're Camile, the taco dancer, aren't you?"

"Former taco dancer," Camile confirmed with a cheerful salute. "But yes." Setting the first steaming beverage on the counter, she recited the order, "Twenty-ounce no-fat stormcloud latte with macadamia milk."

"That's me." Emma grinned. "That was awesome the way you told that Bobby guy off. My entire office watched the video like twelve times."

"Omigosh!" Katie added, "I'm so excited to meet you. Janice Strudle is Howard Klintz's aunt. She wants to invite you to speak to her women's group. Everyone is talking about it. He totally deserved it. Way to go, girlfriend!" Katie thrust an arm across the counter, offering a fist bump.

"Thank you," Camile said, tapping her knuckles in kind, now used to the attention she'd garnered. If only these people knew the trouble she'd caused herself by fighting back. Still no official word about the lawsuit, but Bailey had said she'd heard buzz that made her believe it was coming. Attorney talk, she'd called it. In keeping with what life had dished up lately, Camile expected the worst.

Emma shifted back to the drug dealer conversation. "Although that would explain why he doesn't want anyone trespassing, wouldn't it? The giant fence and the gate. I heard he has Doberman pinschers—classic drug-dealer dogs."

"Totally. Plus, it seems more realistic than the bigamist thing."

Camile finished the second drink and set it down. "Twenty-ounce iced Americano with room for cream. And I'm sorry, I don't normally do this, but what bigamist thing?"

"Oh, you know that guy who lives out by the old lighthouse, Rhys McGrath?"

"Yes," Camile said.

"Someone who works in Katie's real estate office was saying he's got like a bigamist compound out there. But we're pretty sure he's a drug dealer."

"What makes you think he's either of those things?"

"He's *soooo* secretive. He never goes out in public. Well, hardly ever. Until last night, apparently. And no one knows him," Katie said dramatically. "I mean, no one."

"I do."

Their matching wide-eyed stares were almost comical.

"You know him?" Katie asked doubtfully.

"How well do you know him?" Emma asked in a way that suggested Camile might know him in the way that Emma's previous attempt at flirting suggested she'd like to.

"Well enough to know that he's not a bigamist or a drug dealer. And he doesn't have a dog." The door opened, and a group of caffeine-seeking tourists ambled inside. A relieved Camile said goodbye and moved on to take orders, grateful not to have to answer any more questions about the man she didn't like whom she'd suddenly found herself defending.

CHAPTER SIX

"ANNE, WE'VE BEEN over this. I had no choice."

"Rhys, you absolutely did have a choice."

"Not the way I see it."

"All I'm saying is that you cannot talk to people that way."

Camile heard the exchange after walking into Rhys's house. When she'd buzzed in at the gate, Rhys had told her the door would be unlocked and to come inside. From across the open floor plan, she could see into one end of the kitchen where brother and sister appeared to be having a standoff. A scowling Anne stood with hands on hips on one side of the granite bar while Rhys leaned on the other. As Camile watched, he slid a hand around the back of his neck and held it there. A gesture of frustration Camile now knew well from their first two dance lessons. She'd agreed to one more lesson as she wanted to make sure Rhys had the basics down before handing him off to someone else. At least, that was what she told herself.

"The woman is a mean-spirited gossip."

Anne glanced in her direction. "Great, Camile, you're here. Please tell my brother that he can't insult people in this town if he wants them to like him."

"I don't care if someone like her likes me."

"It's prominent people like her who influence other people."

"Um…" Camile pointed toward the door. "Should I wait outside?"

"No," Rhys fired off. Softening his tone, he caught her gaze and added, "Please don't." Focusing on Anne again, he said, "She insinuated that I'm a bigamist."

"I'm sure she was joking," Anne countered.

"She tried to present it that way, but she was irritated that I won't let her daughter get married here."

"Keisha Williams?" Camile asked, thinking fast. Katie worked at Keisha and Tom's real estate office. This was making more sense now.

"Yes," Anne answered. "How did you know?"

"I heard you were at their party last night. And everyone knows that Bethany is after the 'it' place to get married. The place *no one* else can get." Camile added an eye roll.

Rhys's eyebrows shot up, and he flashed Anne the classic "I told you so" look.

Anne sighed. "No one is going to believe that you're a bigamist."

"Probably not," Camile said. "Not when drug dealer is so much easier to believe."

"Drug dealer?" Rhys repeated. "Who said that?"

"I heard it this morning at the coffee shop, in addition to the bigamist thing."

"The coffee shop!" Anne cried. "This is just great!" Throwing her hands up in the air, she immediately let them fall to her sides. "Instead of getting better, it's getting worse. We need a body double for you."

Frustration emanated from a now-pacing Anne. Even Rhys appeared troubled by the news. Camile felt awful, her gaze darting between them. "I'm sorry. I shouldn't have said anything."

"No! I mean yes, you should say *all* the things," Anne countered, stopping and facing her. "I need to know what people are saying about him. What else have you heard?"

"Who said that I'm a drug dealer? Specifically, who were these people?" Rhys asked, blue eyes locked on to hers.

Camile answered Rhys first, "Um, Emma Vale and Katie Manning. They came into Blue Carafe this morning, and I overheard them talking. I asked them about it and assured them that it wasn't true."

"Thank you," Rhys said, although Camile could see the reassurance didn't help much. Making it that much more difficult to answer Anne, who was staring intently at Camile, waiting for the answer to her question.

"Okay, well, as you know, I haven't been back in town very long. But when Nina heard that you'd hired me, she told me that people have been gossiping about Rhys since he moved here. She said she's heard that you're an ex-spy, a mafia hit man and in the witness protection program."

"Because that's what you do when you're in the witness protection program," Anne said sarcastically. "Draw attention to yourself by irritating the community members where you live."

Rhys said, "I don't try to irritate anyone. I try to do the opposite. That's the point."

Voice softening, Anne said, "I know, Rhys. This is just…not going as well as I'd hoped."

Camile glanced from one distressed sibling to the other. What was going on here? Their reaction to this silly small-town gossip seemed a little over the top. Rhys did not seem like the type of guy who cared what people thought of him, a trait that Camile rather envied, and one he'd presumably been living with for better than two years. So why was this suddenly bothering him? Surely he'd heard some of these rumors before now?

"What are we going to do?" he asked.

Anne took a step back to lean against the counter. "We're not going to give up."

Give up? On what? What did that mean?

A loud buzz sounded. Rhys and Anne both frowned at a tablet sitting on the countertop between them. Rhys reached for it.

"Who could that be?" Anne asked crossly.

"I have no idea," he said, tapping on the display. His glower transformed into a huge smile. "It's Mom and Willow."

Anne let out a gasp. "What! They weren't supposed to be here for two more days."

"Remember, we need to keep Willow out of my wood shop. I'll sneak in there later and put everything back to the way it was before."

"Right," Camile answered hurriedly. "But what about your lessons?"

Rhys and Anne looked at her. "The studio," Camile quickly supplied as if she were an eager coconspirator. Definitely not the time to tell them she wasn't going to continue teaching him. "If you don't mind driving into town, we can use the studio. Late nights or early mornings are a safe bet."

Anne graced her with an appreciative smile.

"Thank you." Rhys's shoulders slumped with relief. "You're sure it's okay? You have a key? Do I need to talk to the owner? Rent the space?"

"I promise it's okay." Camile said reassuringly. "I live there in an apartment right above it. Gia lets us use it for private lessons. Text me later, and we'll work it out." Camile hitched a thumb behind her. "I think I'll go so you guys can catch up."

"No, stay," Rhys said quickly. "You can meet our mom and Willow."

"Yes, please stay," Anne said.

"How are you going to explain me?" She gestured at herself in leggings, short skirt, tank top and heels. "This is maybe an odd outfit if I'm not a dance instructor?"

"Take off your shoes," Anne said. Removing her own cardigan, she handed it to Camile. "Put this on."

She must not have appeared convinced because Rhys added, "I've been wanting to tell Willow about you. It's difficult keeping you a secret. This way if I slip and mention you, she'll just think you're a friend and nothing more."

Another odd statement. Why would he talk about her to his fiancée in any aspect other than as his dance instructor? The dancing was supposed to be a surprise. Hence, there should be no talking about her at all. The thought of meeting Rhys's fiancée had her insides twisted in knots. The reason behind those knots caused even worse knots. Basically, she was a mass of confusing and baffling knot-feelings. She just knew the woman was going to be beautiful beyond belief. And highly intelligent, like Rhys. She was probably a doctor or a physicist or in some other equally revered profession. But before she could decline, voices and footsteps sounded from the porch.

She felt Rhys's eyes on her as she smoothly stepped out of her shoes and, with one foot, slid them under the nearby side table. She slipped into the sweater. The grateful smile he gave her left her with a warm glow. Tentatively, she returned the gesture. His eyes seemed to be asking her a question, and she was baffled as to what it might be. The door opened. She planted a smile on her face, spun around and prepared to be intimidated.

That was not what happened.

Not at all. One look at the young Willow and Camile wondered if Katie and Emma's most ridiculous speculation might be true. Willow had long, curly, auburn-colored hair, porcelain-pretty skin and very blue eyes. Eyes that flashed with excitement as she bolted across the room. Her dimpled smile was so bright that not even the braces on her teeth could diminish it. Braces! The girl—the *girl*!—could not possibly be more than sixteen years old. As she came closer, Camile realized that even for an immature sixteen-year-old, that estimate likely was a stretch. She looked more like twelve or thirteen. What in the name of all that was good and sane was going on here?

The girl reached Rhys first and threw herself into his arms the way *children* do—eyes squeezed shut. He hugged her tight like she was the most precious of treasures while Camile contemplated calling the police or her new attorney or Aubrey and her Coast Guard cavalry or…someone. The sensation of being trapped in a creepy psychological thriller stole over her. Next, they'd lead her and the child Willow to the bigamist compound located in the deep woods out yonder and lock them both inside with their sister wives.

"Mom!" Anne embraced the older woman with an enthusiastic ferocity before letting her go. Then Willow and Anne exchanged hugs while Rhys similarly greeted his mother.

Anne cried, "What are you guys doing here? Wait, before you tell me, let me introduce you to our friend. I'd like you guys to meet Camile

Wynn. Camile, this is our Mom, Roberta Mc-
Grath. Everyone calls her Bertie or Bert."

The woman stepped forward to shake Camile's hand. She had thick silvery-gray hair
with waves reminiscent of Rhys's, but longer
and much tamer. And the same shatteringly
blue eyes as her children. Like Anne's, hers
were full of life and curiosity. "Nice to meet
you, Camile. What a lovely name."

"Thank you, Bertie. Nice to meet you, too,"
Camile managed.

Anne kept one arm around the child's shoulder. "And this is our niece, Willow."

Niece? Niece! How had she missed this? Willow had Anne's complexion and the McGrath
eyes, too, she realized, peering at her more
closely. They just looked different contrasted
with her much darker hair. Rhys was not engaged to this teenager, thank the stars above.
Rhys was not engaged at all… Camile felt her
pulse slowly decelerate even as warmth bun-
dled right at her core. The heat began to radiate
outward when she noticed Rhys's focus on her
again, approval and affection in his dazzling
smile. And this time Camile smiled right back,
ignoring the multifaceted reasons for her relief.

Then she showered her attention on Rhys's
adorable *niece.* "Hi, Willow! I've heard tons of
good stuff about you. I'm so happy to meet you."

LATE THAT EVENING, Rhys pulled up outside the large brick building in Pacific Cove where Camile's apartment was located. When she'd left that morning, he'd walked her out to her car and they'd made a plan to meet here for his lesson. As instructed, he took out his phone and texted her: I'm here.

When he'd gone back inside the house, Willow had asked if Camile was his girlfriend. Now, staring at his phone like an anxious teen waiting for a response, he wondered if his feelings for her were that obvious or if Willow was simply being a curious kid?

Meet me at the front door. I'll be right down. Her response sent his pulse racing, tipping the scales toward the former.

Gathering the container he'd brought, he exited his pickup and headed toward the entrance. A light flicked on in the entryway, and a few seconds later, the door opened.

"Hey, come on in."

Rhys stepped inside.

"You're early," she said with that full-on smile that always left him a little dazed. He found it difficult not to stare at her mouth. He'd never met anyone who conveyed so much with a smile. What would she do if he kissed her? That might be the way to resolve the question of mutual attraction. Because there were moments like this when he thought she liked him, too—instances where chemistry seemed to jolt them both.

"I am," he said, without explanation. The truth was he'd been anxious to see her again. Admitting that would probably make her uncomfortable. Holding the carton aloft, he said, "I brought you something."

Smile dissolving in a way he didn't like, she narrowed her gaze suspiciously and asked, "What is it?"

"Why are you looking at me like that?"

"Like what?"

"Like you don't trust me." *Why don't you trust me? I want you to trust me. I want you to like me.*

A flicker of something appeared in her eyes. She opened her mouth to reply and then shut it again. "I don't trust you. I hardly know you. Besides, no one in their right mind would trust a bigamist drug dealer," she joked.

He laughed. She was good at lightening his mood. Like the sun suddenly appearing after a rainstorm, she seemed to have that effect on everyone.

She was still smiling when she reached out and took the carton from him. "It's warm." She gave it a sniff. "And it smells really good. Like chocolate."

"Willow and I made cookies."

"You brought me cookies?" Her tone was filled with disbelief, and her eyes searched his face like she couldn't believe he'd done it.

"I did. Willow and I like to bake together. Harper said you like sweets."

"Thank you. I do. I like pretty much anything that's fast and that I don't have to cook myself. And if these are anything like your muffins, they will make a perfect dinner."

"Dinner? It's almost nine. Haven't you eaten?"

"Nope. But suddenly I'm super excited about the prospect. Do you mind coming upstairs to my place for a few minutes? I'm not quite ready. I just got home from a shift at Tabbie's."

"Sure," he said, and she pivoted around. Rhys happily followed; he wanted to see where she lived. "Tabbie's has great food. Why didn't you eat there? Don't they give you free food or at least a discount?"

"I know, and yes, they do. Their seafood chowder is so good it brings tears to my eyes." Her shoulders pulled up into a shrug. "So I don't know why. Busy, I guess."

"Too busy to eat?" he asked as they climbed the stairs. "How many jobs do you have? Harper said several."

"It's more that I start thinking, and then I forget to eat, if I'm being honest. Until I'm super hungry and then I eat everything in sight as fast as I can. I have six jobs."

"You have six jobs?" he repeated and knew his voice held an edge. She'd left the door to her apartment open, and they went inside. "No wonder you forget."

She set the bag on the table and removed the container of cookies. He liked how she took a second to study the lot and choose a specific one as if they weren't all the same.

"Where do you work besides Blue Carafe, Tabbie's and the dance studio?"

"Clean Breeze Car Wash and Fast Lanes, the bowling alley. I also do product promotions. But those jobs are usually temporary. Like a day or a weekend, or a few consecutive weekends. I did more of that in college when I lived in Portland and before..." She took a bite of cookie and immediately gushed, "Oh, wow. Delicious."

"Product promotion is like the taco dancing?"

She cringed. "You saw the video?"

At his nod, she groaned and shook her head. "Has anyone not seen the video?"

"In this town, doubtful." Brushing a hand across his jaw, he let out a chuckle. "I don't do social media myself, but Anne saw it and showed me. And Mom and Willow. If you divide the number of views by the population of Pacific Cove, then everyone in town has watched it multiple times, or nearly every person in the state has watched it once."

"Are you kidding me?" she cried. "It has four million views?"

"Just over," he said. "You were honest and brilliant. It made me proud to know you and…"

Camile appeared too distraught to grasp the compliment, and he was growing concerned by how pale she'd gone.

She braced her hands on the chair in front of her. A touch of despair emanated from her as she said, "I should have known better, right? Everyone has a camera these days, don't they?"

Rhys took a step closer. Why was she so upset about this? She hadn't done anything wrong. He wanted badly to touch her, to comfort her, to reassure her. "He deserved it."

"He did. It was very satisfying to let him have it. But unfortunately, it's going to cost me."

"Does a job like that really pay that much?"

"No. It's not about that. It's…" she trailed off as if trying to decide how to answer.

"What is it about?"

Head slowly shaking, she reached for her third cookie.

Concerned about her physical state and wondering if not eating was messing with her blood sugar, he said, "Cookies aren't the best choice for dinner."

"You sound like my sister Aubrey." Her chuckle sounded forced. "That depends if by best, you mean not convenient and delicious."

He walked over and opened her fridge. Happily surprised by what he found, he said, "You have food. Will you eat something else if I fix it for you?"

CAMILE HATED THE word *surreal*. She'd always thought it was like saying circumstances were not real when in fact they were just bizarre or difficult to believe. To her, the term sort of took the punch out of an authentically strange experience by giving it a dreamlike quality. But it was the word she kept coming back to as she sat at the table and watched Rhys McGrath moving around her kitchen preparing her a tuna melt with a side of sliced apple. His concern and thoughtfulness had her reeling. Obviously, she'd never experienced conditions that truly met the surreal criteria before.

"How do you have groceries but not cook?" After placing the sandwich under the broiler, he shut the oven door and moved so his hips were resting against the cupboard beside it.

"I don't usually. Aubrey brings me groceries sometimes."

His brow creased like he was thinking about that. "I take that to mean she doesn't approve of your eating habits?"

"Yep."

"Does it have something to do with what you guys were discussing at the restaurant the other night? You were in the hospital, right?"

Camile thought for a moment. They'd pretty much finished discussing the topic when Harper had appeared with Rhys and Anne, but now that she thought about it, Aubrey had brought it up again before she'd left. "You are one of those people who appear not to be paying attention when they actually are."

One shoulder lifted in a little shrug. "My sister has told me that, too. To me, I'm just..."

"Just?" she prodded.

"I mean, I don't look bored on purpose. It's just...me. Like it's... I also...think a lot. I tend to tune out everything except what I'm interested in. For example, if I find one person particularly interesting in a conversation, I'll only hear them or what pertains to them."

What? Camile took a second to ponder that, grateful when he returned to tending the oven. Because did that mean he was interested in her? But how could that be? Why would he be interested now and so very...*not*, two years ago?

Back at his task, he removed the pan and slid

the tuna and cheese-laden bread onto a plate, added a slice of tomato, and then placed the plate before her. Taking a seat across from her, he said, "Thank you for staying and meeting my family today. They loved you."

Camile smiled. She'd stayed for breakfast and a longer visit than she'd anticipated. Willow was funny and outgoing in a way that reminded her of Anne, while her curiosity and intelligence were all Rhys. Camile also discovered the uncle and niece shared a competitive drive when Camile and Willow teamed up to annihilate Rhys in a video game of *Castle Gate*. Willow confided that she'd never bested her uncle at it before and could Camile come back tomorrow so they could do it again? Rhys joked that she'd worn out her welcome and would never be allowed in his house again.

"I thought they were pretty awesome, too. Willow is a doll. She's a brainiac like you, isn't she?"

"Yes, she thinks a lot like me. Evan and I had that in common, too. Fortunately, she inherited her mother's sweet nature. She also seems to have been blessed with my mom's and Anne's wit. The combination gives her social skills that Evan and I lack, or lacked, I guess in his case." He cleared his throat and

Camile felt sympathy tighten her chest at the glimpse of latent grief. "Most grateful for that."

"Your sister is like a carbon copy of your mom."

The statement seemed to cheer him and Camile was glad. "Yes, with Evan gone, I don't stand a chance against their schemes."

"Can I ask you a couple of questions about them?"

His eyes found hers then and held on. "You can ask me anything you want." The sincerity in his tone intensified the gravity in his expression, leaving Camile with the feeling he was trying to convey something extremely important. The man was a puzzle. And since he didn't seem to mind the query, she couldn't resist a bit of solving.

"Anything?"

"Yes, absolutely. But if you don't get the answer you're after, please rephrase the question and try again."

"What if it's a really embarrassing personal question?" she teased.

His brow furrowed like he was pondering the implications of that possibility. "I thought the questions were going to be about my family."

"They are," she rushed out the words. "I was just joking because you implied that you'd answer honestly."

"Oh," he said but it didn't dispel the furrow.

"I take it that means the subject of you is off-limits, question-wise?"

"No. I didn't mean to imply that. You can ask anything about me, as well. What I was referring to before is that sometimes I miss subtleties and end up misunderstanding the intent of the question. In other words, I, uh, fixate on an unimportant detail or go off on a tangent or however you want to term it."

"I see."

"But you should know before you start asking questions that dishonesty is very difficult for me. Anne always tells me that there's a place in this life for *hedging* the truth, but I've never mastered the art of it. Probably because I don't want to. I don't understand the purpose, beyond creating confusion and misunderstandings. I either tell the truth, or I don't say anything at all."

Camile felt a prickle of unease dance up her spine. That meant she could ask him why he'd left her on that date, and she'd get an honest answer. But she knew she wouldn't ask. She didn't think she wanted to know. The notion was both disappointing and a little depressing. She didn't want to hear him say the words. It would be like getting rejected all over again.

Which meant that she liked him way more than she should.

"I'll stick with my original family-related questions for now," she affirmed, forcing a lightheartedness she no longer felt.

"Fire away."

"Anne mentioned the other day that Willow's parents have both passed away. So she's your late brother's child?"

"That's correct." Seeming to warm to the topic, he leaned toward her, placing his forearms on the table and intertwining his fingers. "Willow is the daughter of our brother, Evan, and his wife, Vanessa. Evan suffered a series of strokes a couple of years ago. The first stroke was relatively mild, and we thought he'd make a full recovery. Odds were in his favor. But then he had another one, much, much worse than the first. He didn't pull through. It was a shock."

"I'm so sorry. You were close?"

"Yes, very. We were very similar. He understood me, as did Vanessa, because of Evan."

"When did Vanessa die?"

"Almost three months ago. Car accident."

Camile felt her chest go tight with empathy and distress. That kind of suffering made her problems seem insignificant. "I can't even imagine. That poor girl. Willow lives with your mom now?"

"Oh. No..." He paused for a beat as if gathering his thoughts. "She lives with me. Evan and Vanessa granted me custody of Willow in their will. Anne has committed to helping and is moving here from Portland so Willow will have a strong female influence in her life. Our parents also live in Portland. They've always been very involved in her life, too."

"Why has she been in South Carolina? And what's this 'practice' you were all talking about?" The McGraths had all discussed it over pancakes. As a purported friend of Anne and Rhys's, Camile had felt like she should know what it was without asking in front of everyone.

"Willow is spending part of the summer in South Carolina with Vanessa's parents because she's participating in the Magnolia Junior Debutante Program there. She'll be flying back and forth until it's concluded."

Camile frowned, thinking. People grieved in all kinds of ways, but did it seem like an odd thing to do in light of her mother's recent death?

Subtlety may not have been his thing, but there was nothing wrong with Rhys's powers of deduction. "Vanessa came from an old Southern family. Willow's great-great-grandmother was one of the first participants in the program. Willow is participating as a tribute to her mom."

Camile nodded, the ache in her chest intensifying. Was there something she could do? Some way that she could help? Of course there was, she realized, as the importance of his goal became clear.

"And the dancing is somehow a part of it all?"

"The ball kicks off with a father-daughter waltz." The combination of vulnerability and hopefulness in his expression had her heart squeezing tightly. "I need to be able to do this for Willow. She's the bravest person I've ever known. Doing this when I know how much she's hurting... I want to make her happy and..." Pausing, he swallowed and glanced away for a few seconds. Then he nodded, clearly struggling to rein in his emotions. After inhaling a deep breath, he focused on her again. "And I know it's what Evan and Vanessa would want."

"Well, Rhys," Camile said, blinking back tears, "I don't think I've ever heard of a better reason to learn to dance."

They shared a smile and Camile knew in that moment she'd give the man as many lessons as it took.

CHAPTER SEVEN

THEY'D BARELY STARTED the lesson when something occurred to Rhys. Watching Camile in the mirror, he asked, "So Anne didn't tell you any of that about Willow?"

"Nope." Tonight's agenda included introducing the natural turn so he could, according to Camile, "gracefully whisk Willow around the *entire* dance floor." He had no idea what that entailed other than it sounded terrifying and impossible. She'd just demonstrated the steps and now prompted him to try. "Left foot forward whenever you're ready."

Half-heartedly, he attempted the steps.

"What are you doing—the zombie shuffle?" she joked. "Pick up your feet, elongate your steps. Show me some life."

He did. "I just assumed when you guys were talking that morning that she'd told you some things."

"No, she didn't. I thought you were learning to dance for your fiancée. I tried to figure out how I made the assumption. At the restaurant,

I asked when the 'big day' was, and Anne said five weeks."

"That makes sense." He glanced at his feet, both of which seemed to be cooperating uncharacteristically well.

"I thought so. All this time I thought Willow was your fiancée. Don't look down!"

The meaning of her words hit him fast and hard. He looked up but the implication behind the statement left him a little breathless. He stopped moving. Did this explain her initial standoffishness? As unfortunate as the misunderstanding was, he liked her even more as a human being if that were the case. This revelation also changed things, gave him hope. But what did he do with it? A mix of longing and fear warred inside him. There were moments, especially when they were dancing and he had his hands on her, when he was sure he could *feel* her attraction to him. But there were also moments when she looked at him as if…as if she wasn't sure.

He hadn't wanted a person to *like* him this much since elementary school. Back before he realized that way more people were not going to like him than did. That had been a painful truth to bear, but he'd always had Evan and Anne. In the military it had been easier to find common ground, and he'd forged some lasting friendships. Now he had Kyle. But those were men. His romantic relationships had all been either unsatisfying or outright failures, usually a combination of both.

He'd never met a woman he'd been comfortable enough with to get close to. Until now. If there was even a chance that Camile returned his feelings, he needed to try. He needed to think, to formulate a plan.

Rhys realized she was watching him, curiosity and amusement fueling her smile. Another point occurred to him. "I bet this is the kind of misunderstanding that's led to most of these rumors about me."

With an exaggerated, comical wince, she nodded. "I'm glad you see the humor."

"I do. And I see some other things, too."

Confusion knitting her brow, she asked, "Like what?"

Opportunity, he answered silently. Thankfully. But that reminded him of a topic that would be far safer for him, at least. "Anne made me promise to ask you if you know of anything fun we could do with Willow while she's here."

"How long will she be in town?"

"Through the weekend."

"There's the Sea Stars Scavenger Hunt on Saturday."

"What is that? How does it work?"

"Exactly like it sounds—a community scavenger hunt. For adults and children alike. You register in teams of up to five people. Then you literally run around on the beach and throughout town as there's no motor vehicle use allowed, attempting to gather all the items on the list. Afterward, there are prizes and a seafood boil in the park. Willow will love it."

"You seem to know quite a bit about it. Are you going?"

"That's because my sister Aubrey is helping organize it. She does a ton of volunteer work in the community. It's sponsored by the Coast Guard and a bunch of local businesses. And I am going, but not participating. When Nina and my friends were forming their teams, I thought I would be working. As it happens, it will be the first day in forever that I literally have *nothing* to do. But I know tons of people who are going. Harper and Mia are competing with Nina on a team against Kyle and Jay—that will be hilarious. Kyle's teenage niece and nephew have a team, too, so I feel confident it passes the teenager cool test."

"This sounds perfect." Pulling his phone out of his pocket, he asked, "Is there a website or a Facebook page? How do I get more information and sign up?"

"I have all that on my phone. I'll text it to

you." She walked over to the bench by the door where she'd left her phone, picked it up and sent him the links.

"Thank you. I'm glad I asked. I'm sending these to Anne and Willow now. Anne will be extremely pleased. And I'm excited about the idea that Willow might be excited."

"Good. Can we get back to work now?"

"Don't worry," he joked. "You'll get paid the same whether we're chatting or dancing." He tucked his phone into his back pocket.

"Rhys," she said on a lighthearted little huff. "It's not about the money. It's about you successfully waltzing with your niece and making her happy and proud. And me. I'm your teacher, and I want to be proud and happy, too. Anne is going to video it for me."

"Oh, good," he said dryly. "Now I'll get to be Pacific Cove's next internet sensation. But not in a good way like you."

"Okay, number one, my way was not a good way. And number two, that's an insult to my skills as a teacher."

"Why does that video bother you so much?"

"I don't want to talk about that video. And if you keep stalling, we're going to be here all night."

Is that an option? The response teetered on the tip of his tongue. But it was overruled by the fact that she didn't answer his question. Rhys knew what that meant. It was his own method of deflecting when he didn't want to lie. What was she hiding? And why didn't she want him to know? He needed to spend some time with her off the dance floor. How could he make that happen?

Stepping over to her, he reached out and took her hand and positioned his other as she'd taught him. Then he smiled down at her and said, "I can think of worse places to spend my evening. But I know you have an early shift tomorrow, so I promise, no more distractions tonight." Then he purposefully peppered in some waltz terms to make her smile. "I'm ready to rise and fall and *hover corte* and perfect my natural spin turn."

It worked. Her eyes sparkled with humor and approval, and her mouth curved in exactly the way he sought. And that was all he cared about.

For now.

"HI, WELCOME TO Fast Lanes. How many are bowling in your party today?" Camile repeated the words, barely glancing away from the computer monitor where she had her eye on a bunch of rowdy teens. They'd asked her to put up the bumpers in the two lanes they'd rented, and now were purposely throwing the balls against the bumpers to see how many times they could get them to ricochet down the lanes. Enough from these yahoos; she hit the button and lowered the bumpers.

The customer hadn't answered, so she glanced over ready to rephrase her spiel only to discover the smiling face of her friend. "Laura! Oh my gosh, what are you doing here?"

"Visiting you!" she responded enthusiastically. "I told you I would."

"You did." It was a long drive from Portland, and she'd assumed Laura would call first. Camile tried not to let the circumstances bother her, but her friend could not have chosen a worse day to drop by.

"You look fantastic!" Laura gushed.

Camile knew this was not true. She was physically exhausted and completely disheveled. And sweaty. She could feel the evidence of the latter soaking the armpits of her bright yellow bowling T-shirt. Tendrils of stray hair were sticking to her neck. Her stomach felt unsettled, too, and had for most of the day. She hadn't eaten since this morning. Maybe she should have had more than two leftover cookies for breakfast. Not that there'd been much time for eating with the workday she'd endured.

In a perfect display of the coast's petulant weather, the day's forecast for calm seas and sunny skies had been blown off course. A summer squall had barreled in from the ocean, leaving the afternoon unseasonably cold and rainy. The bad weather forced indoors packs of teens, families with kids and groups of tourists, all of whom should have been playing on the beach. This left the bowling alley unexpectedly crowded with a shorthanded staff. Camile had been running, literally, around the place for four hours, fetching errant pins, fixing wonky pinsetters, resetting computer scorecards, and fulfilling requests for heavier bowling balls, lighter bowling balls, left-handed bowling balls, and "that purple and gold bowling ball" that had brought Mr. Thyne good luck last week. She'd exchanged shoes, disinfected shoes, tied shoelaces, untangled knotted shoelaces left by obnoxious kids, fixed the vending machine, cleaned up spilled messes and unclogged a toilet. All of this between assigning customers to their lanes, answering questions, answering the phone, ringing up purchases, monitoring the cameras and babysitting rowdy teens.

Making matters worse, after the late dance lesson with Rhys the evening before, she'd been consumed by thoughts of him, his family and his orphaned niece. To distract herself, she'd attempted to assess her neglected thesis, failed miserably and only managed a few hours of sleep. Despite her advisor Dr. Youngworth's continued offers of help, Camile still couldn't bring herself to tackle the project—or to face Dr. Youngworth. Her cowardice was beginning to wear on her, as well.

Up at 4:00 a.m., she'd worked the morning at Blue Carafe thinking she had midday free. But then Maryanne, a fellow waitress at Tabbie's, had called in sick. Camile adored Maryanne, so she'd agreed to work her lunch shift at the restaurant. She'd barely had time to change her clothes in the bathroom after arriving at the bowling alley. And now, here Laura stood before her, looking perfectly poised and put together. As usual. Undoubtedly with plans for Camile to entertain her for the evening. And spend money she didn't have.

Camile reminded herself that Laura had no idea what it was like to pay her own way in life. Her parents footed the bill, all her bills. Laura had never even had a job, until very recently. When she'd accepted the assistant professor position that would have been Camile's if she hadn't tanked her research. Laura's smiling face made her feel like an ungrateful jerk. She reminded herself that Laura was a good friend.

They'd met soon after Camile had switched her major to psychology. They'd taken tons of classes together, braved the challenges of the master's program together, and she'd been there for Camile through the crushing disappointment that was her thesis failure. If Laura wanted to spend time with her, she needed to reciprocate.

"What time do you get off work?" Laura asked.

"I've got about another half hour."

"Great!" she chirped. "I'll wait. Then you can show me around this quaint little town you're always raving about. Did you know this place has a Michelin three-star seafood restaurant?"

Camile agreed. Laura headed to the café and came back with a snack pack of carrot sticks and a cup of coffee. She took a seat at the counter overlooking the lanes. Camile was almost ready to clock out when she looked up and felt her day plummet from bad to worse. A cramp twisted hard in her gut. Interestingly, it seemed unrelated to the fact that Rhys and Willow stood at the counter before her.

"Hi, Camile!" Willow said. "Uncle Rhys

said you worked here, but he didn't know if you'd be here today."

"Hey, guys!" she said, barely managing not to cringe with pain. "You just caught me. I clock out in a few minutes. But I can get you set up on lane number six before I go." She inhaled deeply and then exhaled, relieved when the discomfort passed.

"That would be great. I'm excited to bowl. I've only been a few times in my entire life."

"Bowling is one of my favorite things. What size shoes do you need?"

"Eight and a half for me, I think," Willow said.

Camile fetched the shoes and handed them across the counter. "These are nines. Let me know if they don't fit. They tend to run a little small."

"Sounds good. I'm going to go pick out a ball."

"I'll meet you down there," Rhys said.

Camile watched a bubbling Willow dash away. After everything the kid had been through, she imagined Rhys savored these joy-filled moments. When Camile faced Rhys again, she realized he was watching her in that way of his that made her feel scrutinized. And that made him appear both extremely serious and extrahandsome—if that was possible. Out of the corner of her eye, she could see Laura checking him out. Camile was sure her friend wasn't the only female in the place similarly affected. Camile felt an unexpected, unwanted pinch of jealousy. Heightened, she knew, by the fact that Laura had recently started dating Rob.

Camile had had a crush on Rob, a fellow grad student, for over a year. He'd scored an adjunct professorship in the sociology department. Thankfully, she'd never confessed her feelings to Laura. After the date debacle with Rhys, she'd gotten into the habit of keeping her romantic interests to herself. She supposed that was one positive thing that had come from her worst date ever.

Matching said date's somber expression, she said, "The largest size shoe we have is sixteen. Do you think you can squeeze your giant man feet into a sixteen?"

He laughed, hard, and Camile realized she was wrong. Laughter made him extra handsome. He said, "I'll try a thirteen."

She fetched the shoes. When she slid them across the counter, Rhys placed a hand over hers and held it there. Lowering his voice, he was all concern as he asked, "Are you okay?"

An unexpected lump of emotion lodged in her throat as his eyes traveled over her. Forcing a swallow, she pinned on a smile. "I'm fine," she lied, feeling a sheen of sweat dot her upper lip. "Why do you ask?"

"You look…off."

I feel off. She resisted the urge to confide in him and went with, "Tired. Long, *looong* day."

Shaking his head, he whispered, "That's not it. Tell me what's wrong."

"Camile, who's your friend?" Laura asked with her attention pinned appreciatively on Rhys.

Camile hadn't even noticed Laura approaching. Great, Rhys still had his hand over hers. Pulling away would look obvious, like she didn't want to be seen holding his hand. Not pulling away seemed worse, like she wanted to hold his hand. The latter was the truth and that left her even more unsettled.

Willow saved her. Jogging toward them, she held the shoes in the air. "These are too big!"

Camile lifted her arms and rolled her wrists inward in a bring-it-on motion. "Well, hand 'em over. Let's try an eight."

Switching out the shoes, Camile introduced everyone.

"It's so great to meet some of Camile's hometown friends," Laura said. "She talks about Pacific Cove all the time. I'm a friend from college. We were in the same graduate program together."

"How nice," Rhys responded politely.

"Are you guys old friends?" Laura asked. Camile wanted to roll her eyes at the obvious attempt to discern their relationship status.

"New friends," Rhys answered, and Camile kind of wanted to hug him for the ambiguity.

Laura waited, clearly hoping for more information. He didn't offer anything further, and neither did Camile. A short stretch of silence ensued until it neared the point of awkwardness.

Willow, seemingly unfazed, looked at Camile. "Are you a good bowler, Camile?"

"Fair." This was a bit of an understatement.

"I love to bowl," Laura gushed. "I used to bowl all the time back in high school. I'm pretty good." Camile did not know this about her friend. How had a shared enjoyment for a hobby like this never come up? Then again, their friendship had been mainly centered around school. Socializing for Camile usually consisted of a makeshift meal, a pot of coffee and a study session. But Laura was always up for it, no matter what odd hours Camile requested. Thinking of that, Camile was once again reminded of Laura's loyalty. She'd enjoyed that, even if their personalities and preferences didn't always match up.

"You guys should bowl with us!" Willow

suggested to Camile. "You could show me some stuff."

"That's a sweet offer, Willow. But I am exhausted after working twelve hours today. Maybe next—"

She'd been about to offer a rain check when Laura chimed in, "I think we can handle *one* game, don't you, Camile?"

At Willow's hopeful look, she answered, "Sure." And then tried valiantly to will her now-roiling stomach into submission.

"CAMILE IS SUPERCOOL, isn't she? Such a guy's type of girl." Laura added a shrill giggle. Rhys noticed that she punctuated all her comments about Camile in the same way. The sound was grating on his nerves like a rusted-over hinge.

"Camile is the coolest woman I've ever met," he answered truthfully. "Hands down."

Camile's friend was a decent bowler. Camile, on the other hand, bowled like she danced: with the unmitigated grace and skill of an expert. And she managed to look gorgeous, be gracious and act funny while doing it. He loved how she made Willow laugh. His niece adored her. Mostly, it brought Rhys a sort of perverse joy to watch the humble and unassuming Camile wipe the floor with her pretentious and condescending friend.

"I love how she's so confident in herself that she doesn't even care how she looks. Look at her scruffy hair! So adorable. Ha ha!"

Rhys was trying to be nice. And he was. Well, nice in that so far, he'd avoided responding to this "praise" in the way that he wanted. The woman had perfected passive-aggressive compliments to an astounding degree, and he was having a difficult time not shutting her down.

The very first frame Camile had bowled a strike, prompting Willow to beg for advice. Whenever it was Willow's turn, Camile stepped up to help with her technique, leaving him alone with this woman. And every time, she had a barb locked and loaded, which she then launched at Camile's back in the same sweet-as-sugar tone. Rhys couldn't believe Camile was friends with her. What he also couldn't believe was that she'd agreed to bowl a game with them after working for twelve hours. Despite her friend's obnoxious demand, he knew she'd acquiesced for Willow's sake. That fact had settled deeply inside him, lighting up all his feelings for her while simultaneously making his distaste for Laura's commentary even more unbearable. He could see Camile didn't feel well. She needed to go home and rest. He wondered when she'd eaten last.

"It's easy to be confident about that when you're as beautiful as she is," Rhys said. "No extra effort required."

"So true!" Laura prattled like a middle schooler and then added, "I've never known anyone who could pull off the *natural* look quite as well as Camile."

"Woo-hoo!" Willow called and high-fived Camile, who'd bowled her third strike in a row. "You are awesome. How are you so good at this?"

"Thank you." Camile sank down next to Willow on the opposite bench. When the game started, Rhys had been disappointed when her friend claimed the spot next to him. He'd quickly changed his mind when he realized it gave him an unobstructed view of Camile as she sat facing him.

Camile explained, "I started working here back in high school. The owner, Hal, let us employees bowl for free when it was slow. He'd give us tips and show us stuff. He's a great guy and an excellent teacher."

"Excellent teachers are the best," Rhys said, pinning his gaze firmly on her. "I'm eternally grateful for mine."

Eyes twinkling, she tossed him a sly, joy-filled smile. Hitting him right in the center of his chest. *His very own secret smile.* Satisfaction settled into him and he took a moment to enjoy the sensation. Willow pointed at the lane, undoubtedly asking a question. Camile leaned toward her while they chatted. He liked how she talked to Willow. She gave the same attention and consideration to his teenage niece that she did to everyone else.

Rhys marveled at her resilience. All her years of customer service experience had undoubtedly taught her to control her outward persona and to perfect her people skills, no matter how she was feeling on the inside. But he'd also learned that she was one of those naturally engaging people. It spilled out of her. She reminded him of Willow's mother in that way, kind, cheerful and generous—probably to a fault. Certainly, at her own expense. The kind of friend that made you feel special, the person everyone gravitated toward at a party, the woman that men wanted to spend time with, the woman every other woman wanted to be—or that they wanted to tear down. Like the woman sitting beside him, her jealous, backstabbing non-friend.

Rhys stood and bowled his turn. Willow consoled him with a pat on the back when he missed a spare by one pin. Camile was next and managed another strike while doing a goofy impersonation of him that caused Willow to laugh. And him, too.

"Camile is actually quite intelligent," Laura said after taking her turn and sitting back down beside him. "Despite her silly antics. I feel terrible about these unfortunate…circumstances she's dealing with."

Okay. Enough was enough. Rhys had been avoiding eye contact, hoping she'd get the message that he wasn't interested in her opinion. But now, he swiveled in his seat and faced her. "What do you mean by that?"

"By what?" she repeated with an innocence so contrived it frayed the last vestige of his patience.

"Aren't you a psychology major, Laurie?"

"Um, it's Laur-a. And yes, I have a master's degree in psychology."

"With an emphasis in passive-aggressive behavior?"

Another giggle pierced his brain stem, this one tapering to a slightly less confident fervor as she pondered his question. "What do you mean?"

"I'm not sure what you hope to accomplish here by running Camile down, but I don't want to hear it anymore."

"Running her down? I have no idea what you're talking about! I just meant it's amazing how well she's bounced back. You know, considering what happened with *her* thesis. Not that she won't fix it, but that kind of failure has to be difficult for someone like her. And then, that awful video. Poor girl. She can't catch a break lately, can she?"

Obviously, Laura was fishing, trying to discover what he knew about this thesis misfortune, and how well he knew Camile. What failure was she referring to? He wasn't about to bite, curious though he was.

"You are good at it, I'll give you that. The fact that you're so good at it leads me to believe that you've had a lot of practice. I suspect it's your personal addiction—putting Camile down to prop yourself up. In fact, I think the reason you coerced her into bowling with us when she's already worked twelve hours on four hours' sleep was so that you could be better than her and show off a bit. That backfired in a big way, didn't it? But I wonder how many ways you've sabotaged her that she's completely unaware of?"

Her bug-eyed gasp held more surprise than outrage, and he could see he'd exposed a nerve. Leaning toward her slightly, he lowered his voice and added, "But you're wasting your time here. It's not going to work with me. If I have my way, and I usually do—" this time he did it on purpose, mispronouncing her name "—*Laurie*. It's not going to work anymore at all. Ever again."

CHAPTER EIGHT

"THAT'S A BUMMER that you have to go," a concerned but mostly relieved Camile lied. "Poor Zeus." Zeus was Laura's diabetic cat. Her friend's roommate had texted to say the cat was acting funny, and now Laura had to cut their visit short.

"I'm sure he'll be fine." Laura hugged her. "You know how he gets when I'm gone." Camile heard a little sniff before she added, "Your deodorant smells good, very fragrant. We'll talk soon."

"Of course." Camile stepped back and watched her friend hustle out the door. "Bye. Drive safe. Text me when you get home and let me know he's okay." Was it her imagination or had a woozy feeling swept through her during the last few frames? The ball had nearly slipped from her hand in the tenth; she'd only managed a spare. Popping a couple of antacids had not helped.

"Isn't she great?" Camile faced Rhys.

"She is something, all right," he answered,

glancing toward the restroom where Willow had gone.

Camile swiped a hand across her brow. "I could tell she was into you."

"I don't think so." Rhys shifted on his feet.

"Trust me—I can tell when Laura likes a guy. I didn't even know she liked to bowl! You saw her run over and sit by you. Too bad she has a boyfriend. Or at least, I think she does. I could set you up."

Rhys frowned. "Set me up?" he repeated sharply. "Why would you think I'd want to be set up? And why with her specifically?"

"Um, I don't know… You're single. At least I think you are? Laura is…maybe single?" She hadn't mentioned Rob. Had she and Rob broken up? Camile supposed she should feel happy about that possibility. But, she realized, she didn't care. School and Rob, and Laura for that matter, seemed a million miles away now. "Well, you met her. You guys are the same, um, have the…" Her thoughts were becoming sluggish along with her body. "The same…" What was she saying?

"I am single. I did meet her," he said firmly. "But that woman and I are not the same."

Camile shook her head. "No, I don't mean you are the *same* same. Your personalities are very different. But you're the same level of…"

She'd been about to say attractiveness but was halted when her stomach twisted with another violent cramp. For which she was thankful, in a way, because saying that would basically be telling him he was good-looking when he already knew. And she didn't mean solely physical attractiveness, anyway; she meant they both had the whole package.

She also didn't want him to think she felt sorry for herself because she wasn't at their level. She didn't. It was just that certain people went together. Beautiful people who had it all together belonged together. Ones who managed to earn their degrees, get awesome jobs and didn't get sued, and still had time to comb their hair. Like apples and apples or oranges and apples? Or…whatever. The thought of fruit suddenly made her want to gag.

But the general subject matter prompted a question she'd been wondering about. "How old are you?"

With a quick grin, he answered, "I'm thirty-two. How old are you?"

He threw the question back to her so fast that she decided he'd been curious about her age, too. "I'm twenty-six."

"That's better than twenty-two."

"It is?" What did that mean?

"From my perspective, yes. I was hoping you were older than twenty-one."

Wait…? Did he mean because there was less of an age difference between them? Her stomach didn't save her from answering this time. "Why?"

"Pretty sure you know why."

Was he saying he *liked* her? That was impossible. He already hadn't *liked* her when he had the chance. Even though he seemed to enjoy spending time with her, in that they had fun at his lessons, and they were sort of becoming friends. She needed clarification and was about to ask for it when her stomach went full rogue.

Pressing her hands to her midsection, she bent at the waist and let out a gasp of pain. "My stomach…"

"CAMILE, ARE YOU OKAY?" Rhys asked the question even though he knew the answer. "I knew something was wrong with you," he whispered roughly. Concern gripped him hard. She'd passed out recently and spent time in the hospital. *Please*, he begged silently, *don't let her have some kind of incurable medical issue*.

"Yes." She shook her head no. "Nothing is *wrong* with me." She doubled over again. "But maybe I do need to sit for a minute."

"Let's do that. And then I'm going to take you home." He curled an arm around her shoulders. His other hand came up to cup her cheek, and he muttered a soft curse. "You're burning up." He led her to a bench near the door and kept one arm securely around her as they sat. Melting against him, she rested her head on his shoulder. Removing his phone from his pocket, he sent a text to Anne.

"No, I'm just hot. It's this shirt. I keep telling Hal he needs to get rid of these polyester shirts. They don't breathe. I should probably breathe…" Pressing her face against his chest, she inhaled deeply and made a loud, snuffling sound. It would have been funny if the situation didn't have him so alarmed. "Oh, man… I really, *really* like the way you smell," she whispered. "I can smell you when we're dancing…"

"You like the way I smell?" Chuckling, he shook his head.

"That's weird, isn't it? I don't know why I just told you that. Maybe because my stomach is trying to kill me, and it helps to think about something else…"

Holding her close to his side so she wouldn't tip over, he whispered, "No, sweetheart, that's not weird." Pressing his lips against her temple, he added, "That's serendipity at its finest."

Opening one eye to look at him, she said, "Did you just call me sweetheart?"

"Yes, I did."

"Why would you do that?"

"Because you're sweet and you've stolen my heart."

"No!" Her fingers grasped a fistful of his T-shirt. He winced when she pulled some chest hair along with it. "Rhys, no, I didn't steal from you. I wouldn't."

Peeling her fingers away, he tucked her hand into his. "Shh, Camile, I know. I didn't mean it literally. And my heart is still safe inside my chest. No need to try to yank it out of there."

"Then why did you leave me?"

"Leave you?"

"Is it because I smell like French fries and sweat and stinky bowling-alley feet?" She gave her head a firm shake. "No, that can't be it. I didn't stink then…"

"Camile, I'm not going anywhere, and you don't stink. In fact—"

"Uncle Rhys, what's going on?" A concerned Willow stood before them. "Is Camile sick?"

"Yes, she's got a stomachache and a fever. Aunt Anne is going to meet us at the hospital."

"No!" Camile cried. "No, you can't take me to the hospital. I'm fine. Just tired. And my stomach—" she pointed an accusing finger in its general direction "—we used to be friends, but now it hates me."

"Camile—"

Struggling, she sat up straighter. There was a stifled sob in her voice as she pleaded, "Please, don't. No hospital. I'm not dying. I don't think. I can't… Also, do *not* call my sister Aubrey! Promise me, Rhys, you will not call Aubrey."

"I promise," he shot back, pretty sure he'd promise her anything she asked of him right now.

"Unless I'm dying. Then you can call her. Which I'm not! I might be sick, though. Probably that stomach bug that Maryanne had. My coworker at Tabbie's was sick and…" She shrugged and it looked completely pitiful. "And I can't talk anymore because I'm going to…"

RHYS TOOK HER HOME, right after she got sick in the trash can and then insisted that she needed to haul the trash outside to the dumpster so that "Jason," her teenage replacement, wouldn't have to do it. After a short argument, Rhys carried out the task. Willow then retrieved yet another trash bag from a concerned Jason who was now working behind the counter, so she'd have it for the ride home. Even then, she insisted that Rhys pull over for her to throw up so she didn't get sick in his "nice car."

Minutes after he got her inside and up the stairs to her apartment, Anne arrived to get Willow. "How is she?" she asked.

"Sleeping. In between vomiting sessions. I got her to swallow two ounces of water, and then she crashed. I don't know what to do... She was adamant about not going to the hospital. Harper is on her way over. Hopefully, she can give me some advice." And answers, he added silently.

"Okay, keep us posted."

A distraught Willow hugged him, made him promise to text updates, and they left.

Rhys paced, checking on Camile with each pass by her bedroom door until Harper knocked.

"Hey," Harper said, stepping inside. "I'm going to check on her." She disappeared inside the bedroom for a few minutes.

When she came out, she said, "Definitely has a fever."

"I know. I feel like I should have taken her to the hospital. She was adamant about not going. That, and not calling her sister Aubrey." And about Rhys not leaving her, but he left that part out. "I know she passed out recently. Is there something going on with her? Is she sick, Harper? Tell me if you know something."

"Oh," Harper said with a frown, seeming to understand his deeper meaning. "No, Rhys, not that I know of. Of course, it's possible that she wouldn't tell me if there was. Despite her outgoing personality, she's a very private person. Nina would know. Let's call her. But I'm pretty sure the reason she didn't want to go to the hospital is because she can't afford it."

"What?"

"All I know is that when she passed out, they took her to the emergency room. She's been freaked out about the huge hospital bill ever since. And now there's—" Harper stalled before adding "—another bill. Anyway, she's been sick about it. Sorry, bad pun."

"She doesn't have insurance? What other bill?"

Harper was clearly uncomfortable with the questions.

"Harper, I'm not prying unnecessarily here."

"I know. It's just… In addition to being private, she's very stubborn. She refuses help, which I get." Harper tipped her head to one side and added, "Even though it seems a little over the top. She wouldn't want me talking about this. But as far as her insurance goes, I believe she has basic, catastrophic coverage with a sky-high deductible."

Rhys thought about her multiple part-time

jobs. No doubt they got her by, but what was her long-term plan? "Didn't she recently graduate from college? Is she looking for a more permanent full-time job? With benefits? Or is she going back for more school? Do you know what happened with her thesis?"

Harper's eyes had gone wide, presumably caught off guard by his questioning. "You need to ask her about all of that. She's been through a lot, Rhys. I'm honestly not sure what her plans are." Rhys let that go for now. But between Laura's snide commentary and Harper's reaction, he knew that something was off in Camile's world.

Rhys nodded and went to sit with Camile. Nina showed up soon after, with Mia in tow. An exam by a doctor of veterinary medicine was fine by him, especially since Harper trusted her. Rhys filled Mia in on Camile's behavior and symptoms, including the information about her ill coworker.

Mia and Nina disappeared inside Camile's room. Rhys winced when he heard vomiting again. He could feel Harper watching him, see the curiosity in her expression. He didn't say anything because he had no idea how to explain how he felt. If he tried, it would undoubtedly come out sounding wrong.

What felt like hours later, they finally emerged

from Camile's room. Mia said, "I'm fairly certain it's gastroenteritis, a stomach bug. Her fever isn't high enough to cause me concern. I'm going to leave this thermometer with you." She placed it on the coffee table. "Take her temperature every hour and if it creeps up past 102, call me. If it spikes to 103, go to the ER and then call me."

"What about the way she was talking? She seemed out of it."

"Do you think she was hallucinating?"

"What was she saying?" Nina asked.

Rhys thought for a second and shook his head. "No, not hallucinating." In answer to Nina, he said, "She was talking about me leaving."

"Ah," she said with a firm nod like this made perfect sense. "She's sensitive about that."

"About what?"

Nina opened her mouth to respond, shut it and then stuttered, "About, um, people…leaving." She was lying, and he knew it.

Rhys narrowed his eyes at her in a way that conveyed this conviction. Nina returned it with a challenging glare of her own, leaving him even more confused.

He let it go for now, when Mia said, "Likely she was just feeling crappy and rambling. Plus, I think she's exhausted. Nina was telling me about the hours she's been working and the stress she's under."

"What do I do?" Rhys asked.

Mia said, "For now, make sure she drinks plenty of water. Dehydration is the number one concern. I predict she'll be feeling better by tomorrow. But then she needs to rest. These viruses come on with the force of a Mack truck, but usually don't last long. It'll wipe her out, though. She'll need to take it easy for a few days to get her strength back."

Nina scoffed. "My little sister does not know how to take it easy. Well, neither of them does, but at least Aubrey takes care of herself while she's working too hard."

The idea of Camile not taking care of herself gnawed at him like a toothache. If anyone thought it was weird that he stayed the night, they didn't mention it. Nina stayed for the first shift of the evening with a plan for Harper to relieve her at 3:00 a.m. Rhys dozed in a chair by Camile's bed.

"Rhys?"

It was nearing the shift change when the sound of Camile's voice stirred him. "Do you need your bucket?" he whispered because Nina was asleep on the sofa.

She shook her head. "What are you still doing here?"

Sitting forward, he picked up her cup. "Torturing you, remember?" Earlier, she'd accused him of "torture by water" when he'd slipped the straw into her mouth and made her drink.

She managed a few sips. Glassy-eyed, she stared at him for a few long seconds like she didn't quite know what to make of his presence.

"I can't believe you're here." Her voice sounded hoarse, her throat no doubt sore from the trauma it had been through.

He pressed a palm to her cheek. Still warm. "Where else would I be?" He smoothed a loose tendril of hair behind her ear.

"Where people aren't throwing up on you."

He chuckled. "I like taking care of you." And he realized how much he meant it. And what that meant. He'd never wanted to take care of a woman in his life—a child in the form of his niece, Willow, yes, but not this.

Despite her now drooping eyelids, she managed an admirable protest, "I don't need anyone to take care of me."

"No one said you *needed* it. I said I liked it."

That got a small smile, the first since her ordeal began.

Eyes closed now, she said so softly that he would have missed it if he hadn't been hover-ing, "You are sweet. When you left, I did not think you were sweet."

Who had left her? Frustrating. Besides the fact that he didn't like being mistaken for this guy, he couldn't help wondering what kind of idiot would ever leave Camile Wynn.

CAMILE ROLLED OVER very, very slowly. And then she waited for the dreaded wave of nausea. When it didn't immediately materialize, she inhaled a deep breath and then waited some more. After another moment, she tentatively pushed herself up onto one elbow. Rhys was sleeping in a chair beside her bed. Rhys! In a chair. Beside her bed. Where he'd been all night, she recalled now. She should have been mortified, but she'd been way too ill to care. And so grateful for his presence. Nina and Harper had been here, too. And Mia at one point.

Tears of gratitude gathered and stung her eyes as she realized she had people in her life who cared this much about her. Who'd held her hair while she vomited, mopped away her sweat, covered her with blankets when she had the chills and uncovered her again when those same blankets threatened to roast her alive. They'd wiped her mouth, pressed cool towels to the back of her neck and coaxed her to drink water. Rhys may have even threatened at one point. Water. It actually sounded good for the first time in what felt like days. She also needed to use the restroom. A good sign, she decided, that she wasn't dehydrated.

Quietly, carefully, she shifted to the edge of the bed. At some point, someone had wrangled her into a pair of pj's. She pretended that it was Nina or Harper and not the handsome sleeping giant slouched in a much-too-small chair next to her bed. She swung her legs around, sat up and almost made it to her feet when her legs buckled. With a little squeal of alarm, she crumpled forward. Rhys scooped her up before she hit the floor and secured her on his lap.

"Hey," she managed to calmly quip despite the embarrassment burning her cheeks, "Good catch."

With a grumpy face and a growly voice, he said, "What are you doing?"

"Oh, I just thought I'd see what was down there on the floor," she joked. "It's dust bunnies, mostly, in case you were curious."

"Did you fall?"

"Not exactly. It was more of a giving-out-of-the-leg-muscles thing."

"I'm sorry."

"For what?"

"For dozing off and missing the show."

"Well, I don't think you can complain too much. You had a front-row seat for the barf and hurl show. Reviewers are spewing their praise. They're calling it a real gag."

He laughed then, and it made Camile smile right through her mortification. And not just with her mouth but inside, like her heart was smiling, too. His gaze traveled over her for a moment as if assessing her condition.

Voice low and smooth as velvet, he said, "I know you're feeling better if you're making jokes."

"Bad ones. Sorry. Kind of gross. I'm a little embarrassed."

"That's quite all right as long as you're not gearing up for an encore performance."

"That's a good one," she said with a weak chuckle.

"You don't have anything to be embarrassed about. We all get sick."

She nodded, appreciating how incredibly kind he was being about this. "Rhys?"

"Yes?"

"Thank you. I can't even begin to thank you for everything and…" Feeling emotional again—what was it about being sick that made a person grateful for every little not-sick thing? For example, she felt a newfound and abiding affection for her pillow, ice cubes and the fuzzy socks on her feet. She took a moment to gather her thoughts and hold back the tears before adding, "I don't know how to repay you."

"Don't worry," he said. "I have some ideas."

"Like what?" she asked, his words rousing a nervous twinge.

"We'll talk about it later. When you're feeling better."

"Deal. For now, since I have sacrificed all of my dignity to the porcelain gods, can you help me get to the bathroom?"

CHAPTER NINE

"FEATHER, SHELL—or a piece of a shell, something metal, seaweed, driftwood, popsicle stick," Anne read from the list of scavenger-hunt items.

Camile stood with Anne, Rhys and Willow on the boardwalk near Pacific Cove's gazebo, the starting line for the Sea Stars Scavenger Hunt. It was the first time she'd left her building in three days, and it felt amazing to be mostly back to herself, physically at least. A reluctant Rhys had left her apartment the next evening only after Nina assured him that she would stay another night to make sure Camile was okay. Camile thought the decision was made easier with Aubrey's arrival. She'd finally texted her and, without a single lecture, her sister had shown up with a ginger smoothie and one of their favorite superhero DVDs. Her concern had Camile tearing up all over again.

Rhys insisted they put the dance lessons on hold, texted her multiple times a day and had called both evenings since. Yesterday, he and

Willow had brought her some delicious soup and homemade bread. Sweet. Ugh. She remembered telling him he was sweet. He had been. He was. She'd said other things, too. Apparently, he hadn't picked up on any of *those* cues, at least not enough to ask about their source. But she was harboring serious concerns about that conversation where they'd made some ambiguous deal regarding her paying him back for taking care of her.

And now her emotions were a jumbled mess where he was concerned. There'd been a definite shift in their relationship. Having a man hold your head while you threw up changed things, she supposed. But it was more than that. He'd gotten to her before that.

Snippets of their conversations kept surfacing, taunting her, confusing her. That comment he'd made about their age difference and how he was glad she wasn't any younger. She didn't understand what was going on. How could she bring it up? She didn't want to bring it up. And now it was like a giant elephant in the room that only she could see. But what if he wasn't interested in her in that way? An offhand comment about their age difference didn't mean anything, *necessarily*. But then there was the sweetheart, heart-stealing thing. Although, she'd had a fever and he'd been worried. She'd gotten sick right in front of him. What choice did he have? Especially when she'd gone on about him leaving. Of course, he'd stayed after that. He'd done what any decent human being would do, right?

Probably it was a little more than decent to sit by her bedside all night, bring her food and text multiple times a day. But he'd said he liked taking care of her. So maybe it was just a simple case of knight's syndrome? She'd been a damsel in distress, and he'd been there to save her. Yes! That could explain almost everything. Surprising for a guy like him, but the psychology of a person was complex and multilayered. She'd pegged him incorrectly because she'd been thrown off by her initial encounter with him. Conclusion: Rhys was a nice guy with a case of knight's syndrome who'd encountered a needy, ill woman. The combination had produced this unique situation. Yep, that was it. That explained it. Almost, because none of this explained his actions on that first date.

Still, even keeping all of this in mind, she knew she was enamored with him. Who wouldn't be? Even now, with him standing beside her, all she could think about was how worried he'd been and how kind he was to her. Okay, and how handsome he looked. In his worn jeans and fleece top, with his golden-blond curls, he could pass for a movie star. And the way he watched her with that concern splayed all over his face made her feel soft inside. Too soft, maybe. Soft meant weak. She didn't want to be weak. She needed to be strong. She needed to take care of herself.

Dr. Youngworth, her thesis advisor, had emailed again the day before to ask when she could meet to discuss her "next steps." The thought of starting over made her panicky. Looming student loans made her sweat. The probable lawsuit was a major distraction. Legal bills. Hospital bills. Her life had gone off the rails, and she needed to get it back on track.

She tuned back into her surroundings where a team consisting of Harper, Nina, Mia, and Mia's friend and office manager, Charlotte, had congregated next to them to study the list. A confident threesome comprising Kyle, Jay and Jay's friend Terrence stood whispering in a huddle nearby. Jay's younger brother and sister, Levi and Laney, were teamed up with Levi's girlfriend, Ty, and a friend of Laney's. The teens seemed unconcerned with the scavenger hunt's objectives as they laughed among themselves.

Harper read, "Bonus points for collecting garbage from the beach in the included paper trash bag. Such a fantastic idea! I despise plastic. Did you know the Great Pacific Garbage Patch now contains thousands of tons of plastic? It's essentially a huge island of garbage floating around our ocean. Heartbreaking." Not only was Harper's father a billionaire businessman and renowned environmental scientist, but she also worked as a wildlife photographer.

"It says here that the proceeds from this event go toward ocean cleanup," Willow said. "That's cool."

"It is! Some studies suggest that as many as a hundred million marine mammals are killed each year from plastic pollution alone. I can't even think about sea turtles without getting infuriated."

"Channel that anger, Harper," Mia gently encouraged. "I really want to beat Jay and Kyle."

Camile laughed. Jay was Mia's husband, and Kyle, her brother. Camile imagined she'd want to best that team, too, if she were Mia.

Camile pointed at Anne's list. "Some of these items you only need photos of, like the bird tracks, the crab and the message in the sand. See the little camera icon? All of those only require a photo with a team member in it. Should be a piece of cake."

"Fun!" Anne said. "Let's get going!"

Rhys and Willow stayed put.

Heads bowed together over their list, Willow explained, "We have to wait for the starting bell."

Rhys said, "I think we need a strategy. We're at a distinct disadvantage with some of these items."

"I agree," Willow said. "And see how certain objects and tasks are worth more points than others? Maybe we should prioritize, go for some of the easier but higher-point items first. If we can figure out what those are..." She tapped the paper. "What's a salty key?"

"I have no idea," Rhys answered. "I don't even know where most of these places are."

"The items around town are worth more and are definitely trickier," Camile said, studying her own copy of the instructions. "A salty key is a piece of salted caramel taffy from Wishing Well Candy. It's their most popular flavor."

"Bonus points for finding a message in a bottle?" Willow added. "That seems impossible."

"Ah, but it's not," Camile explained. "Some off-duty Coast Guard volunteers and fishermen released a bunch of bottles offshore so they'd wash up along the beach for this event." She glanced at Harper, who was listening intently. "Don't worry, Harper, they're biodegradable. Aubrey said they are made of seaweed or something. Inside are coupons and gift certificates."

Harper stepped over to join them. "Camile, you're not working today, are you?"

"Nope. I've got the whole day free. I'm excited to watch the action unfold and chow down on some seafood after. I need to make up for some serious calorie deficits." Her attention was drawn to Kyle, Jay and Terrence, who'd moved a ways away as if they didn't want their strategy overhead. "Kyle's team looks ready to win this thing."

"Pfft." Harper waved a breezy hand through the air. "I'm not worried about Team Intensity over there. Did you see number five?"

Camile ran a finger down the list. "Build a sandcastle and take a photo," she read. "I don't get it."

"Kyle won't be able to build a tiny but adequate castle and move on. It'll be a *castle,* like with turrets and a moat. There are too many items like that on here. He's a perfectionist. Jay is the same. They'll get caught up in the details. I predict a team of women will win this. They're better at prioritizing and multitasking. Ideally, it will be us. I do have the camera advantage."

"Yes, to winning!" Mia cried.

"Right on." Camile chuckled at her friends.

Harper leveled a pointed stare at her. "But Rhys's point is valid. He and Anne and Willow are never going to be able to compete without some insider knowledge. Why don't you help them? Then you can be a part of the action, too."

"That's the best idea ever! Can she do that?" An enthusiastic Willow bounced on her toes. "Is it too late to add a member to our team?" Then she paused, peering at Camile. "Wait, are you sure you're feeling okay?"

"Yes, she definitely can," Harper said.

"She's fine," Nina Under-the-bus-thrower chimed in.

"I love this plan!" Anne said. "Why didn't we think of it sooner?"

Threading an arm around Camile's elbow, Willow asked, "Can you help us, Camile? Will you be on our team?"

"I don't know if there's still time to register," Camile said, trying to get out of it but unsure about exactly why. That wasn't true; she knew why, and he was standing here, piercing her with those blue eyes like he could read her mind.

"You can register right up until the starting bell," Harper offered helpfully, and Camile couldn't help but wonder if Harper was pushing her toward Rhys on purpose.

The hopeful yet concerned expression on Willow's face was her undoing. "Sure. Let's do this. I'm feeling great, Willow, I promise."

Pulling out her phone, Harper then quickly swiped and tapped on the screen. "You can manage your team online. I'm adding you to Team McGrath right now."

"Team McGrath," Willow repeated. "I like that."

"Me too," a very satisfied-looking Rhys added softly. "Very much so."

As FAR AS Rhys was concerned, the scavenger hunt could not have worked out better. He got to spend the day with Camile away from the studio and he didn't even have to ask her. Once again, Harper had put her right in his lap, so to speak. Plus, she was very, very good at this game. They were ticking items off the list right and left. Anne and Camile were making them all laugh. And Willow was loving every second of it.

"Okay," Camile said, pointing at the now-crumpled and slightly damp paper clutched in her hand, "if we head for Kassie's Kite Shop we can get our 'share of string,' then grab a coffee sleeve from Blue Carafe—evidence that we've 'quenched our thirst somewhere in The Cove.'" She'd explained that was what locals often called their town. "That covers numbers sixteen and twenty-seven. Down the street and around the corner, we can snap a photo of the pond in the park for number thirty's photo of 'a body of water that's not the ocean.' I'm guessing most people will head for the river close to the jetty. That gives us an edge timewise because while we're there, we can also collect a wildflower, take a photo of a rodent—there are tons of squirrels over there—and maybe even find a Frisbee. People play with their dogs there a lot because it's not as windy as the beach. And then we can attempt a few more bonus items before time's up."

Rhys was impressed with her ability to strategize. She would have made a great soldier. When they neared the park, Willow immediately spotted a squirrel, and she and Anne jogged ahead to try to get a photo.

Rhys glanced at Camile. "Thank you for this. Willow is having a blast."

"No problem. I'm having a great time, too."

"I don't know about the no-problem part. I know this was supposed to be your day off. You told me it was the first day you had nothing to do in forever, forced sick days notwithstanding. How are you feeling? If you need to take a break, just say the word."

"I'm fine. And I just spent three days doing

nothing. I don't know if I remember what it's like to do *nothing* anyway."

"Why is that?"

"Working. Or school. For years, it was both."

Rhys had been waiting for the opportunity to get some answers from her. "So how long were you in college? Harper said you just finished graduate school."

"Seven years. I switched my major at the end of my junior year from premed to psychology. That tacked on an extra year or so. Then I had to wait another semester to start graduate school." She made a noise that sounded like a chuckle of despair. "I know what you're thinking—who switches from premed to psychology, right?"

"Someone who doesn't want to be a doctor?" he answered gently. "Better you figure it out then than in the middle of med school."

The look of appreciation she gave him made his heart ache because it was so obviously laced with pain. Beneath her cheerful bravado there was unmistakable anguish. He wanted to fix it. "Why do you seem disappointed in yourself for being brave enough to do what was right for you?"

"It's complicated. At this point, I'm not sure if it was right for me. For one thing, my dad was extremely disappointed. He was so excited that I was going to be a doctor. It crushed him when I changed my mind."

"Why? Why doesn't he become a doctor if it means that much to him?"

Camile snuffled out a laugh. "Good point. My dad is a retired Coast Guard officer. He sees the world in black-and-white, good and bad, successful and not successful. My sisters are both unequivocally successful in his mind. Psychology is not a profession as far as he's concerned."

"Hmm. I'm not a biological parent, but I can say that as Willow's guardian and doting uncle, I just want her to be happy. Sure, I'd like for her to live up to her potential, but I realize that her idea of success and mine might not mesh."

"She's very lucky to have you. Remember those words if she someday tells you she wants to join the circus."

Rhys chuckled but stopped when he noted her troubled expression.

"My dad said that to me. He said, 'I'd be less disappointed if you told me you were going to become a circus acrobat than a psychology major.' That's how strongly he feels about it."

"That is rough."

"It was."

"But it's your life."

One side of her mouth pulled up like she

wanted to smile. "That's exactly what I told him. That, and that I did not need his approval. Or his help."

"Good for you." Rhys stopped near a patch of brush. Bending over, he picked two daisies and handed her one. "Wildflower, check."

Staring down at the flower, she brushed a gentle finger over the petals.

"So now you prove him wrong by being wildly successful."

Wincing a little, she said, "That would be nice, but…"

"But what? What are your plans? Are you looking for something full-time, maybe with benefits? What kind of job can you get with a master's degree in psychology? Or are you considering going on to get your PhD?"

Camile kept her attention on the flower, twirling the stem between her fingers and nibbling on her cheek like she was thinking this over. Just say it, he thought. *Talk to me. Tell me what your wicked friend wanted me to know. And then I'll fix it and ask you out on a real date. I will make you happy, and I'll never leave you.* All of which he realized made him sound slightly stalkerish. But it wasn't that. He just wanted to be with her and make her smile as much as possible and give her some of the joy she brought to everyone around her, especially him.

Finally, she sighed. Standing straight, she squared her shoulders and met his gaze. "Well, Rhys, here's the thing. I don't exactly have a plan. I do not have my master's degree. I um… I messed up on my thesis. And right now, the thought of doing it all over again makes me want to curl into a ball and hide under my bed. I've never really had a clear-cut career goal in mind…" Shrugging her shoulders, she winced. "A degree was important to me, but I could never decide what I wanted to do. You know, like how I wanted to spend my days? I like science and medicine but not enough to commit my life to a lab or a hospital, you know? I'm better at…moving around."

"Dancing," Rhys supplied.

"Well, sure, yeah, that's my true love. I will always dance in some capacity. But in real life, here I am, stuck in this limbo of part-time jobs with no benefits and—" She ended the sentence abruptly, and Rhys knew she was trying to decide how much to reveal. "And thinking about running off and joining the circus." Her attempt at a smile only wound up looking grim and sad.

"What do you mean? How did you mess up on your thesis? Specifically?"

"Why are you so curious about this?" she asked, clearly avoiding his question.

"I'm going to tell you exactly why, because as I'm certain you've already learned about me, I'm not great at subtlety. I'm sure it's obvious to you by now how much I enjoy being with you. And I don't enjoy most people. It's too difficult to even get to know them enough to try. They don't get me, so I don't bother. But you... You do seem to get me, or at least accept me for the way I am. And I like you, Camile. Very much. And I want to spend time with you under different circumstances, outside of dance lessons and stomach bugs."

CAMILE WASN'T SURE her heart had ever beat so loudly. Rhys McGrath had just confessed to *liking* her. So much for her knight's syndrome theory. And everything he claimed on her part was true: she liked him, and she understood him—or at least, she was on her way to that—and she wanted to spend time with him, too. Despite warning herself away from him and wishing otherwise. But she was also terrified and overwhelmed by...him. Silently, she cursed that awful, soul-shattering date. And the messed-up state that was currently her life.

"Rhys, I..." She swallowed nervously. Then began again, "You're right, I do like you. I'm not going to deny that. But my life is a mess right now. I am in no place to have a relationship with anyone, especially someone who so clearly has it all together like you."

"Is this your way of telling me you don't return my feelings? Because you don't need to make an excuse. If that's the case, please just say so. The truth is always preferable to me."

"No! I wouldn't do that. I'm an honest person. Maybe not as honest as you, but that's not it. I promise. I have so much…negative stuff going on right now."

His smile was gentle but unconvinced. "How bad could it be?"

"Trust me, it's bad. I've only touched on the highlights here."

"Do you want to provide me with some details?"

"No."

"Camile, sometimes when you're in the midst of unfortunate circumstances, things can seem much worse than they are."

"Is that so?" she asked dryly, growing annoyed by his indifference.

Missing her sarcasm, he seemed encouraged, and added, "Yes, maybe you just need some perspective."

"Perspective?" She frowned.

"Let me help you. If you tell me what's going

on, maybe I can help. If there's anything I can do for you, I'd like to—"

"Rhys," she interrupted firmly. "There's nothing you can do to help, and even if there were, I wouldn't want you to. You've already done enough for me. I appreciate it more than you could ever know. Taking care of me when I was sick, making me food, your kindness and concern, the job, everything. But I have so much going on right now, and I'm the only one who can solve my problems. Trust me—they're mine." *And a little bit yours, too, maybe.* But she didn't want to talk about that.

Camile had seen a young man approaching from the direction they'd come and assumed he'd keep walking. Instead, he stopped and peered deliberately at Camile. "Camile Wynn?"

"Yes, that's me."

He handed over a manila envelope. "Consider yourself served." Then he spun on his heel and marched away.

"Thank you!" she called after him with way too much enthusiasm. "Have a nice day." With a wry grin and one quirked brow, she faced Rhys and managed much more bravado than she felt. "So I'm being sued. Is that detailed enough for you?"

ALL DAY, CAMILE had been aware of the speculative glances Rhys was getting from townsfolk. Gathered on the grassy expanse of lawn at the city park where the scavenger hunt's after-party and award ceremony were being held, it was even more noticeable. It didn't seem to bother Rhys, who, now that a mob of people surrounded them, had clammed up. He hadn't left her side since they'd crossed the finish line. Willow was thrilled that they'd placed in the top half. As Harper predicted, her team had come first. Camile was fine with both Rhys's reticence and his proximity. Taking her turn at playing knight, she found she rather enjoyed the duty.

The official serving of her legal papers had waylaid their conversation with timing that was both completely perfect and embarrassingly unfortunate. It had made her point and rendered an answer to his question unnecessary. She tried to ignore the pang of disappointment at his obvious lack of follow-up. Why did she want him to try to change her mind when she wouldn't change it? She couldn't. It wouldn't be fair to him.

There'd been no point in trying to keep the lawsuit from him, but she'd only had time to give him an overview before an excited Willow had run up to them with objects and photos they'd sought. His outrage and derision at Bobby's allegations had cheered her considerably. If it only lasted for the afternoon, then so be it. Dwelling on what might have been would not clean up the chaos that was her life. Doing her best to make sure Willow had a good time was an excellent distraction and her current objective.

Rhys and Camile were on their way to a picnic table with heaping plates of steaming clams, crab and shrimp when an obviously drunk Sam Garr approached. Camile knew Sam. A year behind her in school, he'd been a football star neither destined for the pros nor a career in rocket science.

"Hey, you're that Rhys McGrath guy, aren't you?"

"Yes," Rhys said, stopping beside Camile.

Reaching out a hand, he said, "Sam Garr."

Rhys shook his hand. "Nice to meet you, Sam."

Sam tossed Camile one of those short, single head-bobs acknowledging her presence. "Hi, Camile. How ya doing?"

"Hey, Sam. I'm all right. How are you?"

But Sam was already zeroed back in on his intended target. Fixated and tense, he glowered at Rhys. "You're the guy who lives out on the lighthouse headland, right?"

"Yes."

Like a belligerent hitchhiker, he flipped a

thumb in the direction of a group of guys huddled nearby, most of whom Camile also recognized. Snickering ensued from the pack. Great, Camile thought, now packs of people were ganging up on him. "I'm hoping you can settle a little bet for my buddies and me."

Rhys seemed unfazed. "Doubtful," he said flatly.

"Doubtful," Sam repeated, his face twisted with confusion. "Why is that?"

"My guess is that you're going to ask me a question that is either A—designed to make me look like a fool, or B—none of your business. Therefore, my response to either type of question will fail to settle any bets."

And, here we go, thought Camile.

Sam went straight-up belligerent. "I've heard about you."

"Have you?"

"Yeah. Mr. Fancy-Pants Navy SEAL Super-Rich-Guy walking around town thinking he's better than everyone else."

"Don't believe everything you hear, Sam. I am an ex-SEAL. I do okay, but I wouldn't say I'm *super*rich. And I wear regular pants. Unlike you." Rhys's gaze flicked down and back up, and Camile wondered how he could put so much derision into a gesture.

Sam glanced down at his ridiculously low-riding baggy pants, the crotch drooping nearly to his knees. Snapping his head back up, he glowered at Rhys. "Are you insulting my pants, man?"

"Maybe."

"What?" he snapped.

"I don't think anyone over the age of sixteen should be wearing pants like that. They're a safety hazard. I hope you're not wearing those at work."

Twin spots of color flamed brightly on Sam's cheeks. "You know what I'm going to do?"

"Buy a belt?"

"I'm going to beat you into next week."

Camile rolled her eyes as Sam made a show of pushing up his sleeves.

"You might want to rethink that," Rhys calmly replied like he was cautioning a child to avoid stepping in a puddle or advising a friend about which entrée to choose. "You've already stated that you're aware of the fact that I'm a former navy SEAL. Not only will such an attempt on your part hurt you much more than it will me, but when I'm finished neutralizing you, I might be tempted to strangle you with your own pants. How would that look to your friends?"

Tense with concern, Anne had descended

upon them in time to catch this last exchange. "Rhys, can you come with me for a—"

"Here, take this." Camile handed Anne her plate. Then she belted out a laugh, clapped Sam on the shoulder and said, "Hey, Sam, remember that time back in high school when Sonny Dowling's sweatpants fell off in gym class?"

CHAPTER TEN

"Do you think I could at least get a cup of coffee?" Rhys sniffed the glass of wine Anne had just handed him. "Instead of this glorified vinegar?"

"No," Anne said with probably more patience than he deserved. "This is a wine tasting. You don't have to drink it." Anne took a sip from her glass. "Just hold on to the glass and pretend like you're having a good time."

"That's—"

"Please, just do it, Rhys."

In dutiful acquiescence, he lifted his glass and gave it a swirl like he knew what he was doing. "How long are we staying?"

"Three hours."

"Three hours!" Rhys checked the time on his watch so he could begin the countdown.

"Shh. Yes, this is the social hour with wine and appetizers, then there's the film screening, and after that is the dessert auction."

Breathing deeply, he reminded himself that at least the event was for a good cause. Sea

Barrel Winery was hosting the charity event to benefit a veterans' organization. He and Willow had baked and donated a cheesecake and a marionberry pie.

An attractive, slender woman in a sparkly dress sauntered over to them. She looked Anne up and down deliberately and declared, "Anne! You look fabulous. I'm so glad you could make it." Pretty with a strikingly pale complexion, the woman wore her black, silky-straight hair in a chin-length bob. Her silver-gray eyes matched her gown, and the deep red lipstick she wore stood out like a splash of color in a black-and-white photo.

"Hello, Gabrielle," Anne said. "Thank you. And thank you so much for the invitation. Everything is so lovely. I'd like you to meet my brother, Rhys McGrath. Rhys, this is Gabrielle Timmons. She and her family own Sea Barrel Winery." Rhys didn't miss the warning look that Anne passed him along with the introduction. She was still traumatized by the near miss of an encounter at the scavenger hunt with Angry Baggy-Pants. Admittedly, Camile had saved him there. A laughing Sam had leveled Rhys with a wary glare and backed down. His posse had joined them, laughing at Camile's remark, and they'd all spent a few minutes reminiscing about the high school PE mishap.

"Nice to meet you," Rhys said. "This setting is extraordinary." And it was. The winery sat on a craggy hillside with spectacular ocean views. This stretch of coastline was known for its windswept landscape and picturesque cliffs, which included some natural cave formations. The astute and industrious Timmons family made good use of the rugged terrain, aging and storing their wines and cheeses in the caverns while offering a picturesque backdrop for customers to enjoy. Their tours were nearly as popular as their wine.

Gabrielle beamed. "Thank you. It's a ton of hard work, but we sure do love it."

"I can imagine."

"We're thrilled that people are responding so positively to our newest vintage." Gesturing at his glass, she asked, "What do you think of the cabernet?"

Rhys glanced at the still-untasted wine. "I'm going to purchase an entire case," he answered diplomatically and hoped she didn't quiz him any further.

Beside him, Anne smiled like a proud sister.

"Thank you." Gabrielle's eyes flashed with appreciation and then traveled over him with what felt way too much like appreciation. Rhys hoped not. He had no interest in any woman who wasn't Camile. Whom he didn't get to see again until the next evening.

Gabrielle turned a sparkling smile on him and briefly pressed one palm flat against his arm. It was a quick gesture, but between that and her lingering perusal, Rhys feared the worst. "That's very generous. I'll have my assistant Molly see to it."

Careful not to make eye contact, he said, "It's a very good cause."

Anne asked a question about wine. Gabrielle launched into an explanation. A relieved Rhys tuned out their chatter and took the opportunity to study the room. To the untrained eye, the high open-beamed ceiling would resemble the timber-frame construction of his home. Knowledge and experience told Rhys the effect was purely aesthetic here. The space was attractively furnished with a pleasing mix of rustic and modern furnishings. Tall windows showcased the ocean view. Rhys estimated there were over a hundred people in attendance, milling around the grounds, checking out the desserts in the reception room and spilling outside across the deck. Anne had told him the amphitheater seated two hundred. Kyle and Harper were supposed to be attending, but he hadn't seen them yet. He hoped they showed up soon. Friendly faces would be appreciated.

Although Anne would tell him he needed to make new friends.

An older man holding a wine bottle in each hand used one to wave at Anne. Laughing, she stepped away to chat with him.

"So… Rhys…" Reaching out, Gabrielle draped a palm on his forearm again. This time she left it there. Rhys tried not to flinch. "Are you here with your wife?"

He answered with a simple "no" because he couldn't think past the desire to peel her hand away from his body. It made him itch with discomfort. These social outings would be so much easier if strangers wouldn't touch him.

"Are you married?" she asked. Nothing like getting to the point, he supposed.

"Uh, no." Avoiding her curious gaze, he backed away, essentially forcing her to pull her hand away. Flagging down a passing wait-person, he deposited his glass on a tray with a group of empties. He remained at arm's length, hoping the distance would discourage any further touching.

"Me, either." The pointed look she gave him felt predatory, and he suspected an uncomfortable question would be next. He hated these moments. He tried not to grimace when she asked, "Maybe we could get together some time? Talk about wine, maybe drink a bottle." She quirked a brow. "Or two?"

"No, thank you. Honestly, I don't like wine."

Lines creased her forehead as she studied him for a few seconds. Tacking on a teasing smile, she closed the distance he'd put between them and lowered her voice, "Well, we don't *have* to drink wine. But I bet I could change your mind."

"I sincerely doubt it."

"Is that a challenge, Rhys McGrath?"

How did she get a challenge out of that? She went on to describe her favorite cave formation and how just outside the entrance was a perfect spot for a picnic for two. Rhys glanced around hoping Anne was nearby to save him. Or maybe for Kyle or Harper to suddenly appear. What he found was better. So much better.

Camile.

Only a few feet away, and all Rhys could think about was getting to her as quickly as possible. She hadn't answered all his questions at the scavenger hunt. But she'd admitted to liking him, and he knew it was true. He could feel it. If issues were standing in their way, he would remove them. No matter how insurmountable she believed them to be.

"Rhys?"

Gabrielle was staring at him, and he realized he'd already taken a few steps away from her. Toward Camile. He paused to ask, "I'm sorry?"

"I asked you if that was a challenge? Are you up for a private wine tasting so I can change your mind?"

"No," he said. "No wine. No picnic. No challenge. No, thank you. Now, will you excuse me, Gabriella?" Then, without a backward glance, he turned and closed the few remaining steps that brought him next to Camile.

"I DIDN'T KNOW you were going to be here," a smiling Rhys said to a stunned Camile. Mouth close to her ear, he whispered, "I can't tell you how happy I am to see a friendly face. No, that's not exactly true. I'm ecstatic that it is specifically your face that I'm seeing right now."

The softness of his tone and the feeling behind his words made her cheeks go hot. "I didn't know I would be here, either. Harper invited me at the last minute. Kyle got stuck on a job. I had an earlier shift at Tabbie's, so here I am."

When she'd arrived a few moments prior, Camile had spotted Rhys and Anne, snagged a drink and then headed in their direction. They'd both been engaged in conversations, so she'd loitered around, waiting for the right moment to approach. She'd observed the interaction between Gabrielle and Rhys the way one does an impending train wreck. It was shocking and unbelievable and yet had happened so quickly she hadn't possessed the presence of mind to intercede.

After glancing around them to make sure she wouldn't be overheard, she lowered her voice and asked, "What was that?"

Camile liked how he looked at her; gaze slightly narrowed and traveling over her in a way that made her feel noticed and seen. Not in a bad way, but in a way that made her believe he was truly happy to see her.

"You look gorgeous. What was what?" he repeated absently, his eyes lingering on her mouth.

Heating thoroughly at the compliment, she glanced down at the sundress she'd hurriedly donned after Harper had shown up at her door. It was almost shabby and borderline too casual for the occasion, but she'd dressed it up with a pair of heels and arranged her hair into an elegant chignon. All her years of dance had made her a champion at the updo.

"Thank you. You brushed Gabrielle Timmons off like she was infected with a bad disease."

"She kept touching me…" Wincing slightly, he gave his head a little shake. "I don't like to be touched."

Hmm. Camile did not know this; she touched him often in dance lessons. Was he tolerating that for the sake of dancing? If so, she needed to dial that back.

"Are you aware that you called her Gabriell-*a*? She hates that."

"No *A* on there, huh? Shoot. I try to avoid using names when I'm not sure, which is most of the time. But Anne told me using names was a way to build rapport and get people to like me, so I thought I'd give it a shot. Was it that bad?"

"It was pretty rough. She's not my favorite person, but I actually felt a little sorry for her."

He pulled one shoulder up into a half shrug. "I didn't know what to do. I think she's interested in me." He delivered this insight with grave dismay.

"You think?" Camile quipped in a sarcastic tone. "And…?" she drawled when he didn't elaborate.

"I do not return the sentiment."

"I see." How was that possible? Gabrielle Timmons was gorgeous, classy and wealthy. Pretty much the most eligible bachelorette in

Pacific Cove. "And did she run into your car or kick your dog before she hit on you?"

Rhys paused, surprise flashing across his face a second before he laughed. She'd noticed he did that often when she teased him. Like he was playing the joke back in his mind, processing her words. "I was just being honest with her."

"You were certainly that."

With one thumb, he reached up and scratched his forehead before settling his gaze firmly on hers again. The earnestness, the desperation in his eyes as he searched her face sent her heart fluttering wildly inside her chest. "Unfortunately, I'm even worse at socializing than I am at dancing. Despite the way it often appears and what my sister believes, I don't mean to treat people badly. I hope you don't think I'm a total jerk."

That was when Camile was struck with several vitally important facts. The first was that he didn't intend to be rude. There was no doubt in her mind that women hit on him constantly. Truly, he was one of the best-looking men Camile had ever met in her whole life. And there was this air of mystery about him whether he wanted it or not. If he rebuffed every interested woman with this same dismal amount of finesse, it explained a lot of the problem concerning his reputation around town.

The next revelation was that while Rhys McGrath didn't seem to care what anyone thought about him, apart from his family, he cared what *she* thought about him. Camile didn't know how to feel about that. She'd been on the receiving end of his abruptness in a manner way worse than he'd just perpetrated with Gabrielle. And now that she knew that wasn't really who he was—how he meant to be—it made her wonder about that date. She needed to think about this.

But first, she needed to try something.

"Hey," she said with an encouraging smile. "Your dancing is coming along just fine." Then she reached out to touch his hand. His fingers felt almost frantic as they curled around hers and held on tight. Giving her the answer she sought. Being touched by her was okay, even off the dance floor. And she realized that she desperately wanted to hold on to him, too, to touch him, offer him some of the same comfort he'd given her.

"And I don't think you're a jerk." After giving him a reassuring squeeze, she released his hand.

"Unfortunately, you're one of the few, huh?" With a grim smile he looked away, disappointment stealing over his features. Which only made her want to take his hand again. Squinting across the room, he expelled a breath and muttered, "Anne is going to kill me."

Camile followed his gaze to where Anne was chatting with the principal of the high school, the mayor and the owner of The Shoals Hotel. Camile had no idea what he meant by that. Did he mean that Anne would be upset with him because he'd been abrupt with Gabrielle? He hadn't been *that* bad. Gabrielle had come on pretty strong. Back in high school, Nina's boyfriend had cheated on her with Gabrielle, a pattern she'd established and never relinquished. Was Anne trying to fix him up with her? A flash of jealousy flared inside her at the thought. Despite his lack of interest, she had no right to be jealous, especially when she'd told him she wasn't ready for a relationship.

He gestured at her mug. "What are you drinking?"

"Coffee. I don't like wine, either."

A slow smile spread across his face and made her forget about asking him anything for now.

"GOOD MORNING, MCGRATHS," Rhys's attorney, Bailey Leeds, said striding into her office where Rhys and Anne were already seated across from her desk. Pulling out her chair, she sat, scooted close to the desk and tucked her sleek brown hair behind her ears. "How goes Operation Reputation Recovery?" she asked, her shrewd gaze shifting between him and Anne.

"Not great," Anne said. "I'll be honest. I thought that getting Rhys out into the community and introducing him to people would help. But so far, the gossip seems to have gotten worse. Of course, it would help if he would quit insulting people and calling them by the wrong names."

"Anne, let it go already," Rhys said. "I apologized to Gabri-*elle*." And he had. When they'd left for the evening, he'd thanked her, apologized—using her correct name—and then purchased *two* cases of expensive wine that he was now stuck with. The interaction had been stiff and awkward, but still, he was on record.

Bailey frowned. "How much worse?"

Anne ticked items off on her fingers. "Bigamist, drug dealer, commune leader, hit man, serial killer, dogfighter, scrooge. I could list the expletives being used to describe him, too, but that seems unnecessary. If it wasn't for Camile at the last two outings, I don't know what

I would have done. Rhys almost got into a fight at the scavenger hunt before Camile swooped in and saved the day." To Rhys, she said, "You know, you—"

"Dogfighting?" Rhys interrupted. "Seriously? I don't even own a dog. And I have nothing against Christmas! I love Christmas."

"Hey." Anne raised both her hands in the defensive palms-up gesture. "Don't glare at me. I'm just telling Bailey what we've heard. Between Camile and me, we cover a lot of ground."

Bailey cocked her head to one side, and drawled, "Camile...?"

"Camile Wynn. Rhys's dance instructor turned friend," Anne explained. "She knows a lot of people in the community. She works several part-time jobs in gossipy places. Her sister Nina owns a berry farm and is very social. Her sister Aubrey and brother-in-law Eli are Coast Guard. Very active in the community. Camile has sort of been my ears on the ground, so to speak."

Rhys frowned at Anne, who shrugged. "What? I need to know what we're facing."

He was uncomfortable with the notion that Camile was hearing these rumors. She hadn't mentioned any of them to him.

An irritated Rhys refocused on Bailey.

"How important is this, though, really? Does a bunch of gossip have any true bearing on me retaining custody of our niece? Custody that's already been granted to me legally?"

Bailey shrugged. "It's difficult to say. In all honesty, your chances would be better if you weren't a single guy. Anne's commitment to move to Pacific Cove might help, but a wife or a stable girlfriend would be ideal. You're not dating anyone, right?"

"No," Rhys said.

"Well, if you decide to, please make sure it's only one woman at a time, that she's drug-free, and not in any trouble with the law."

Rhys nodded, secure in the knowledge that Camile's frivolous civil suit didn't count as legal trouble.

"Do you have any idea what Vanessa's parents will say? As of this morning, they still haven't submitted a statement."

"I don't know. Evan loved them. I've always gotten along well with them. Heather was kind of the black sheep of the family. Still, it was a surprise when she decided to fight for custody."

Bailey thought for a moment. "So you don't know if they knew that Vanessa and Evan intended for you to have custody of Willow? If they were shocked and outraged by the terms of the will, that could bode unfavorably for you."

Rhys did have this in his favor. "Yes, they knew. Or, at least, Evan told me that they knew. After his first stroke, we were joking about it in the hospital. I arrived at the hospital first, and he said if Vanessa died on the way, then I'd need to get Willow to her soccer game the next day. Then he told me that they'd updated their will to ensure that I would have legal custody." He glanced at his sister, who had tears shining in her eyes. "Anne came into the room right then, and Evan asked Anne if she would help me raise Willow. Of course, we joked about it at the time. You know, like siblings do?"

Anne agreed, "This is true. I knew. Our parents knew. Evan told us that everyone knew—including Heather."

"He mentioned her by name? You're positive?"

"Positive," Anne and Rhys replied at the same time.

Anne added, "Evan said they'd announced it at Easter dinner with Vanessa's parents and Heather."

"That's good news. If they'd been against you having custody, Evan probably would have mentioned it."

"I still don't understand why the fact that

they named me in their will as Willow's guardian isn't enough."

"I know. And most of the time it is. As it should be." Bailey offered him a commiserative sigh. "But there are times… There was a woman in Maryland who left the care of her three small children to the family dog. In her will."

"She was obviously crazy."

"No, she wasn't—that's my point. At least not that anyone could prove. She earned a six-figure salary as a sales rep. Friends and co-workers and the pastor of her church all adored her. By all accounts, she was a productive member of society. Her children appeared to be nice, intelligent and well adjusted. The dog was an agility champion and exceptionally brilliant, according to his trainer. But not even he believed the dog was fit to raise the kids. Fortunately, as in this case, the courts have the discretion of something known as the best interests of the child."

"Point taken," Rhys said.

"My advice is to keep doing what you're doing. Eventually, people will start to see the real you. Or at least come to accept the real you, the way that the people who know you and love you do. If that doesn't work, at least you are proving that you're *able* to socialize.

Heather's assertion makes it sound like you're a clinically diagnosed agoraphobe. We need to show that that is not the case."

Rhys sighed. Anne nodded thoughtfully.

They thanked Bailey and left. Anne was uncharacteristically quiet in the car. Rhys knew she had something on her mind.

They were almost home when she asked, "What about Camile?"

"What about her?"

"Why is it that you can socialize with her?"

"I don't know." He shrugged a shoulder. "She's different. I know her. She…knows me."

"She hasn't known you very long."

No, she hadn't.

He could feel Anne staring at him. When he didn't respond, she said, "You're different when you're with her."

Rhys couldn't disagree. There was definitely something about Camile. He'd been heading into a fight with Baggy-Pants. He hadn't wanted it, but the guy had been gearing up to throw a punch, and Rhys would have had no choice. She defused the matter in record time.

"Your lack of denial tells me that I've nailed this. You like her."

"Of course I like her. Everyone likes her. Somehow she manages that feat without even trying."

"How much do you like her?"

"Anne, where are you going with this?"

"You heard what Bailey said. This custody thing would all be so much easier if you were married or if you had a girlfriend."

"But I don't."

"But perhaps you could."

"Are you suggesting that I date Camile to help secure custody of Willow? Or, better yet, whisk her off to Vegas for a movie-style fake marriage?"

"It sounds bad when you put it that way."

"What other way is there?"

"The way that gives you the edge you need over Heather."

"The answer is an unequivocal no. It's dishonest, and I would never use her that way. Besides, she doesn't want to date me."

"Rhys, I can tell she likes you."

"I didn't say she doesn't like me. I said she doesn't want to date me." At the scavenger hunt she'd told him as much. But at the wine tasting she'd taken his hand. So maybe... Had her "messy life" just been an excuse? He intended to find out. Which he planned to do by helping her solve some of these external issues complicating her life. Just the mere thought of her rejection made him feel empty inside.

"Do you want to date her?"

Heat crept up the back of his neck. He knew Anne wasn't trying to torture him, but it felt like it. He wanted to do more than date her. He wanted to marry her and live happily-ever-after, but that would also sound movie-esque. And probably cause his sister undue concern. But trying to explain what was going on between him and Camile was too complicated. And none of his sister's business.

"That's irrelevant. I understand the concept you're proposing, but I don't want to do it. Even if I wanted to pretend-date her, we both know I'm not good enough at pretending to pull something like that off."

"Hmm. True. If this endeavor has taught us anything, it's that you are a terrible, *terrible* actor."

CHAPTER ELEVEN

"GORGEOUS." ANNE'S GAZE bounced around the vast expanse of sandy shoreline. "What a great idea. Being so close to the beach is still something of a novelty for me. I love it."

Earlier, Anne had texted to see if Camile could get together after her morning shift at Blue Carafe "to talk about something." Hoping everything was all right, Camile had immediately agreed and suggested the location. They'd met at the gazebo and descended the wide cement stairs that emptied onto the beach.

Strolling toward the water's edge, Camile stopped to slip off her shoes. "Me too, believe it or not. Growing up, we always lived close to the ocean. You think I'd be over it, but I'm not. I don't want to go swimming in it like my sister Aubrey." She paused to add a wry grin. "But I love pretty much everything else about it, the scenery, the sand, the salty air, even the temperamental weather."

"Rhys, too. He's always loved it. When he was about twelve, and he told Mom and Dad that he wanted to be a SEAL, they thought he meant an actual seal because he was obsessed with the ocean. Imagine their concern over their seemingly intelligent twelve-year-old fantasizing about being a marine mammal."

Camile laughed. "You can see that about him in the way he built his house, can't you? And I don't just mean because it's situated on a cliff overlooking the ocean. It's the way that he captured the views with the ocean as the focal point. No matter where you are, you can either see the ocean, or you're just a few steps away from being able to see it. And Rhys almost always stands or sits where he can see it."

Anne slipped her a quick sideways glance. "He did that very thing on purpose. He went to incredible lengths to make sure of it, including endless measuring and calculating and laying out of the floor plan." After a chuckle, she asked, "Did he tell you about it?"

"No, he didn't. I just…"

"Know him," Anne finished her sentence with complete certainty. And then added with what sounded like a twinge of awe, "You know my brother and that's no easy feat."

"I don't know about *that,* but I've definitely observed a few things about the guy."

Anne's smile held the soft edge of satisfaction. "I'm going to ask you a question, and I want you to answer as truthfully as possible, okay?"

"Okay," Camile agreed slowly, feeling a flutter of nerves without knowing exactly why. "Does this have to do with what you wanted to talk to me about?"

"It does."

"Ask away."

"What do you think of Rhys?"

Oh. Good question. How did she explain to Rhys's sister that she'd grudgingly accepted that she liked the guy she'd hated for the last two years? "Um…"

"Pretend he's not my brother. I should have prefaced the question with that proviso in the first place. I promise there's a reason why I want to know. So go ahead and tell me how you would describe him to someone else."

That was easier. "Kind, interesting, thoughtful, talented and completely brilliant. I think he's the smartest person I've ever personally met, and… But he's also…"

"Rude, annoying, odd?" Anne suggested.

"No," she answered firmly. "Honest, shy, eccentric—yes. Annoying—absolutely not. And, I mean…"

"Go ahead." She waved a hand, encouraging Camile to continue.

"Well, it's difficult to see at first and even

harder to explain. But the way I see it, him, is that his honesty collides with the shyness and produces this awkward guy who then comes across as abrupt." She cocked her head, contemplating her description. "And, I'll concede, that sometimes comes across as rude."

"Uh-huh," Anne said, nodding in agreement.

"The mystique that has emerged around him due to his reclusive habits doesn't help matters. The property, the lighthouse, the bunker—him being off-limits only heightens the collective curiosity. People don't understand. They want to know why and who he is and what he's up to. Then there's the added difficulty of him being so…physically appealing. People wonder how a guy that nice-looking could not be in love with himself. But for Rhys, his looks are a liability. He doesn't want to draw attention to himself. He doesn't want attention, period. And he doesn't like getting it for the wrong reason, does he?"

"No, he doesn't."

"I never in a million years thought I could feel bad for someone who looks like him. I feel bad about my own preconceived notions where he was concerned." Camile chuckled and shook her head. "Is that a thing? Beautiful-people problems?"

Anne grinned appreciatively at her. "You're psych major is showing."

"Probably, but I'm not sure that it makes me any more insightful."

Anne bent over to pick up an empty limpet shell. "You like him."

It was more of a statement than a question, but Camile answered it anyway, "Yes, I do."

"How would you feel about spending more time with him?"

"Um…" Anxiety constricted her chest, a bitter leftover she knew from the date. But it was also coupled with the stark realization that she wished she was in a place where she could explore a relationship with him. She'd been thinking about this, and the simple fact was that she wasn't ready for a relationship with anyone, especially not Rhys. If she was, she would want it to be Rhys, but what she'd told him held true: no way would she foist her problems onto him, no matter how much he claimed he wanted to help.

The "helping" made her slightly uncomfortable. She'd witnessed his take-charge attitude when she'd been sick. But she'd noticed he hadn't mentioned another word about helping or dating since they'd had the conversation and she'd been served with Bobby's lawsuit right before his eyes. Presumably, she'd managed to scare him away, and that was a good thing. Even if it didn't feel very good.

Anne exhaled a loud, breathy chuckle and said, "I'm sorry. Apparently, Rhys isn't the only one who can be a little abrupt. I'm not usually. It's part of my job to be diplomatic and persuasive, but I'm doing a terrible job of it here. It's different when something is so... personal and important."

This wasn't the first time Camile had felt like she was missing something important where this family was concerned.

Anne stopped walking and faced her. Camile mirrored her actions, and Anne said, "I'd like for you to spend more time with my brother."

"I don't...you mean, like dating?"

"If that's what you want, that'd be fantastic! It would help so much."

What! "Anne, maybe I wasn't clear enough before. Or maybe there is some sort of sister-brother mind distortion going on between your optical nerve and your brain that doesn't allow you to see him clearly. Rhys is gorgeous. Like a fairy-tale prince. And last night, the most beautiful woman in, in...in all the kingdom made it very clear to Rhys that she'd like to date him. He could date any woman he wanted."

"What if he wants you?"

"He doesn't," she answered quickly and then tried to explain. "He definitely… It's possible he may have thought he did for a brief moment, but that was before…"

"Before what?" Anne asked with blatant curiosity.

Camile knew she was waiting for an explanation, but she held her ground and answered with an ambiguous, "Before he knew me better." Shaking her head, she swallowed nervously and said, "It's difficult to explain, but he knows I'm not interested in a relationship. I do like him, and I'm enjoying teaching him how to dance. He's a great student, just like you promised. And he's a fun guy to spend time with."

"Huh." She frowned. "Rhys told me this morning that you didn't want to date him, but I didn't believe him."

"If you discussed this already, that means Rhys doesn't think this is a good idea, either."

"No, he knows *dating* is a good idea, in theory. Our attorney told him that. He doesn't like the idea of dating you for the sole purpose of improving his reputation."

"Wait a minute, your attorney? Anne, what is going on?"

Gazing out toward the water, Anne nibbled

on her lower lip, and then seemed to make a decision. "What did Rhys tell you about Willow?" she asked quickly. "About her living with Rhys?"

"That she's your niece. Her parents, your brother and his wife, have both passed away. Rhys is her legal guardian. And he's learning to dance for her cotillion, for the opening father-daughter dance."

"But nothing about Willow's aunt Heather, or the lawsuit?"

"No…" Lawsuit? Camile felt a swirl of dread forming right at her core.

"Legally, Rhys has custody. But Heather, Vanessa's sister, is contesting the will and suing for custody. She's trying to take Willow away from him, from us."

A bolt of shock ran through her. "What? But why? If Evan and Vanessa wanted Rhys to raise her, why would she do this?"

Dread and confusion gave way to anger when Anne explained, "Her claim is that Rhys is unfit to raise Willow. That he lives a highly unusual and reclusive lifestyle. That his behavior is questionable. Shutting himself, and Willow, away from the world would be detrimental to her well-being… Et cetera."

"That's completely ridiculous and unfair! It's not like he's a weirdo hermit or something."

Although, she had heard that very term to describe him at the wine tasting yesterday. Frustration twisted inside her at the injustice and the stress he must be feeling.

That was when it all came together: the sudden social outings, odd conversations between Rhys and Anne, the seemingly exaggerated reactions to situations. "That's why he's been going to these events, isn't it? Dinners and parties and the fund-raiser? To prove that he isn't these things?"

"Pretty much. It's all part of a larger plan to improve his reputation and show that he's an active, productive member of the community. But it's not going quite like I planned."

"I see." And she did. She'd been listening to the gossip herself and reporting to Anne what she heard, with no idea about why Anne needed to know. Or why it was so important. This was way more serious than she'd imagined. No wonder Rhys had backed off when he found out about her lawsuit. Likely he'd realized what Camile already knew: he didn't need her baggage weighing him down, too. Not when he was grappling with a lawsuit of his own, one that was much more important than what she was facing.

"What does Willow want?"

"She wants to stay with Rhys. She's old

enough to voice her opinion, but Bailey says the court isn't required to consider it. Especially if Heather can prove that Rhys is unfit."

"Unfit?" Frustration ground into her along with the mention of that word again. "Are you kidding me?" No matter how many people he offended or dates he'd abandoned, he did not deserve this. And poor Willow. As if the child hadn't suffered enough trauma in her life. Now there was a custody battle waging over her. It had taken Camile about two seconds to see how much Willow adored her uncle, and vice versa. It had only taken her slightly longer to ascertain the depth of Rhys's love and devotion.

"I know." Anne scraped at the sand with the toe of her shoe. "That's why I've been dragging him around town asking him to pretend to be someone he's not. He's trying so hard. But he's miserable, and he's very bad at schmoozing and making friends." One hand flipped up toward Camile. "Well, you've seen him in action. Evan was the same way. But with Rhys, there is the added problem of him being virtually incapable of subterfuge."

"He does give new meaning to the term 'honest to a fault,' doesn't he?"

Anne barked out an approving laugh. "I've told him that very thing many times. Yesterday, the attorney mentioned that in these cases, it can help to have a wife or a steady girlfriend. I started thinking about how much smoother his interactions have been recently. You saved him at the scavenger hunt and then again at the wine tasting. That's when it dawned on me. It's you. He's different with you, more relaxed, more…himself. The real Rhys. The one I know and the one you've gotten to know. The man we need for other people to see. He smiles when he's with you."

Camile couldn't disagree. Rhys did seem better when she was with him. His demeanor was less stiff, his speech not quite as abrupt, and he did smile more—all of this making him appear friendlier. Camile had introduced him to many people last night, and she'd only cringed at his remarks a few times. Even then, she'd been able to help clarify his meaning and smooth things over.

"Anne, I'd love to help. I would. I already adore Willow, and I can't stand to think about her or Rhys, any of you, having to go through this, but I'm not sure what you want me to do, exactly?"

Reaching into the bag strapped over her shoulder, Anne removed a piece of paper. "I have a list of outings and things that I'd like him to participate in. The dates and times are all on there."

"But if Rhys isn't comfortable having me as a fake girlfriend, I don't see how this would work."

"Well, you're already real friends, right?"

"Yes." That, she could both accept and admit.

With an easy shrug, Anne said, "That's all you need to be. Just go with him to these events and activities and do what you did last night. You know practically everybody in this town. I've asked around, and I doubt there's anyone as well liked as you are. Introduce him around, help him navigate it all."

Camile studied the list. "Wow. This is a lot. Honestly, I don't know how I'd fit all this in. Evenings are tough. Even without checking my calendar, I can tell you that I have to work on most of these nights teaching dance classes or waiting tables at Tabbie's. And Saturday and Sunday afternoons, I'm at the bowling alley."

"Is there any way you could quit Tabbie's and the bowling alley?"

"I'm so sorry, Anne. I can't afford to do that."

"No, I mean, I'll pay you to quit those jobs and work for me. Double what you're making now."

"You want to pay me to be your brother's friend?"

"Yes. But let's not call it that. Let's call it compensation for lost wages. And we can't let Rhys know that I'm paying you. He'd never agree. In fact, we'll have to be careful about how we go about this."

Camile studied the list again and thought. Hal would be disappointed, but she could appease him by working one weekend day, especially if Jason worked out like she suspected he would. She'd want to stay on the schedule at Tabbie's, but she could reduce her hours and possibly trade for lunch shifts. What was she thinking? This felt…extreme. And yet she knew Anne was right; she could help. She wanted to help. Another part of her wanted to agree for selfish reasons, too. Because who was she kidding? She wanted to spend time with him, to protect him from the gossipmongers and bullies in this town who misunderstood him. And clearly Anne was desperate. What if she said no and Anne asked someone else to do it? Like Gabrielle.

"Please, Camile. I can see you're considering it. You know I'm right about this. I need help. Rhys needs help. Willow needs to stay with us. Rhys needs you. We all need you."

CAMILE GATHERED HER courage as Rhys led her around the dance floor. He seemed stoic and thoughtful and maybe even a little sad. And no wonder. An ache formed in the pit of her stomach at the reminder of the stress and worry she now knew he was feeling.

After a complete rotation, she dredged up a gentle smile and said, "You are doing fabulously."

His answer was a relieved grin that made her want to hug him. "I am, kind of, huh?"

"Yes," she confirmed with a chuckle. "I can tell you've been practicing. Anne said you guys were thinking about going to the Chowder Challenge on Saturday. She needs to go to Portland for work. I was planning on going. Do you want to go with me?"

He stopped moving but kept his arms around her.

Staring up at him, she asked, "Why did you stop?"

"I can't talk and dance at the same time."

"I think if you'd let me play some music, you'd find that easier."

"I wouldn't." Rhys sighed and let his arms drop to his sides. "Then there would be one more thing for me to keep track of. Stepping, counting *and* music."

"Music brings it all together."

"Maybe for you."

"You do realize you're going to have to dance with music at some point, right?"

"Of course."

"Can we put a timeline on that?"

Slowly, his gaze narrowed in on her as if thinking it over.

As was often the case, his response seemed to come from the intersection of left field and outer space. "What if I wore earplugs?"

Camile stared up at him, ready to laugh, but then realized he might not be joking. "You want to wear earplugs while you're dancing?" she attempted to clarify.

"Yes. If I wore earplugs, the music would be muted enough that it wouldn't distract me. I could count out the steps. Deaf people do it—the counting, I mean. I doubt they wear earplugs."

Camile folded her arms over her chest. "Yes, they do count, but you're not deaf. So what's the deal?"

Shifting on his feet, he shoved his hands into his pockets and said, "I don't enjoy music the way most people do."

She recalled him mentioning this before but hadn't thought he'd meant it then, either. Pausing, she pondered this revelation before asking, "What is it that you hear that you don't like?"

"Noise. Chaos in my head. It's distracting, but not in a good way."

"Interesting."

Shoulders lifting, he cringed a little. "I'm sorry."

"Why are you sorry?"

"Because I know you like it."

"I do, but the fact that you don't is not something to apologize for. I'm sure there are things that you like that I don't."

"This is a strange one, though. I've found myself apologizing for it my entire life. I've been stalling because I didn't want to tell you. Stalling is kind of like lying, and so that's been bothering me, too."

"Why? Is there something I've said or done that makes you think I would judge you for this?"

"Of course not."

"Good." She added a sincere, encouraging smile. "Don't worry. We'll fix this. Let me do some research."

He looked stricken by her words.

"What's the matter?"

"It's a neurological condition. It can't be fixed."

There were times when she couldn't help herself; she had to tease him. Scrunching her face into a mock look of thoughtful skepticism, she asked, "Are you sure? Not even with brain surgery?"

"No, it's not considered a medical issue. As far as I know, there's no elective procedure, either."

"Rhys!" Camile reached out and gave his arm a squeeze. "Would you lighten up about this? I was joking. I meant that we'll find a way to work around it."

"Oh." A slow smile spread across his face. "You're taking this so much better than I thought you would. I was afraid you'd like me less because of it."

"You know all that computer equipment that you have set up in your office?"

"Yes."

"Just looking at it makes my eyes glaze over. If you forced me to sit down and learn how to use it, I would probably cry. Do you think less of me because of that?"

"No."

"If anything, I think even more highly of you for taking on this dancing project under the circumstances."

"I would do anything for Willow."

Admiration and affection welled inside her. His devotion, his love for his niece, left her a little awed. It was exactly what she needed to hear to dispel the lingering doubts she had about the plan she and Anne had devised. No one could possibly love that child more than Rhys. Camile would do whatever she could to make sure he got to do exactly that.

"Now, do you want to go to the Chowder Challenge with me or not?"

"I have no idea what that is, but honestly, I don't care. I'll go anywhere with you."

"In that case—"

"Almost anywhere," he amended. "No concerts or karaoke." With a wink and that grin that made her heart smile, he pulled her back into his arms and started counting.

CHAPTER TWELVE

CAMILE WAITED IN the reception area of her attorney's office and mentally calculated the amount of money in her checking account. Even with Rhys's dance lessons and Anne's future payments, no amount of adding and subtracting could conjure the funds necessary to afford this fiasco. Even if she won, and Bobby had to pay her legal fees, the ordeal would take months to conclude. Bobby was suing her for loss of income and defamation of character. If she lost and added the judgment to her student loan debt, it came to more than she could ever dream of paying off.

A mountain of debt before the age of thirty. She'd never recover. As it was, all she had was an unfinished master's degree in a field where decent-paying jobs required at least that. If she'd stuck to her original plan and become a doctor, at least she'd have the means to pay off her medical school bills. *Don't go there*, she told herself. She didn't want to be a doctor. Then again, she didn't know if she wanted to be a psychologist, either.

Despair flooded her thoughts. How had her life come to this? Tears burned and pooled in her eyes. Even though Nina had been sworn to secrecy, it was only a matter of time before Aubrey, and therefore her dad, found out about the lawsuit. The thought of facing her dad's disappointment again was nearly unbearable. Thank goodness, her parents were still on vacation. It was easy to dodge phone calls and fake that everything was fine when they did converse.

In her heart, she knew she was a good person. She didn't deserve this. But bad things happened to good people all the time; everyone knew that. Rhys's situation was a perfect example. Those things only defined you if you let them. She would not let this define her. That philosophy might be something of a platitude, but for now, it would have to be enough. That, and the fact that her agreement with Anne meant she was officially engaged in something positive. A little good to balance out the bad. Spending time with Rhys without the added pressure of a relationship was a bonus.

Tricia, Bailey's assistant, looked up from her desk. "Camile? Bailey will see you now."

Rhys GRINNED WHEN his friend Brandon Sawyer answered his call, "Rhys! Buddy! How are you? Are you in town? Please tell me you're in town and you have time for a golf game tomorrow. I need to play against someone who challenges me, but who I can still beat."

"Sorry, man, I'm at home in Pacific Cove." Rhys admired the view from his living room. The sight of the ocean stretching endlessly before him never failed to ground him, calm him, make him grateful and remind him to keep life in perspective.

"How long has it been since you left that home of yours?"

"Day before yesterday."

"The grocery store doesn't count."

"I spent the evening at a wine tasting, film festival, dessert auction fund-raiser. Tomorrow, I'm going to a chowder cook-off." *And tonight, I have a dance lesson.* But that felt like more than he wanted to share at the moment, probably ever.

"Liar."

"You know very well that's one thing I'm not. I'm serious, you wouldn't recognize me lately. I am a veritable social butterfly. Butterfly might be overstating. More like socially awkward moth?"

Brandon barked out a laugh. "No, you already said butterfly. I like butterfly," he joked. "You're too pretty to be a moth. But if you are going out, does that mean it's with a lady friend?"

"It does." Rhys didn't bother to clarify the fact that he hadn't technically gone to the wine tasting with Camile. But he'd spent the evening glued to her side, and she didn't seem to mind. Then, this morning, she'd invited him to the chowder thing. Progress. Which made him think her feelings for him might be overriding her protestations. Regardless, he was going to eliminate as many of these obstacles as he could. Starting now.

"Well." Brandon paused. "I can honestly say I've never looked forward to meeting another human being as much as I'm looking forward to meeting this woman. But mostly, I can't wait to tell Jane."

"Ah, good. I'm glad you brought up your wife, who is smart and beautiful and way too good for you. She is the reason I'm calling. How is my favorite English professor?" It hadn't been difficult to find out which college Camile had attended. When he'd learned it was St. Killian's, the same university where Jane worked, it had seemed like a good starting point.

"Tenured and pregnant. And married, too, in case you forgot that part."

Rhys laughed. Brandon had met Jane at a baseball game. He'd been with Rhys and a few other SEAL buddies. Initially, Jane had been interested in Rhys. A preference that had lasted only until Brandon began telling jokes. "Congratulations, my friend! I'm seriously thrilled for you guys. I'm coming to Portland soon, for sure. We need to celebrate."

"Only if you promise me a round of golf and bring your lady friend. I want to meet the woman who has captured my lonely butterfly friend's heart."

"All right. That's enough. Is your wife home? I need to ask her a favor."

"TABBIE'S SEAFOOD CHOWDER has won best chowder for the last several years. It's the pride of Pacific Cove." Camile handed Rhys a steaming cup filled with a sample from Surf's Up Grill, a restaurant located several miles down the coast. She'd informed him on the way that the annual competition was held in nearby Remington, but entrants traveled from locations all along the coasts of Oregon and Washington, and even northern California. Chefs prepared a pot of chowder for the judges and vats more for festivalgoers to purchase and sample.

Rhys dipped a spoonful and tried a bite.

"What do you think?" An aproned man behind the table in the booth asked him. "Best chowder of the day so far, right?"

Too much thyme and rosemary and there aren't enough clams, Rhys opened his mouth to say and simultaneously glimpsed Camile's pointed expression. How could she say so much with just a look? It reminded him of Anne.

Rhys thought for a long second and went with "Interesting choice of spices."

"Hey, thanks, man." The guy beamed. "My grandfather invented this recipe. He always used fresh spices, so that's what I do."

"I can tell," Rhys added. "It's very…obvious."

Camile ushered him away as another group of eager chowder samplers approached.

"Well done," she said. "I could tell you didn't like it, but he couldn't—that's the point."

"I didn't like it. It tasted like a hot thyme-and-rosemary smoothie."

Camile laughed. "I am so glad you didn't say that to him. Ready for the next one?"

"Yes, this is fun. Willow would have enjoyed it."

Willow had flown back to South Carolina the day before for her final round of practice.

"She seems excited about the ball, so that's good."

Rhys smiled down at her. "She does. And that reminds me about something I want to ask you."

"Of course."

"You don't have to say yes. I know you're busy."

"I've lightened my schedule a bit." Camile didn't feel quite right about keeping the reason from him. But Anne insisted. Anne was paying her to make time for Rhys, and she wouldn't be able to do so otherwise. She'd drastically reduced her overall work hours, switched to two lunch shifts at Tabbie's and retained three mornings at Blue Carafe, mostly so she could keep her finger on the pulse of town gossip.

"That bodes well for me, then. I was wondering if you'd want to go to South Carolina with Anne and me for Willow's ball?"

"Really?" she repeated, not bothering to squelch her eagerness.

"Yes. I would feel so much better about the dancing if you were there. I know you don't like taking time off work, but maybe—"

"Yes, Rhys," she interrupted with a happy smile. "I would love to go to South Carolina with you."

"BAILEY, I KNOW that Camile Wynn is your client, too."

Bailey did an excellent stone-faced attorney visage. She used it on him now. "Rhys, you know very well information about who may or may not be a client falls under attorney-client confidentiality. Is that what this meeting is about? Because I'm billing you the minimum regardless."

Rhys leaned back in the chair where he sat across from Bailey's desk and crossed one leg over the other, ankle on knee. "Camile told me about the lawsuit."

"Privilege," she shot back.

"Are you aware that Bobby Veroni uses fillers and ungraded beef in his taco meat, but advertises it as one hundred percent organic?"

Bailey huffed out an exasperated breath. "Are you dating Camile Wynn?"

"Would it matter if I was?"

"I specifically warned you against getting involved with someone who was in trouble with the law."

"A frivolous civil suit is not trouble with the law."

"I know." Bailey sighed and rubbed a hand across her brow. "I'm torn here. I cannot discuss this with you."

"Can you recommend a private investigator?"

"The best ones are not cheap."

"I'd like the best one in the entire state. Can you tell me who that is?"

Bailey stared at him for a long moment, indecision evident on her face. "I'll give you three names." Sliding a notepad close, she began to write. "These are in order of who I'd call first."

"Thank you."

She tore the paper from the pad and handed it over. "I'd feel sorry for Bobby if he didn't deserve it so much."

"I apologize for the cut in pay that could conceivably result from this endeavor where you're concerned."

"Don't worry about me. She doesn't deserve this. And if you make this go away, that will be payment enough."

Rhys nodded.

"Rhys, I hope you…" She started to say more and then stopped. Finally, she settled for a resigned smile. "Camile is a lucky woman."

Rhys could only hope that she saw it that way, too.

LAURA HAD BEEN relentless in wanting to make up for her untimely departure from the bowling alley a couple of weeks before. Camile had suggested meeting for lunch at her favorite brewpub in Astoria, both because her evenings were now booked solid and because it would give her some control over the length of the visit. She and Rhys were attending a semiformal fund-raising dinner for the mayor tonight, and she wanted plenty of time to get ready.

The pub was housed in an old converted fishing warehouse on the Columbia River. Sheet metal covered the walls of the spacious interior and the floor consisted of a thick slab of concrete. Camile thought the impossibly high ceiling was its best feature, with its eye-catching tangle of copper pipes intertwined with the exposed rafters. A stage made up one end of the dining area where they showcased live entertainment on the weekends.

There was a ton of seating and consistently great food. They served gourmet sandwiches and salads, creative pasta dishes and hand-tossed sourdough pizza topped with interesting combinations like smoked razor clams, locally farmed goat cheese and Oregon bay shrimp.

"You're his *dance* teacher?" Laura said flatly.

They'd already ordered, Camile the "skipper's choice" pizza loaded with seafood toppings and a Caesar salad. For an appetizer, she'd gotten the house specialty called "po-tatoes on the docks," hand-cut French fries topped with gravy, shrimp and cheese curds. Laura was having grilled chicken and a tossed veggie salad with light balsamic dressing.

Because Laura asked, Camile had just fin-ished telling her how she'd met Rhys. And was it her imagination, or did Laura say dance like it was a disease? This wasn't the first time she'd detected derision for Camile's love of dance; Laura had often pointed out that Camile would have a lot more time for school if she didn't spend so much time in the studio. Ad-mittedly, the assertion was true, but that was her choice, and she'd still managed to graduate at the top of the psychology department, even above Laura. She told herself it was difficult to understand someone else's passion unless you shared it. Camile couldn't think of anything Laura was passionate about outside of school.

"Yep."

"I hope he's paying you well."

"He is. But that's not why I'm doing it. You know dancing and teaching dance have always been my favorite things." She took a sip of her coffee.

"I do know that." Laura sounded sympa-thetic, but for the life of her Camile couldn't understand why. "What kind of dance lessons?" Laura plucked the lemon wedge from the rim of her glass and squeezed it into her water.

"Waltz." Amazing how that one word now filled her with so much pride. Rhys had almost mastered the steps, including the turns. The only thing missing was music. And she'd been working on a plan for that.

Wiping her hands with a napkin, Laura asked, "Why does he want to learn to *waltz*? He's not getting married, is he?"

"No. His niece is participating in a debutante program."

"Wow. They still have those?"

"They do."

"Huh. Aren't they rather, um, sexist by today's standards? Isn't the whole point to introduce a woman to society so she can get married? Is that the kind of message we want to send to our teens—that it's 'time' to get married when you reach a certain age?"

This conversation felt off. The waiter delivered her appetizer, and Camile was glad to have the distraction to consider her response because she realized the reason why their friendship felt so strained lately. They'd never had one outside their little world of psychology: projects, research, tests, papers. If they were going to continue the friendship, they'd need to find some mutual interests beyond bowling.

Camile explained, "It's really not about that. It's a lovely tradition, and it means a lot to Willow's mom's family. The girls learn some very valuable skills." Curious herself, Camile had discussed the details with Willow at length.

"Like what?"

"Etiquette, manners, public speaking, how to be a leader and to set a positive example for their peers, ways to get involved in their communities through volunteer service. And, of course, ballroom dancing." She picked up a fry and gave it a twirl. "Which is where I come in."

"That's sweet. But it seems a little over the top, don't you think? To pay a private instructor for dance lessons for one night in a child's life?"

"No, it doesn't. Not in this case. Not if you knew why it's so important to Rhys, and to Willow for that matter."

"Oh?" Laura looked interested. Of course she did. See? They could do this. Camile needed to get over this resentment or whatever it was that she was feeling for her friend and find that common ground. That was why, in that moment, she impulsively decided to confide in her friend. A mistake she'd come to regret for the rest of her life.

LOCATED OCEANFRONT ON the outskirts of Pacific Cove, The Shoals Hotel was one of the oldest, largest and grandest structures on the entire coast. The Victorian-style architecture lent itself beautifully to the grand ballroom comprising nearly half of the entire second floor. The space would be an ideal location for an elegant political fund-raiser like this one, if not for the atrocious acoustics.

Rhys could see the guy's mouth moving, he could hear words, but the room was so loud he couldn't concentrate on their meaning. Something about the mayor, maybe? And a new ordinance he wanted to get passed? Couldn't anyone else hear the echoing pings of silverware scraping on the dishes? The inordinately loud clop of heels on the hardwood floor had him wondering why people insisted on purchasing loud shoes. Rubber soles were an option. And the squeaking hinge on the door leading into the kitchen needed about a quart of grease. Every time one of the waitstaff entered or exited, it made his teeth clench.

His jaw ached and he missed Camile. She'd texted to say she was going to be a few minutes late. How many constituted a few where she was concerned, he wondered?

"Don't you think so?"

Rhys stared at the guy and gradually realized a response was expected. Sweat broke out on the back of his neck, prickling his skin and irritating him even more. A headache was forming behind his right eye. Glancing down, he studied the appetizer-laden plate that Anne had handed him several minutes ago. The pale pink salmon on crusty bread slices had him recalling an earlier snippet of the conversation.

"I don't like the ordinance about seafood farming."

"What do you mean you don't *like* the ordinance about seafood farming? It's perfect."

"The risk of disease and decimation to native seafood populations is too high."

"But we need this. The town needs growth. Do you have any idea how many jobs this could create?"

"Burning nuclear waste in the town square would create jobs, too."

The man's face scrunched and slowly turned red. "Are you comparing seafood farming to burning nuclear waste?"

"In a manner of speaking, yes. Statistically—"

He felt a hand slide between his arm and rib

cage, and he knew it was her before she even uttered the words, "Rhys, hi! I've been looking everywhere for you."

All it took was the sight of Camile's smiling face. That fast, and the distractions, the myriad of irritations chipping away at his brain with their tiny, vicious ice picks fell away. She was gorgeous as usual but also…different. Her hair, for one thing, was down around her shoulders and curled in waves. And that dress… The cinnamon-brown color was a perfect complement to her green eyes and brought out the warm gold tones in her hair. A flicker of a memory swam before him, but it was gone before he could place it. He rested his hand on top of hers, hoping she wouldn't pull away. The feel of her skin against his heightened the calming sensation about a million times. He couldn't explain the phenomenon, but he relished it. He'd begun to count on it.

"I think what Rhys means," Camile said, smiling at the man, "is that he believes—as do you, Mayor Hobbes—that the focus should remain on sustainably harvested seafood whenever possible. But he's open to the idea of farming if it's done responsibly. Right, Rhys?"

Ah. The mayor. Made sense, seeing as how Anne had dragged him to this fund-raiser for the man himself. He'd read about this harebrained seafood farming scheme in the news. Camile's summation of his opinion wasn't accurate, but he picked up on her cue and said, "Possibly." If about six hundred items were added, removed, and/or clarified.

Before the mayor could ask him to elaborate, Rhys leaned close to her ear and said, "Hi, Camile. I am very glad you found me." That was when he realized that something was different. She looked different. He realized he'd never seen her hair styled this way or known her to wear quite so much makeup. It wasn't a lot, but there was lip gloss and eyeshadow. No glasses… Had she done this for him or because the occasion called for it? Him, he thought. At least, he hoped that was the case because he liked the way she was searching his gaze. He didn't dare move because he wanted her to find what she was looking for, hoped that she saw how he felt about her.

Anne joined them. Reaching out a hand, she introduced herself to the mayor.

Camile asked Rhys, "Can I borrow you for a minute?"

"Yes, please," he said. They moved away, and he bent close to her ear, and said, "You can borrow me for as long as you'd like. Especially if it gets me out of here."

Camile chuckled and, as he'd anticipated

she would, tried to remove her hand from his elbow. Rhys held tight, and then slid her hand down his arm where he entwined their fingers. And left them that way.

CHAPTER THIRTEEN

CAMILE WASN'T SURE exactly what had just happened, how much of the ill-fated conversation between Rhys and Mayor Hobbes she'd missed. What she did know was that the mayor was seething, she felt warm and flustered, and a good share of the crowd was watching her walk across the ballroom hand in hand with Rhys McGrath—dogfighter, bigamist, hit man and drug lord. The important point being that Rhys held tight to her hand.

She didn't attempt to free it as she led him out the door and onto the patio, where a set of stairs led down to the beach. She knew they'd be in plain view if she went that direction, so she headed to the left, into the hotel's garden, and didn't stop until they were behind the large fountain in the middle. A concrete likeness of the Greek god Neptune posed with his trident in the center of the large pool.

Rhys turned and rested his hips on the thick edge of the pool. Then he exhaled a pained sigh. "Thank you for saving me. Again. I think I may have offended the mayor."

Camile grinned and gently tried to extricate her hand.

He held firm. "Why don't you want me to hold your hand?"

Eyes squinted, she returned quickly, "Why do you *want* to hold it?"

With light pressure he pulled at her hand, urging her to come closer. "Because I like touching you. It calms me down."

"Did you just compare me to a sedative?" she teased even as her heartbeat began to pick up speed. They were often this close when they were dancing but this was different. Much different.

Moving over to him had brought their faces so much closer together, and she liked how she could see the many shades of blue in his eyes, all of which were blazing with full force now. He brought his other hand up to trail a finger along her collarbone to her neck, where her pulse was now racing beneath his fingertip. He flattened his hand, spreading his fingers, and she let out a little gasp. Eyes on hers, he curved his mouth at the corners like he was satisfied by her reaction, and looped his hand around the back of her neck. His other hand loosened the hold it had on her fingers to slide up her arm and curl around her shoulder.

Leaning forward until his lips were almost grazing hers, he whispered, "Not exactly," and then pressed his mouth to hers.

Camile didn't hesitate. His touch, his kiss, felt so right, and all she could think was, *finally*. And *yes*. She'd wanted this kiss for so very long. And it was…perfect. She felt cherished and adored in a way that only Rhys made her feel. It seemed that in his arms, honest was the only way she could be with her feelings. Her doubts and insecurities slid away and melted into oblivion where they belonged. No doubt his excellent technique helped. The guy might be awkward when it came to most forms of interpersonal communication, but not this one. He was very, very good at this one, conveying everything she wanted to know. And she wanted to kiss him forever.

At some point, his hands moved to her waist. She looped her arms around his shoulders, bringing one hand up until, finally, she got to touch his hair. It was every bit as soft as she'd imagined, and he let out a low moan when her fingers threaded through the silky mass.

Eventually, he pulled away and pressed a kiss on her collarbone. Drawing back enough to see her face, he said, "Thank goodness, I read this one right. I've wanted to kiss you for so long. But I didn't know what you'd do. When I saw you in there tonight, the way you looked at me... I had to try." He brushed a thumb along her bottom lip. "And you kissed me back."

"Yes, I did."

"I'm very proud of myself right now."

Despite the reality slowly creeping in, she had to laugh. "I'm glad I could help."

"Camile." His eyes turned serious. "You have helped me in ways you cannot possibly imagine. The feelings I have for you terrify me and electrify me. I feel like I didn't know how to...*be* until you came into my life. Where have you been? Why did it take me so long to find you?"

It didn't, she wanted to say. *You could have had me two years ago, but instead you left me sitting in a restaurant all by myself.* Maybe if he had, her life wouldn't be in such shambles right now. That thought was both unfair and unreasonable. None of her problems were his fault. But she didn't think she could do this. She'd thought she was over this. And she could be, maybe, if they were only friends.

"Rhys, I think you're confusing your feelings for me with gratitude."

His head tipped back as his mouth formed a

small smile, like he was waiting for the punchline. "Gratitude? For what?"

Camile shrugged. "For teaching you how to dance, for being honest with you."

"That's ridiculous. I'm grateful for that, of course. Grateful, but not confused. I know exactly what I want, and right now, what I want is to get out of here and kiss you all night."

Camile wanted that, too. So much. She wanted to be more than friends. But she didn't trust these feelings, his or hers. And she realized in that moment that she had to know. As much as she feared the answer, she wanted to hear it. Because she knew this insecurity that he'd planted two years ago was at the center of her misgivings. If there was any chance of a future between them, she had to deal with it.

"I don't get it. I don't understand why you're interested in me now."

"What do you mean *now*? I've been interested in you from the first moment I saw you in that restaurant. I grew ever more interested as you spent the evening making everyone around you happy." He dipped his head to place a quick kiss on her neck. Then he straightened again and continued, "I fell in love with your smile that night. I wanted to get to know you better even as I was terrified for you to know me. But then, when you started teaching me to dance and making *me* happy, I was lost. No one, no *person*, has ever made me happy before. Holding you in my arms without *holding* you the way I wanted, that was pure torture and—"

With her eyes glued to his, she ignored the sweetness of his words and interrupted with a whispered, "Which restaurant?" More doubts immediately poured in. Why was she doing this to herself? Why couldn't she just get over this? Forget about it and move on? She made him happy; he'd just said so. But she couldn't be happy with him, could she? Not with this between them.

A crease of confusion formed between his brows, the one that tugged at her heartstrings when he realized he'd offended someone but wasn't quite sure how he'd done it. Or what to do about it.

"The loud and crowded Mexican place where we first met. In my mind, I called you the pretty one until I learned your name. Camile— I repeated it over and over again because I thought it suited you so well. Do you know how much I love your name, by the way?"

"Rhys," she said with a firm shake of her head. "You already knew my name."

"No, I… What do you mean?"

"We'd already met before that night. At a

different restaurant, a little over two years ago. May 10. I remember the date because it was the last day of finals week. We had a date at Stovall's Seafood Bistro. You ordered crab cakes and a gin and tonic, both of which were still untouched when you got up and left me there." She gestured at herself. "I was even wearing this dress."

"MAY 10." RHYS repeated the date while the memories crushed in from all sides, hard and fast, squeezing his heart with love and regret and grief. Then he understood. The dress, and all that hair curling around her shoulders, the woman he'd abandoned in Stovall's. The one promising date he'd had in years, brief as it had been.

On the worst night of his life.

He dipped his forehead down until it touched hers. Her name was a whisper on his lips, but it might as well have been a shout for all the emotion, the love, he felt for her. "Camile." Then he inhaled the lilac scent of her and re-alized he'd never hoped for anything as much as he did right then. *Please, let her forgive me.*

"Rhys, I'm…" Her voice slayed him because he could feel her hurt, see the tears that she was struggling to keep at bay. "You hurt me so deeply when you left me there that night.

I sat at that table like a fool for I don't even know how long. Until the waiter finally came over and told me you weren't coming back. The valet saw you leave. And I know it sounds silly because I didn't know you, but it crushed me. It took me so long to get past it. You were so… I thought you were interesting and smart, and I was having fun. Later, I told myself you were just a jerk who didn't know me and didn't deserve me. But now that I do know you, I couldn't handle it if you treated me that way again…" One hand came up to cover her mouth as if to smother a sob.

Rhys had never felt so excruciatingly terrible about himself in his entire life. *Left her.* This was where her sickbed ramblings about leaving came from. He'd been the jerk who'd left her. No one's opinion had ever meant as much to him as Camile's. The irony was not lost on him; that he'd accidentally, unsympathetically at the time, hurt the woman he'd come to care most about in the world. And he hadn't even remembered it until now. That day and the days following were still a blurry nightmare.

But despite the circumstances, he shouldn't have left that way—he knew that, whether he liked the person or not.

All this time, he'd done his best to forget that horrible night. No, that wasn't true. He hadn't had to forget it. It was already gone, crowded out by tragedy and heartbreak.

"Camile, I am so sorry."

"Just tell me the truth," she said, her voice hoarse with tears and emotion. "I know you can't lie." Rhys felt her trembling. He went to pull her close, but she placed her palms firm against his chest and wouldn't budge. "Get it over with. Tear off the bandage. I'm comfortable with who I am now. Mostly. I want to be. The point is, I can handle it."

Rhys felt another wave of loathing directed at himself. "Wait a second—you think I left that night because I didn't like you?"

"Of course. Why else?" She gestured at him. "You are the most perfect-looking male person I have ever known." She motioned at herself. "I am not your equivalent in that way. What else would I possibly think? Gah!" she growled. "This is just humiliating all over again. I shouldn't have said anything."

Rhys felt his jaw drop open, and, feeling like a buffoon, he closed it again. "Camile, that is the most…absurd statement you've ever made. And you've made a few doozies. You can be extremely illogical at times."

She glared. "You're not helping your case."

"I know. I'm trying to decide which subject to broach first and how. I can't believe you didn't tell me until now. I can't believe you agreed to be my dance teacher when I'd done that to you. I'm glad I offered you so much money."

"Money didn't have anything to do with it!" she cried. "I went to your house that morning and told Anne I was turning down your offer. She plied me with your muffins and said all these nice things about you and tried to talk me into it. It didn't work. But then you showed up, and you two started talking about Willow, and I could see how desperate you were, how much learning to dance meant to you and I… That's why I agreed. I did need the money, that's true. And it might have made saying yes a little easier. But initially, I only agreed to two lessons, and then three. I planned to hand you off to a different teacher, but then I met Willow. I wanted to be the one to teach you because it was important, and I knew I could."

Reaching out, he cupped her cheek. "It kills me to think that you believed that I could leave you like that without a real reason."

She shook her head like she didn't understand. And, of course, she didn't. But she would. Hopefully.

He took both her hands in his. "I'm going to tell you a story, okay? In my way. Please."

She whispered a ragged, "Yes."

"Roughly two years ago, on May 10, I was in a restaurant in downtown Portland having the best first date I've ever had. Generally, my dates don't go well, as I'm sure you can imagine. But, all my life, women have put up with my…idiosyncrasies for other reasons. Superficial reasons like you just mentioned. When I was younger, I didn't mind these reasons as much. But as I grew older, I realized how unimportant and unfulfilling these reasons are. Because of my physical appearance, which I didn't have anything to do with, and my brain, also not my doing, I am made up of this extremely unfortunate dichotomy. Good-looking, but terrible personality."

Camile started to protest, and Rhys shook his head. "You promised, remember?"

She nodded.

"After a couple of disastrous relationship attempts early on in my life, I realized I had a serious problem. I'd never truly know if a woman liked me for me. Or how much of the bad she'd put up with to get the superficial, unimportant parts."

Camile's eyes flashed with irritation.

He grinned. "Back to that night. I was hopeful for the first time in a very long time. Because sitting across from me was this beautiful, enchanting woman who hadn't asked me to marry her, didn't take my picture to send to her friends, or ask me to take her home before getting to know me. But what she did do was look at me like I was a person, make me laugh, and even insult me a little. I don't recall the exact details because I don't remember a lot about that day and the days that followed. But I do remember how good it felt to talk and laugh. It had been a while since I'd been so relaxed. My brother had just gotten out of the hospital, and I'd been under an immense amount of stress. But that night, I was having a really, really nice time.

"So nice, in fact, that when my phone buzzed in my pocket, I ignored the text. And I ignored the next one, too, and a few more. But when it started ringing, I got a little concerned. And when I saw that it was Vanessa, I panicked. Without another thought, I headed to the entry for some privacy to take the call. That's when I learned that Evan had suffered another stroke. He was in a coma. I don't remember exactly what happened next. I know I left the restaurant, but I don't remember the drive or getting to the hospital. Later, I learned that I'd parked illegally, and my car had been towed. I barely left my brother's bedside until he died two weeks later."

THE COMBINATION OF guilt and relief and joy and sadness collided right in her center, stealing the breath from her chest. Stunned, Camile whispered, "Why didn't I put this together sooner? You told me, and Anne said it, too, that Evan passed away two years ago. For some reason, I didn't connect the two events."

"Why would you? I doubt either of us ever mentioned the date or even the month when he died."

"I know but… Rhys, I'm so sorry."

He wrapped his arms around her and nuzzled her neck. "Why would you be sorry?"

"For thinking the worst of you."

"Sweetheart, I think anyone would have."

She gripped his shoulders, squaring them solidly with hers. "But I shouldn't have. Can't you see? I'm guilty, too. Just like those other women you mentioned, I assumed things. Granted, they were different things. But I assumed them, too, because of your looks. That you were a jerk because you're so hot. That wasn't fair."

He chuckled. "Camile, I *know* you like me. I can tell."

"I do like you! So much." Too much, maybe, because she was having a difficult time processing all of this; she wanted to laugh and cry and wrap herself around him all at the same time.

"That's enough for me."

"You believe me, right?" How could she prove this to him? "I don't care what you look like. I don't see your looks now. I don't see them now. I mean, of course, I see them. But I see them second—no, not even second. More like tenth."

"Tenth?" he repeated skeptically. "You like nine things about me better than my looks?"

"Your brains, honesty, kindness, integrity, love for your family, determination, courage, self-discipline, your neat penmanship, muffins and cookies—I'll even combine those last two into one and say baking. Which brings up a myriad of other impressive and enviable skills you possess, like woodworking and drawing. I'm not counting, but I know that's more than ten, and right off the top of my head."

"Impressive. I think my penmanship is a bit of a stretch, but I'll take it."

"Thank you." She grinned. "It's not—your handwriting is like artwork. I wanted to add your hair, but I was afraid that fell under the category of physical characteristics."

He chuckled. "It might, but I'm glad you like it just the same. Do you want to know what I like about you?"

"I'm not sure."

"You're not sure?"

"Well, I know that lying is difficult for you and I'm afraid that I might not—"

This time, he cut her off with a kiss. A really good one that left her breathless. When he pulled away to look at her, his blue eyes were scorching. He brought his hands up to cup her cheeks, and his expression confirmed the truth as he said, "Everything. I like everything about you. And I love how you're honest with me, too. Please, promise that you'll always be honest with me."

CHAPTER FOURTEEN

"BYE, MOLLY! See you soon." Camile and Harper waved to the tutu-clad little girl holding tightly to her dad's hand. She was the last of the summer ballet session's five- and six-year-olds to be picked up for the day. The other regular ballet instructor's grandmother had passed away, and Gia had asked Camile to fill in. She'd had the morning free, so she'd happily agreed.

"Wow. That was super fun," Camile said. "What a bunch of cuties."

"You're great with kids," Harper said.

"I'm great with tiny dancers," Camile lightheartedly corrected. "There's a difference. Kids are so much more manageable when they're engaged in an activity they enjoy, have you noticed that?" With a laugh, she headed to the studio's closet to retrieve the large dust mop. "Did they eat any of those crackers?" she joked. "It's like they just crunched them up and danced on them. Maybe we should offer a cracker-dancing class?" The mop handle was taller than the doorjamb; she always struggled to angle it out of the closet.

"You're good with all dancers." Harper retrieved a cotton towel and disinfecting spray and moved to wipe down the barre.

"Thank you," Camile said. "That is a very nice compliment. Especially when I love dancing so much. I'd like to think I impart some of that to my students."

"No, I mean, you are a genuinely gifted instructor, do you know that?"

"Have you been talking to Rhys?" Camile chuckled, pushing the mop across the floor.

"I'm serious, Camile. Sometimes, I think, when we're amazing at something, we don't realize how truly good we are at it because we don't struggle. If something comes easy, we tend to brush it off as not important or not useful."

"I guess I can see what you mean. In other people. Like how Nina has such a head for business. She thinks it's nothing that she's turning Quinley's little berry farm into Nina Marie's empire."

"Did you know Gia is thinking about selling the studio?"

Camile paused in her step as yearning blossomed right in the center of her heart. "No, I didn't."

Harper eyed her carefully. "Camile, I don't know what your plans are now. But is owning your own studio something you've ever considered?"

Another stab of longing followed, this one painful in the way it was to want something that was impossible. In an effort both to hide her feelings and to change the subject, she joked, "Sure, yeah, I've considered it in my lottery fantasy. You know, the one where you think about what you would do if money wasn't a consideration? Well, not you, obviously, so you might not be aware that the lottery fantasy is a common one that people who are not billionaire heiresses have."

Harper grinned, but she would not be deterred. "I'm serious. This is a fantastic opportunity. Gia wants to sell the building, the business, everything. You know how we've talked about ways she could expand."

Camile shook her head and let the disappointment of reality squelch the desire. "I could never afford it."

"You could get a loan."

Sweeping again, she said, "Harper, I appreciate you thinking about me, wanting this for me. But there is no way I could get a loan. I have a mountain of student loan debt looming over me that I'm supposed to start paying on this fall with a degree that I have failed to earn. Not to mention a lawsuit, the outcome of which isn't looking great."

"What about your family?"

"Out of the question. I refuse to ask my family for help with anything. Besides, my dad would never agree. In his eyes, dancing is a nice hobby, not a real career. When I was younger, along with you and about a million other ballerinas I wanted to join a ballet company. He refused to even let me try."

Harper's head tilted thoughtfully. "You'd be an incredible acro-dance performer. You're so athletic, and you have the perfect body type."

"Harper." Camile stopped again to make sure she had her attention. "I think you might be the coolest person I've ever met. And a stellar friend. Possibly, the best one I've ever had. That's saying a lot because you're competing with my sister, Nina."

Harper blinked rapidly like she might be fighting tears. "Camile…that means so much to me. I feel the same way about you. I don't have that much to compare with because I haven't had very many friends, but it feels wonderful to have one now."

"If nothing else, I'm grateful to this studio for bringing us together. Hopefully, Gia will sell to someone who wants to keep the business. If not, we'll find somewhere else to teach together."

Harper put a hand on her hip. "Speaking of this studio and dancing… What's the deal with you and Rhys?"

"What?" The mop handle slid from her hand and smacked against the floor.

"Rhys told Kyle that you are going to South Carolina with him for Willow's debutante ball."

"Oh, um, yeah. He said that he'd feel more comfortable about the father-daughter dance if I was there. You know, to coach him."

"I'm sure he would. Is that the only reason you're going?"

"For Willow?" She hadn't meant for it to sound like a question, but it was such a weak response that it came out that way.

"Mmm-hmm." Harper bobbed her head and went on in a voice laced with sarcasm, "Yeah, because she'll only have Rhys, Anne, her other aunt and uncle, and her grandparents there to support her. How could she get through it without you?"

Camile couldn't help laughing.

Harper laughed with her, and then said, "Camile, you don't have to tell me what's going on. But please don't make something up. Just say that you don't want to talk about it, and I'll respect that."

"You sound like Rhys."

"Yes, we do have that in common—an extreme dislike for prevaricating. I just serve mine up with more sarcasm."

Not for the first time, Camile felt a twinge of guilt stir inside of her. Now that she and Rhys were…whatever they were, her work for Anne felt wrong somehow. She needed to tell Rhys. But first, she needed to talk to Anne.

"What are you wearing?"

Camile glanced down at herself. "Uh…"

Harper snickered and tossed the towel aside. "To the ball? It's formal, right?"

"Oh, great," Camile said with a groan. "I didn't even think about that. A dress. There's another thing I can't afford. And I have zero time to go shopping."

"How about some shopping at my house?" Harper suggested. "I have a closet full of fancy gowns that I've only worn once or twice. You can borrow one."

"I HAVE A SURPRISE for you." Camile stood before Rhys in the same studio classroom where she and Harper had taught ballet the day before.

With Willow back in South Carolina it meant they could dance at his house again, but Rhys had to come into town for an early meeting, so he'd suggested they have a morning lesson here. "It's good news and a surprise combined. I called the coordinator for the Magnolia Junior Debutante Program."

"Okay." Rhys had no idea where she was going with this, but she seemed pleased, so that pleased him.

"Turns out, they use the same playlist every year. She emailed it to me."

"Ah."

"Yeah, so this morning we practice to music, to the song that you and Willow will dance to. Isn't that cool?"

"It is," he said and realized how much he meant it.

"I'm glad you think so." Her grin was contagious. "There's more…" She walked over to the bench where she always set her stuff. "I'm guessing you don't have a digital music player or a music app on your phone?"

"That would be correct."

Removing something from her bag, she then walked back over to him. "This is one of mine. I downloaded the song they'll be playing for your waltz on here." She reached up and slipped an earbud into his ear. The other she placed in hers. "It was actually your earplug suggestion that gave me this idea. I was thinking you could take this home and listen to the song, become familiar with it, practice counting to it, and even practice the steps in your workshop if you want to. At the same time, you'll be sort of desensitizing yourself, getting a handle on the 'noise.'" She paused to add air quotes. "You'll be a step ahead of the game, or three steps in this case." She added a wink. "What do you think?"

Rhys stared down at her. The hopeful, tentative smile on her face had his heart squeezing hard with love. How could a person be so thoughtful? Specifically, to him. He could *feel* how much she cared about him, and he could barely contain the words he wanted to say. He loved her. He thought there was a solid chance that she loved him back, but he was pretty sure she hadn't acknowledged her feelings yet. She was still too fixated on the external issues weighing her down, had convinced herself they were an obstacle to having a relationship. He knew she needed time, which he was giving her while he solved the issues that he could. And so, as difficult as it was, he would wait to tell her how he felt.

Slipping a hand around the back of her head, he dipped his face until it was close to hers. "I think it's brilliant and incredibly sweet. You're brilliant and sweet. This might be the nicest thing anyone has ever done for me. I know this is against the rules, but I have to…" He brushed a quick kiss to her lips. "Thank you."

Camile had instituted a professional behavior policy for the duration of his lessons. "Hands are for dancing and mouths are for counting," she'd told him. "Otherwise, we'll never get you ready."

He'd protested good-naturedly, but secretly he admired her discipline and dedication to her craft. And he knew she was right.

Now her hands came up, and she shifted slightly toward him. Thinking she was amenable to bending the rules, Rhys went to kiss her again. She placed her palms flat against his chest, and the soft notes of a percussion ensemble began to play in his ear. He realized the movement had been to switch on the MP3 player.

Grinning, she positioned her hands and patted his shoulder in a pleasingly affectionate way. "Nice try, big guy. But it's time to dance."

AFTER THE LESSON, Camile headed upstairs to her apartment so she could change her clothes for her lunch shift at Tabbie's. Rhys kissed her goodbye with another thank-you and a promise to call her later. Then he walked across the street to Blue Carafe, where he'd agreed to meet Jay Johnston, Brady Markel and Tony Forster. Brady had been hired by Rhys to oversee the establishment of the youth center. Jay was a building contractor, and when Rhys had approached him about possibly constructing the building, he'd not only agreed, he'd offered to do it at cost. Tony was a real estate agent, thankfully not affiliated with Keisha Williams, and was showing the men potential building sites.

Rhys spotted Brady walking down the sidewalk, and he stopped to wait.

Brady approached, and the men shook hands. They continued inside, where Jay and Tony were already waiting. After greetings were exchanged, they all ordered coffees and then argued briefly about who would pay. Rhys insisted since it was his meeting and they made small talk while they waited.

"So," Tony said when they'd all received their drinks and were gathered outside. "I have several properties to show you guys. But first, I'd like to throw an idea at you that's different than your initial vision."

Rhys and Brady traded easy shrugs. "Sure. We're still in the planning stages here."

"Great. A building is about to go on the market here in downtown. I think it would be an easy remodel. It would give the youth center more of an urban feel—as much as you can manage here in Pacific Cove, anyway."

Everyone laughed. Tony went on, "But that would have advantages, too, I think. It's got the square footage, it's conveniently located to all the amenities our town has to offer, and it's within walking distance of the school. And the best part is, it's priced to sell. Of course, that means that once it's on the market, it won't be there for long. The owner happens to be my cousin's wife, so I've got an opportunity to show it to you guys before it's officially listed."

"Sounds interesting," Brady said.

Rhys agreed. "Let's take a look."

"Excellent." Tony pointed. "As it happens, it's right across the street."

Rhys spun toward the building where Harper stood outside the dance studio's entrance gazing in their direction. Smiling, she lifted a hand and waved before opening the door and disappearing inside.

SITTING ON THE edge of the Ashley River, the Pomona Country Club was "the pride of the small South Carolina town that shares its name." Anne was reading from her phone and infusing her tone with a touch of cutting humor. But as they walked from the car to the grand entryway, Camile thought there might be ample reason for the collective boasting. Like a storybook illustration, a massive magnolia tree draped with Spanish moss shaded the courtyard. Carolina jessamine wound around metal lampposts that lined the cobblestoned walk, its sweet fragrance mixing pleasantly in the humid air. Enchanting, Camile thought for about the millionth time. It was a reaction she'd become familiar with since they'd landed in South Carolina the previous day.

Anne went on to recite that the large colonial-style building had originally been the county's courthouse. "Yada yada, much history. Colorful past. Ooh," she then added in a voice thick with what sounded like genuine intrigue. "Possibly haunted. Tours given daily."

Once inside, they headed into a huge ballroom decorated so elegantly that Camile stopped in her tracks to take it all in. Beneath their feet, the wood floors were buffed to a high sheen. Silver and white centerpieces decorated round tables draped with white sateen and set with china, crystal and gleaming silver. Shimmering candles abounded, twinkle lights cast a warm glow and cheerful classical music played at a volume so subtle she thought that even Rhys might find it soothing.

In every direction, there were elegant women in extraordinary gowns. Camile sent a silent thank-you to Harper for loaning her the dress. Emerald-green satin delicately embellished with tiny rhinestones; she'd thought it might be too much. How wrong she was. It had been a little too big and way too long, but Harper had solved that problem, too, somehow managing to have it altered in record time. Now it fitted her like a glove. And when she'd put it on earlier, she'd agreed that Harper was right that it made her eyes look "impossibly green."

All the men wore tuxes, but none wore one as well as Rhys. Despite his calm demeanor, Camile could tell he was nervous. He held her hand even tighter than usual.

Willow's maternal grandparents, Olivia and Les, turned out to be friendly, engaging people. Les was handsome, tall and lean, and if it weren't for his thick head of silver-white hair, he could pass for a decade younger than he was. Olivia was a perfect match for her husband in a floor-length flaming red gown that showed off her generous, attractive curves. With her porcelain-perfect complexion, extra-long eyelashes and dark brown hair twisted up into a chic bun, she reminded Camile of a movie star from a more glamorous era.

An easy, dimpled smile lent her a down-to-earth quality, and her low, soft voice with its melodic accent contributed to her appeal. "The girls and their escorts will come through that door there." She indicated the direction with a flowy wave of her hand. "That way, we can all take a nice long gander at their pretty gowns. That was the worst part for me when I was a deb, walking in those high heels past all these people—my word! That was nerve-racking for a country girl like me!" A chuckle of delight followed before she went on, "One at a time, the girls go up on stage there, turn around and face the crowd, perform their best curtsy, and then form a line on each side of the podium. When everyone has been introduced, we'll all take our seats for dinner and give them a chance to show off their fancy table manners." She paused to add a wink. "During dessert, there will be a short speech by the director of our program, followed by an inspirational talk by Pastor Corbin. Don't worry, it won't be like a boring, long-winded sermon. The pastor is a riot and just a wonderful speaker. Then the fun begins."

A woman joined them. Olivia said, "Oh, Heather, honey, there you are. I was getting worried you were late."

Heather, on the other hand, was a surprise. Camile had studied the photos of Vanessa in Rhys's house, and Heather looked nothing like her sister. Vanessa had been extremely pretty with soft features and a curvy figure. She had striking brown eyes and hair and her mom's cheerful smile. Heather wore her straight, platinum blond hair in a razor-sharp A-line bob. She had hazel eyes and a pointy nose that dominated her long face. She was extremely thin, which dramatically accentuated the sharp edges of all her features. Camile could see the bluish circles under her eyes even though Heather had a thick layer of skillfully applied makeup. She couldn't help but wonder if the woman was ill or just plain exhausted. Camile could relate.

"Not late." Her smile was as cool as the icy blue dress she wore. "I just snuck in the back to wish Willow good luck one more time." She turned away from her mom, her gaze going from Rhys to Camile, and then briefly flickering on their joined hands, before focusing her attention firmly on Rhys. Shoulders rigid, nostrils flaring slightly, she said, "Rhys. Glad you could make it." Then she acknowledged Anne with a tip of her head and a frosty "hello, Anne."

"Hi, Heather," Anne said, doing a much better job of faking enthusiasm than her counterpart. "Nice to see you again."

"We wouldn't have missed it," Rhys responded politely. "Heather, I'd like you to meet

Camile Wynn. Camile, this is Heather Dupres, Willow's aunt."

"Pleased to meet you, Camile." Heather managed another tight semismile. That was when Camile realized that she was nervous, too. Rhys had every right to be nervous because of the dance. But what were Heather's nerves about? For Willow? More likely, Camile speculated, because she was face-to-face with Rhys.

Olivia got right to the point. "Now, I know this is awkward, but who will be dancing with Willow for the father-daughter dance? Les, of course, would love to do it, but Troy has also volunteered. Heather and I were thinking they could split the dance. Les could start, and then Troy could cut in? Or vice versa. It's done sometimes with dads and stepdads and grandfathers raising children and whatnot. Now—"

"I am," Rhys interrupted. "I will be dancing with Willow."

The flash of fury that crossed Heather's face was unmistakable. Camile realized that she'd miscalculated her uptight demeanor. There was anger and hatred mixed in with that nervous energy. What was up with that? If anything, Rhys should be hating on her.

"You?" Heather snapped. "You're going to dance with my niece?"

"Yes, me," Rhys returned calmly. "I am the legal guardian of *our* niece."

Olivia interjected, "He's right about that, Heather dear. Legally, he has the right. Now, we discussed this possibility." Was it Camile's imagination, or did Olivia seem pleased by this revelation?

Heather's scoff was as cold as her glare. "Yeah, but I never thought…" Facing Rhys, she said, "Is this a joke? Everyone knows you can't dance."

"Not a joke," he answered. Camile squeezed his hand. In the same even tone, he added, "And I find that strange."

"You find what strange?" Heather said with snide impatience. "Don't play your word semantics with me, Rhys. It's very tiresome."

Interesting, Camile thought, that she'd give her insecurities away so easily; she was intimidated by Rhys's intelligence.

Rhys answered, "I find it strange that everyone knows I can't dance when no one has ever seen me dance before." With sparkling eyes and an enigmatic grin, he glanced down at Camile, and said, "Except Camile."

AND, OH MY, did he dance.

Brilliantly.

From her front-row spot on the edge of the

crowd, Camile blinked back tears of joy and pride as she watched Rhys whisk a beaming Willow around the dance floor. As a dance instructor, she'd had some proud and incredibly wonderful moments. In fact, she had them regularly. None could compare to this one. Because of the dancing, but also because it was the moment she realized that, for the first time in her life, she was in love. She loved Rhys McGrath. She'd been making excuses to keep from getting too close, but she knew now that all she really wanted was to be closer.

Beside her, she felt Anne's hand find and clutch hers. Her whispered words were teeming with admiration and awe. "Camile, you are a genius. I cannot believe that's my brother out there."

"Oh, my stars…" Olivia came up to stand on her other side. Camile glanced over to see she'd pressed one hand flat against her chest. "What a lovely, lovely sight that is," she gushed. "Rhys is an excellent dancer. I suspected that boy had something up his sleeve. I haven't seen our Willow this happy since…" Trailing off with a sniffle, she dabbed a tissue to her eyes. "Vanessa would be so proud of them both."

And Willow did look happy and absolutely radiant. In her stunning peach-colored gown, she shone like a moonbeam in Rhys's arms.

Rhys appeared poised and completely comfortable as he expertly guided Willow around the room. There were only a couple of other men who could compare with his skill. No one would ever guess he'd only been dancing for five weeks.

Way too soon, the song came to an end. The room erupted with applause as the dads, or other similarly adored escorts, guided their girls from the dance floor. Les intercepted Willow for the next dance.

"Rhys!" Camile said, looping an arm around his elbow when he reached her side. "You were incredible—you and Willow both. Like you'd been dancing together forever. I am overjoyed."

Rhys's smile was full of relief and pride. Camile could only imagine how he felt right now.

"I wish I could kiss you," she said.

Leaning close, he whispered, "Why can't you?"

"I don't think it would be a proper example of etiquette for these young ladies."

"If I escort you out onto the patio, will you kiss me? I've been waiting a long time for this moment."

Camile laughed. "You've kissed me lots of times now, Rhys."

Dipping his head so that his lips grazed her ear, he whispered, "But you've never kissed me."

Camile felt her face go hot. This man and his mouth. There was definitely an argument to be made for his brand of extreme candor. Threading her fingers through his, she said, her voice a little breathless, "Let's go fix that."

They were on their way outside when Heather's husband, Troy, intercepted them. "Rhys, could I have a word?"

Camile gave his hand a squeeze. "I'll meet you outside," she said and exited through the French doors onto a large patio.

Where she was promptly ambushed.

"Who even *are* you?" Heather demanded from where she stood a few feet away by a low brick wall.

"I'm sorry, Heather. We were introduced earlier. I'm Camile."

After one final drag, Heather crushed her cigarette out on the edge of a flowerpot and stepped closer. "You know very well I'm not talking about your name."

Camile did know that, but she wasn't about to get into a verbal sparring match with this woman. "Then you'll have to be more specific."

Throwing an arm out, she pointed toward the building. "You're responsible for that, aren't you?"

"For what?"

"For the new Rhys—smiling and talking and *dancing*, for pity's sake! Are you kidding me?"

How could she possibly respond to that?

Heather stepped closer, her glare menacing and speculative. "Are you and Rhys serious?"

"Yes."

"How serious? Are you engaged?"

"That's none of your business."

"It is my business. I'm suing for custody of Willow. He's not fit to have her. She's going to be mine."

Camile shrugged. "There's absolutely no reason to think you'll be successful in that endeavor."

"On the contrary, I will be successful. And whatever is going on here, whatever game Rhys is playing with you, it won't work. Willow is *my sister's* child. Mine. Do you understand that? I'm the only one who lost a sister here! *Everything* that Vanessa had should be mine. Rhys has enough. He shouldn't get this, too." With a final challenging glare, she marched inside the building.

CHAPTER FIFTEEN

THE COTILLION'S COMPLETION seemed to lighten Rhys's spirits. It helped that Willow returned home with them from South Carolina. Camile spent the following week ticking off Anne's list of activities. Most evenings were spent out at one social event or another.

The two nights Camile had dance classes they opted for a daytime outing of some sort. Saturday morning, Camile, Rhys and Willow volunteered at Lucky Cats, Mia's cat shelter. After lunch, they headed to the kite festival and then spent the afternoon browsing for vintage treasures at an outdoor flea market. On Sunday, they spent the entire day working for Helping Homes, an organization that built houses for the needy.

That was a good day as Kyle, Jay, Levi, Eli and a few other friends and acquaintances were there as well. Rhys was in his element and enjoyed spending time with people he knew. Willow hit it off with a group of teenage volunteers that included two of Jay's siblings.

At the end of the week, Camile and Anne met to discuss their progress.

"I think it's going well," Camile said, pouring coffee for herself and Anne. "He seems more comfortable all the time. And even when he's not, he's learning to hide it better." They sat at the table in Camile's kitchen.

"As long as you're there to temper him," Anne said with a frown. "Did you hear him tell that woman at the kite festival that she needed to pick up her trash?"

"Yes, luckily, it was windy and difficult to hear." Camile had fudged and told the woman that Rhys said he thought she dropped some cash. "To be fair, the woman did litter on the beach."

Anne sighed. "I know. It's just his delivery is so off-putting. But Mayor Hobbes did talk to him at the VFW luncheon, so that's good. Turns out, the mayor looked into Rhys's comments, and he's not quite as sold on seafood farming now. He told Rhys he owed him one."

"That is good news." Camile tapped a finger on the table. "You know what still bothers me, though, is the gossip. Yesterday, at Tabbie's, I heard people talking about the hit man rumor again. So weird. It seems to die down for a day or two and then comes raging back."

Anne nodded. "I know what you mean. It's

like we put out a fire and another one flares up." She sipped her coffee. "The mediation session is in a few days. And overall, we've gotten Rhys into a better legal position. Bailey is pleased with his efforts. She seems to think Rhys's past, before Willow, won't matter quite as much as Heather and her attorney are trying to emphasize. Making an effort in the present and then showing a commitment going forward is more important, and we can show that."

"Bailey?" Camile asked. "Is Bailey Leeds your attorney?"

"Yep. She's your attorney, too, right?"

"Yes. How did you know that?"

Anne waved a breezy hand. "Oh, Rhys mentioned it."

Camile thought back to the scavenger hunt when the courier had served her the papers. She'd relayed the highlights of the case to Rhys and mentioned Bailey. Since then, she'd been careful not to discuss the case with him. It was her problem; she refused to make it his, too. Especially when he had the much more important issue of Willow's guardianship to contend with.

"It's nice that you two are more than friends now. It makes a lot of this easier, doesn't it?"

"That's something else I wanted to talk to you about." They'd gone beyond friends, far-

ther and faster than Camile could have anticipated.

"Oh no." Anne's face scrunched with distress. "You're not breaking up with him, are
you?"

"No. It's just that our relationship is causing a complication I didn't anticipate. I don't
think I'm comfortable with Rhys not knowing
anymore. It feels...deceitful."

"Ohh... Phew! Well, it's not."

"Then why do I feel guilty?" Because she'd
promised Rhys she'd always be honest with
him. Even though, technically, she'd made the
arrangement with Anne pre-promise. Somehow, she didn't think that excuse would fly
with Rhys if he found out.

"No clue. You shouldn't. Listen, Camile—
you're not doing anything wrong. Trust me.
This is what I do. My job is to improve a client's
image. I advise them on where to go, and, often
more important, where not to go, who to socialize with and how to act while they're doing
all of it. I even manage their social media accounts. I pay for all kinds of things to facilitate
this process—clothes, haircuts, manicures, pet
grooming, tickets to events. You name it, if it's
legal, I've probably bought it. And let me as-
sure you that it's not uncommon to find, or pay
for, a suitable date for a client. I've done that,

too. With famous people, fake relationships happen all the time. When you accepted this job, you didn't know you'd end up falling for Rhys, right?"

Not *quite* right, Camile thought. She'd already been falling. "But we're not famous, and our relationship isn't fake. I think we need to tell Rhys." Somehow, having this discussion only made it feel worse, as if she'd jumped off a cliff without a parachute or any kind of plan on how to land. Even though Anne made some good points.

"No! You can't tell him even if you wanted to."

"What do you mean? Why not?"

"I won't let you. You signed a contract."

"You won't *let* me?" Camile repeated. "I can quit, which is what I'm considering anyway. Then you can get in line and sue me." She followed that with a harried-sounding laugh.

An expression of horror transformed Anne's features. "Wait, Camile, I'm so sorry. That came out wrong. But this is about way more than your feelings here, or Rhys's for that matter. This is about Willow. And keeping her from going to live with that viper, Heather. I know my brother and he won't... Look, you care about Rhys, right?"

"Yes, of course. I..."

"Then trust me here. What purpose would it serve to tell him now? And what if it upsets him? That's the last thing he needs right now. Whether you tell him or not, the outcome will be the same, right? You'll be together either way. So you can be together and keep Rhys happy, or you can be together and potentially upset him, disrupt your relationship and cause him undue stress right before the most important event of his life."

Camile knew Anne was right. She'd have to wait and tell him after the custody hearing.

CAMILE WOULD NEVER forget the moment she received the most shockingly good news of her life. Partly because she almost sent the call to voice mail and partly because the timing was so fortuitous. She was in the middle of updating her résumé. With Rhys's dance lessons complete and the custody hearing on the horizon, she needed to start searching for another job. A real job with, as Rhys suggested, benefits. Then, of course, there was the news itself.

"Camile, it's Eva Slater."

"Hi, Dr. Slater, how are you?" Dr. Eva Slater was the head of the psychology department at St. Killian's. She oversaw the master's in psychology program. Camile assumed she was calling to see why she hadn't been in to speak with Dr. Youngworth, her advisor. Camile didn't have an answer to that question. Hence the reason her finger had almost silenced the call.

"I'm pretty great. Do you have a minute to talk?"

"Yes, I do."

"Excellent, because I have some good news for you."

"Dr. Slater, if you're calling to discuss a date for me to reschedule, I'm not sure I—"

"That won't be necessary. Before I explain, I need to tell you that you passed your thesis, after all. Congratulations."

Camile reached out a hand and gripped the edge of the table in an attempt to steady the vertigo-like sensation. "I don't understand. How could I fail and then pass?"

"We received a tip urging us to examine the circumstances surrounding your failure. Well, you know how crushed Dr. Youngworth was when you didn't pass—she was all over it." That explained the recent influx of emails urging Camile to respond. "The short version is that your original sources were correct."

"Original sources? I don't know what that means."

"I'm afraid it means that someone sabotaged

your work. They went into the database and changed information."

Camile tightened the phone in her hand as Dr. Slater's words sank in. "Who would do something like that? Why?"

"We've got a computer forensics expert working on that first part."

"You're positive about it being sabotage? It's not just some kind of error?"

"I'm afraid there's no doubt about that. The why is a puzzle that we may have a difficult time deciphering. I can't help but think it's like something from a psychological thriller come to life."

Camile felt a chill go through her. Was there really someone out there who despised her this much? If asked, she'd claim she didn't have an enemy in the world. Except for maybe Willow's aunt, but she hadn't known Heather nearly long enough for her to be a suspect.

"Anyway, Camile, I'm looking at your degree right here on my desk. Would you like me to send it in the mail or do you want to pick it up here?"

"I um… Can I get back to you on that?"

"Certainly."

"Dr. Slater, thank you so much. To say that I'm in shock doesn't even begin to explain how I feel."

"You don't need to thank me, Camile. I hope there's happiness mixed in with that shock because you did the work. Finally, it's paid off, as it should have all along. I'm sorry you had to go through this. I can only imagine what an ordeal it's been for you. If it's any consolation, Dr. Youngworth says you're one of the brightest students she's ever had the pleasure of teaching."

"It is. That's been one of the most difficult aspects of all of this. I felt like I let her down. That's why I've been avoiding her."

"I understand, and so does she. Congratulations, Camile. I hope you'll consider going on to get your PhD. You'd make an excellent psychologist."

"Thank you, Dr. Slater. I'm not sure about my future plans yet, but it feels wonderful to know I have options."

Hands trembling, pulse pounding, Camile texted Rhys to make sure he was home and then asked if she could come out for a visit. She wanted to see him, tell him in person. His answer took less than three seconds to arrive: Yes on all counts.

Followed immediately by a: Please hurry. Now that I know you're coming I can't wait to see you.

She was still staring dreamily at that message when the next one arrived: Do you like cabbage?

Chuckling, she texted an affirmative response.

Then she called Nina who, like the excellent big sister she was, screamed her congratulations and immediately started planning a dinner to celebrate. Camile convinced her to wait until their parents were back in town. A call to Laura went straight to voice mail. She left a message asking her to call as soon as possible. Laura would be thrilled. This would help cement their friendship, for sure. In case she didn't check her messages, Camile followed it with a text: Hey, Friend! Guess what? We finally get to have that master's celebration we dreamed about... Call me ASAP!

Finally, she messaged Harper: Turns out I passed my thesis after all. Weird story. I'll call you later. Yay me!

Camile knew there were more people she needed to tell, but they could wait. She couldn't wait to see Rhys.

Rhys was busy mixing coleslaw when Camile buzzed in at the gate. Anne, who was sitting next to the control panel, tapped the unlock button. He could tell from the happiness on Camile's face when she came through the door that she'd heard the news. Jane had called an hour ago to tell him that the matter he'd asked her to inquire into at the psychology department had resulted in the best possible outcome. For Camile anyway, not so much for her non-friend, Laura. At least, Rhys felt confident they'd find the proof she was behind it.

"You guys! You're not going to believe this… The head of the psychology department at St. Killian's just called. I passed my thesis! There was a mistake. Well, not a mistake exactly, but…something."

"Are you kidding me?" Anne jumped out of her chair, rushed to Camile and hugged her tight. "Congratulations!" Anne's reaction was perfect and genuine because Rhys hadn't told his sister what he'd done. When he'd asked Jane to explore the matter, it had only been a suspicion.

Anne let her go and said, "I wish I could stay and celebrate with you guys, but I'm on my way to Portland for a meeting with a potential client. I am thrilled for you, Camile." Anne gathered her bag and her keys, said goodbye, and headed for the front door.

Rhys took his turn. Wrapping his arms around her, he kissed the top of her head and tucked her in close. "Congratulations, sweetness. I knew it couldn't be true. You're way, way too smart to fail like that."

"You are so nice." Cheek pressed against his chest, she added, "You haven't heard the weird part yet."

"Let me guess, someone hacked into the university's cloud where your thesis was stored and altered your sources?"

"Rhys, how could you possibly...?" She took a small step back so she could see his face. She followed that with a little gasp. "You did this?"

"Well, no. I mean, I facilitated an inquiry, yes."

"How? Why...?"

"When we were bowling that day your..." Rhys hesitated, not wanting to call the woman a friend. "Laura said some things that made me wonder exactly what happened."

"Laura?" Camile's face twisted with confusion and Rhys realized that she hadn't even considered her as the perpetrator.

"She talked to you about my thesis?"

"Yes. That's why I asked you about it."

"Oh. I can't believe this... Someone did this to me, sabotaged me. Dr. Slater said they have computer forensics people working on it and they feel confident they'll figure out who did it. Why would someone do this to me?"

"Camile." With gentle hands, Rhys took her

by the shoulders. "Have you considered the possibility that Laura did this?"

"Laura?" Camile reached out and gripped his biceps as if to keep herself steady. "What are you talking about?"

"Let's sit." Rhys looped an arm across her shoulders and led her across the room to the sofa. He left to fetch a glass of water. He returned and placed it on the coffee table before sitting beside her.

Camile took a sip and then asked, "What else did she say to you that day at the bowling alley?"

"Comments that told me she was jealous of you. She seemed almost pleased about your failure."

"And that was enough to prompt you to... What did you do, exactly?"

"Not that much, really. I got lucky. My friends Brandon and Jane Sawyer live in Portland. Jane is an English professor at St. Killian's. I explained what I knew and asked her if she could find out why you hadn't passed. She had a conversation with Dr. Youngworth, who offered to let her read your thesis. Jane noticed some inconsistencies in your references. Apparently, you cited the same source several times. In most instances, it was cited incorrectly, but in one place, it was correct. When read in conjunction with the content, which was excellent, according to Jane, it struck her as odd. It reminded her of a similar issue she faced in the English department where a student hacked into the university's cloud and corrected his own sources. She followed up on her suspicion and discovered that indeed someone went in and changed yours, incorrectly, though."

"But you don't have any proof that Laura did this?"

"No."

"I agree it's an interesting coincidence, but just because she told you about my…failure doesn't mean she's responsible. Laura wouldn't do this. I know she can be a little much at times, but she's my friend."

"Camile, if you peel away that sugarcoated delivery, all that's left is insults. That woman is hostile and bitter. She is no friend of yours."

CAMILE STARED AT RHYS, a mix of anxiety and consternation forming inside of her.

"Rhys, I don't mean to sound ungrateful about what you did because I'm not. I'm thrilled. But…" How did she say it? This felt extremely uncomfortable because how could she be upset with him when the result of what he'd done had such a positive outcome? And yet, he'd inserted himself into her life in a way that she'd specifically asked that he not. She'd been clear about declining his offer of "help."

"But you asked me not to help, and I did anyway?"

"Yes."

"I understand if that distresses you. I know how difficult it can be to accept help."

"It is very difficult for me."

Rhys put his arms around her and hugged her to him. "I'm sorry that you're upset. That's not what I intended. But I'm not sorry I did it. I'm hoping that you can understand that helping you with this is my way of showing you how much I care. I really care about you, Camile. I know how much this was bothering you, and I don't want there to be anything standing in the way of your happiness. Sometimes it's okay to accept help from people who care about you."

Camile nodded against his chest because what could she say when she and Anne were doing the very same thing for him?

CHAPTER SIXTEEN

THE CUSTODY MATTER was being settled in Oregon rather than South Carolina. From the beginning, Bailey had decreed this was a positive. The decision affirmed Rhys's standing as legal guardian and reinforced the appearance that Willow was already comfortable in her new home. Rhys tried to believe it, but he couldn't alter the most important fact: at the end of the process, some judge who didn't truly know any of them would choose between him and Heather.

The attorneys and both parties had agreed to a mediation session before the official hearing with the judge. It wasn't required, but Bailey advised that he participate, pointing out that declining might give the impression that Rhys wasn't open to compromise. He wasn't. And they all knew the only compromise that interested Heather was the one where Rhys relinquished his rights. But trusting Bailey's judgment, he agreed to go through the motions. They'd worked out the terms of the session beforehand. Both parties agreed to have their attorneys present as well as one support person.

On the morning of the meeting, he and Anne arrived at the family court's designated resolution center ten minutes early. The building was a functional three-story rectangular-shaped structure with square windows framing the lobby, where they found Bailey already waiting for them. Camile had graciously offered to spend the morning with Willow. They planned to go bowling and then head to the beach. Rhys couldn't help but wish he was with them.

"We already have a room," Bailey said, and directed them toward the elevator. On the third floor, they exited into a wide hallway and traveled all the way to the end.

Bailey showed them into the small conference-style room where there was a rectangular table with six padded office-style chairs neatly arranged around it. Against the back wall, a one-cup coffee machine stood on a narrow side table along with an electric teapot, cups, napkins and an assortment of drink offerings and fixings. A plate of cookies sat in the middle of the table.

Once they were settled, Bailey said, "Just so you're aware, I received a phone call from Griffin this morning." Griffin Santos was

Heather's attorney. "He gave me the impression that they are going to make a proposal."

"What kind of proposal could they possibly make?" Anne asked. "We've already said that joint custody is off the table."

Not that Heather had ever suggested the option. But neither had Rhys ever threatened to keep Willow from Heather or anyone in Vanessa's family. On the contrary, after Vanessa's death, Rhys had told Olivia and Les, and Heather, that his home was open to them anytime they wanted to visit Willow. He'd also promised to fly Willow out to visit as often as schedules permitted.

"I don't know." Bailey smoothed a hand across the table. "But I don't like it. I didn't care for his tone. He's a snake, and I'm afraid he has something up his sleeve."

A soft knock accompanied the slow opening of the door. A woman entered. She had black hair pulled up into a loose bun, a big, bright white smile and kind, expressive brown eyes. "Hi, I'm Sarah Stuart. I'll be your mediator today."

Bailey performed introductions.

Sarah took a seat and smoothed a strand of loose hair behind one ear. "So, I won't waste time. We all know why we're here. You've already submitted documentation refuting Heather's claims that Rhys's reclusive lifestyle precludes him from being an effective parent." Anne had kept a detailed calendar of Rhys's activities over the previous weeks. She'd even included a list of future obligations to prove his intentions and commitments were long-term. "You've maintained an impressive social calendar."

Rhys nodded. Thanks to Camile, the socializing hadn't been that bad. Going forward, with her by his side, he felt he could handle a lifetime of outings of almost any type.

Steepling her fingers, Sarah inhaled a deep breath, and said, "The problem is that Heather is claiming that you've participated in most of these events under false pretenses. Further proof, she claims, that you suffer from a form of mental illness. Your agoraphobia, as she terms it, has become so severe that it's forced you to these lengths, which are not a positive influence for Willow."

Bailey scowled. "Can you tell us, specifically, the pretenses that are allegedly false? What lengths?"

"According to this, all of the outings that Rhys has attended with Camile Wynn."

Rhys said, "What are you talking about?"

"Heather is claiming that Camile Wynn is being paid to be your…escort."

"My escort? I paid her to be my dance instructor. She taught me how to waltz for Willow's co-tillion. That's how we met and ultimately got together."

"She alleges that Camile is a bad influence on Willow, too—unstable, recently fired from a job, resulting in a legal dispute. They've included a video of her engaging in a tirade against a respectable businessman named Roberto Veroni. The claim asserts that Camile is in financial trouble and is only interested in Rhys for his money." Sarah read from a sheet of paper: "A romantic relationship whereupon one party is being financially compensated for their time is not a positive example for Willow."

Rhys felt anger flare so hard and fast inside him that he curled the fingers of one hand around the edge of his chair to keep from bolting to his feet. Inhaling slowly, he forced himself to keep his tone even. "This is absurd." He looked at Bailey. "Can she get away with fabricating scenarios like this? Will the court consider this as evidence?"

"Only if there's proof," Bailey said, but the statement seemed to be directed toward Anne.

Rhys turned toward his sister, who'd gone very, very pale. At that moment, he realized how uncharacteristically silent she'd been considering the accusation.

Bailey, who was thinking much quicker than

Rhys at this point, said, "Sarah, we do not know where Heather has come up with these allegations. Can you give us a private moment to discuss?"

Sarah stood. "Of course."

Several seconds of silence ensued after she left the room. Finally, Anne held Rhys's stare and said, "I have no idea how she could have found out. I didn't tell a single person. Not even Mom."

"Anne, you did this?" Rhys's blood went cold as his hot anger chilled to shock. Camile had agreed to this? He forced himself to think about the timeline. How Camile had told him she wasn't interested in a relationship, how her life was a mess, and she needed to get it in order. He'd believed her. Then he hadn't, or more to the point, he'd believed she'd reconsidered. Because suddenly she was asking him to go to the chowder contest… One outing followed another, and he'd been too happy, too confident, too much in love to be suspicious of her change of heart. The fact was she hadn't changed her mind. Anne was paying her to spend time with him, to be nice to him, her socially challenged brother who couldn't make friends on his own. Who'd never been able to find a woman who truly loved him. Why had he believed that he'd suddenly, miraculously managed that feat now?

Especially with a woman he'd treated badly in the past.

"Rhys," Anne's tone was pleading, "I'm so sorry. I thought I was helping. I was helping. Camile has been nothing but good for you. They've twisted this in the ugliest way. I never—"

Rhys wasn't interested in excuses or apologies. "When did you hire her?" he interrupted.

"The day after the wine tasting. We'd been at the scavenger hunt the day before. You were so relaxed and having fun and then she saved you from that fight. Then, at the wine tasting, she saved you again. I could see the effect she was having on you, and I thought if only she could be with you all the time. You are a different person when you're with her, in public anyway. Then Bailey mentioned the advantage of having a steady girlfriend. That's when I came up with the idea—"

He was right. About all of it. "You suggested this, and I distinctly told you no."

"No, think for a second. I suggested you *date* her, and you all but said you'd like to, but that you wouldn't use her in that way. I thought if *she* dated *you*, then we'd both get what we wanted."

"And you had to pay her?" Bailey interjected, frowning at Anne. To Rhys, she said, "I'm sorry. I thought she liked you."

"She does like him! I paid her because it was the only way she could afford to do it. My list was vast and time-consuming, and I wanted it done right. She was working almost every night. She quit one of her jobs and had to cut way back on her hours at the others, so I compensated her for that loss so she could pay her rent. That's all."

"That's all?" Bailey repeated the words on a burst of laughter that didn't possess even a trace of amusement. She dipped her head down and squeezed the bridge of her nose. "And you didn't think to mention this to me? That you'd hired Rhys a *companion*, that you'd purchased him a *friend*? Worse than a friend—a girlfriend. You realize how this appears, right?"

An ache had started right in the center of Rhys's chest, and now it hurt to breathe. It hurt even more to think. He'd been such an idiot to believe he'd finally found a woman who loved him. And Camile of all women. He should have known better. She was so outgoing. Everyone liked her. Why would she want to be with a man who was the exact opposite? A man who regularly said and did the wrong things? Someone she had to extricate from embarrassing situations?

Why did this have to happen with her? The only woman who'd ever held his heart in her hand? He'd given it to her willingly and she'd crushed it. Rhys felt the fragile fantasy he'd been building in his mind come crashing down around him, his hope for something approaching a normal life disintegrating right along with his happiness.

"Or me?" Rhys added. "Why didn't you tell me, Anne?"

"I didn't tell anyone because no one was supposed to find out!"

"I CAN'T FIRE HER, Rhys," Anne said as they walked across the parking lot toward his car. "And you can't break up with her."

There was no breaking up to do, Rhys thought, not when they'd never really been together. Not in an honest sense. There was only letting her know that she didn't need to pretend anymore. No doubt, she'd be relieved.

When he didn't answer, Anne went on, "You heard Bailey—it will seem even worse if you split up now. If you suddenly stop seeing Camile and prevent her from spending time with Willow, it will look like you were guilty and got caught. Or give the impression that you think she's a bad example for Willow."

Rhys cast her a meaningful glare and unlocked the doors.

They climbed inside and Anne kept talking. "Glare at me all you want—you know I'm right. I admit I royally screwed up here. Now we have to figure out a way to fix it."

There was no fixing this where Rhys and Camile were concerned. He'd acquiesce for Willow's sake, for the short term. He didn't see any other way around it.

"This is not her fault—you do know that, right? This was my idea."

He did know that, but the facts didn't change her feelings; she'd spent time with him for money. Maybe it was payback for him not remembering their date? He couldn't imagine her being that cold. Then again, he could never have imagined this at all. At the very least, it was karma.

"Are you going to talk to me? What are you going to tell her?"

He put the key into the ignition and looked at his sister. "The truth, Anne. I'm going to tell her the truth because that's what *I* do."

WILLOW DREW HER arm back and chucked the tattered tennis ball down the beach. Marion, Nina's border collie, took off after it in a sprint that suggested the fate of humanity was on the line. The dog gave new meaning to the word *intensity*.

"This dog is amazing!" Willow gushed.

Camile exchanged smiles with Nina. Her sister had called this morning, and when Camile had revealed her plans for the day, she'd suggested they meet on the beach. Now that berry season had wound down, it was easier for her to get away from the farm, and she'd been taking advantage.

"She is pretty spectacular," Nina agreed.

A triumphant Marion dropped the ball at Willow's feet. She reached down and scooped it up. The dog backed away, brown eyes zeroed intently on Willow as she zigzagged through the sand trying to anticipate which direction it would fly. Ready to save the world one fetch of the ball at a time.

"I would love to have a dog—or a cat. Uncle Rhys likes cats."

Of course he does, Camile thought. Cats were quiet and deliberate and independent like him. "Have you talked to him about it?" Camile asked.

"Yes. He says we should adopt two cats from Lucky Cats, one for each of us." Willow grinned.

"Sounds like a good idea to me."

"He hasn't said it, but I know he's waiting until after the hearing."

Nina's phone rang. "Sorry, I need to take this. I'm trying to find a new supplier for my fertilizer." She stood and headed up the beach out of the wind.

Willow went on, "Aunt Heather doesn't like animals, so if I have to live with her, I won't get either."

Camile so badly wanted to ask the question, but didn't think it was her place.

Willow saved her from having to by saying, "I wish Aunt Heather would listen to me. I love her, I do. But me and Uncle Rhys, we have this…bond. We're sort of the same, like my dad and I were. No one understands me like he does, do you know what I mean?"

"I do," Camile said. "It's the best feeling in the world when another person understands you and accepts everything about you."

"Right? Aunt Heather keeps saying that I should stay in South Carolina where all my new friends are, and Mom's family lives, but Pomona is just a place. Now that Mom is gone, it hurts me to be there. Portland isn't that far away from Pacific Cove and I still have my old friends there." Camile knew Willow had lived in Portland when her dad was still alive. Vanessa had moved back to South Carolina with her parents after Evan's death. "Pacific Cove already feels like home. I love it here so much. I love the ocean."

"And you've told your aunt all this?"

"I've tried." Willow sighed deeply, and the sound was filled with so much anguish Camile dug her toes into the sand to keep from going to her and wrapping her in a hug. "She just says that once I'm hers, she'll redo my bedroom and get me a computer and anything else I want. She keeps talking about how we'll go to Hawaii for Christmas and Mexico for spring break. I don't want to go to Hawaii or Mexico. I don't like the heat. I don't like that about South Carolina, either. Look at my skin! Just like Aunt Anne, I fry like an egg in the sun. I want to go skiing with Uncle Rhys and Aunt Anne and Grandpa and Grandma McGrath for Christmas. And you, too, I hope. Do you know how to ski?"

"I do. I love to ski," Camile answered while Heather's words from the night of the cotillion rushed through her with the force of a tidal wave. *Everything that Vanessa had should be mine. Rhys has enough. He shouldn't get this, too.* The statement hadn't made much sense at the time; she'd written it off to emotion. Camile analyzed it now and wondered just what, specifically how much, was included with custody of Willow? How could she find out? She would need help. Funny how it didn't feel quite so difficult to ask for help when it benefited someone else.

Picking up her phone, she texted Harper: Remember when you told me to ask if there was anything you could do to help?

Harper responded immediately: Name it. Whatever you need.

Camile believed her, and she treasured the feeling. Laura would have demanded to know what she needed and given her unsolicited advice before agreeing. Rhys's assertion about Laura flashed through her mind. She pushed it away and messaged Harper again: Can you drop by my apartment tonight after class? Evening ballet classes for advanced students had started up again.

I'll be there by 8:15.

RHYS AND ANNE had been home for about twenty minutes when Camile returned with Willow. Rhys engineered a plan that allowed him to talk to Camile alone. Anne didn't like it, but she agreed. She intercepted Willow on the way inside the house, commandeering her to ride along into town to pick up a pizza for dinner.

Rhys stood in the kitchen and watched Camile enter the front door and cross the spacious living room toward him. Frustrating, that he still couldn't control his emotions. Knowing what Camile had done, that her feelings were contrived, should have been enough to shut his off. It wasn't. Not even close.

The coming days until the hearing were going to be torture. Her skin had that sun-kissed glow, and she'd pulled her tousled hair back into a messy braid. The moss-green sundress she wore made her eyes glitter like a set of matching emeralds. Her tentative smile, full of concern and what he would have previously mistaken for genuine affection, was nearly his undoing. Everything about her was beautiful. Except for her dishonesty, he reminded himself. As far as he was concerned, that was the ugliest trait a person could possess.

She'd just reached him, was coming in for a hug when he spoke. "I'll double what Anne was paying you if you continue our pretend relationship until the custody hearing."

With a quiet swoosh, her arms fell to her sides. Rhys had to concentrate so as not to reach for her. The gesture was already a habit, and his heart ached from wanting it, her, and the physical contact and the comfort she provided. He realized there was a part of him that wished Anne's scheme had worked, that he hadn't found out, that they could go back to the way it was. He needed to get a grip here. That *way* wasn't reality; she'd been acting. Lying. How could he have been so wrong about her?

Frozen before him, her smile faded to a look of confusion and distress. "What?"

"Heather found out about Anne's scheme involving you. It will come out at the hearing that I paid you to be my companion."

"Anne paid me," she shot back and then winced a little as she seemed to realize how that sounded.

"Do you think the judge will care where the money came from?"

"Rhys—"

"The bottom line is that this looks like I can't make friends—or get a girlfriend, in this case—on my own. I am so socially inept that I have to pay a woman to spend time with me. And I can guarantee that Heather's attorney will imply that I paid you for other services, as well. They're already calling you my escort. How do you think that will look to the court when deciding whether or not I'm fit to be Willow's parent?"

THE AIR HAD whooshed from Camile's lungs, leaving her cold and shaking. She'd been right about not getting involved with him. Her talent for attracting chaos had done exactly what she hadn't wanted it to do; it had spilled over onto Rhys. She'd done this, however inadvertent and well-intentioned it had been.

"Rhys, I'm so sorry. I would have done it for free."

"Even better," he said in a tone laden with sarcasm and bitterness. "You would have made me your charity case. At least, that would have played better with the court."

"No! That's not what I meant. I agreed because I wanted to be with you. I wanted to spend time with you."

"Can you see how that's a little difficult to believe? Anne told me she asked you after the wine tasting, right after you turned me down. If you'd wanted to do it for free, you would have said yes to me then or told Anne that you didn't want the money. End of story."

"I couldn't afford to!" she protested, even though a part of her knew he was right. "I mean, not the way Anne presented it, and she was right because…"

"Oh, I know. I am very well aware of your financial difficulties. I've…" His voice trailed off, and he lifted both hands to scrub them across his cheeks.

"Can't you see that I wanted to help? That I was trying to help you keep Willow?"

He shrugged. "Maybe. Someday. It doesn't matter. Right now, I can't see past the damage you and Anne have done. I wish I didn't ever have to see you again."

Camile flinched as her heart shattered into about a million shards of the most painful anguish and regret that she'd ever felt. What had she done? Bringing a hand up, she placed it on her aching chest and tried to breathe. He didn't want to see her again. Of course he didn't. She didn't even want to see herself. She nodded and blinked through her tears. It wasn't fair for her to cry. She wasn't the wounded one here.

Swallowing more apologies and excuses that she knew he didn't want to hear, she managed to force out the words, "I understand. I'm going to go. You don't have to worry about seeing me again."

"That's another problem. I do, actually."

She faced him again and it was excruciating to look at him, to see the disappointment, the pain in his expression.

"If we 'break up' now, it will only look like Heather was right. That's why I need you to stay in my life until after the hearing. But don't worry, it shouldn't be much longer. The hearing is scheduled for next week."

CHAPTER SEVENTEEN

RED-FACED AND RUNNY-NOSED, Camile wiped her tears and opened the door of her apartment. She was expecting Harper but was surprised to find Nina standing beside her. She almost lost it all over again at the sight of her two favorite people.

"You look awful," Nina declared.

"Are you okay?" Harper said at the same time. Her hand flew up to rest on Camile's forehead.

"Are you sick again?" Nina asked, stepping inside. Her bag hit the floor with a thud.

"She doesn't feel warm," Harper said.

"You guys, I'm not sick."

Harper peered at her. "I can see now that I'm closer that you've been crying. What happened?"

"Did something happen with Rhys?" Nina asked. "I know the mediation session was earlier. I was on my way home, saw your car, and decided to stop by and see how it went."

Camile held up one finger to indicate she

needed a sec. With the other hand, she pinched the bridge of her nose in an attempt to stop another bout of tears. After a few deep breaths, she made a sweeping motion with both hands toward her sofa. Together, the two women moved there and sat.

Camile lowered herself between them, inhaled deeply, and then told them everything.

When she finished, Harper said, "Oh love, I'm so sorry. Why didn't you tell me earlier? I would have come when you first texted. Why didn't you say you needed help *now*?"

"Oh." Camile shook her head. "This wasn't the help I needed. When I texted you, I was all happy and in love."

"Wait." Nina peered at her carefully. "You're in love with Rhys?"

"Yes. Absolutely. Unequivocally. One hundred percent in love with Rhys McGrath." She paused to chuckle, and it sounded as helpless as she felt. "I didn't even get a chance to tell him. When he told me he'd found out what we'd done, he said he wished he never had to see me again. He looked at me like he hates me."

"Oh, sweetie, he didn't mean it," Nina said.

"But he does. That's the thing about him, Nina. If Rhys says it—he means it."

Harper dipped her chin to stare at her lap.

"See?" Camile pointed in her direction.

"Harper knows it's true. He's brutally honest. It's hard to get used to at first, but then it's... pretty wonderful. He's wonderful."

She shook her head and blew her nose. "At first, I refused to admit my feelings because I was a little intimidated by him. I used the excuse that I wanted to straighten out my life before I made room in it for him. And that was true to a degree. It didn't seem fair to weigh his life down with all my baggage. Later, after we were involved anyway, I should have told him how I felt. Then he would have known and I—"

"Whoa, wait a sec." Nina sat up straighter. "What do you mean you were intimidated by him? Did he do something that we need to talk about?"

Despite the fact that despair was radiating painfully throughout her entire body, even to her lips, she managed a small smile at Nina's defensiveness. "No, it was nothing like that. He's the kindest, gentlest guy I've ever known. Maybe if I'd realized that he left me that night for a good reason I wouldn't have been so insecure and then—"

"Left you," a confused Harper interrupted. "It's like you have a fever all over again. What does that mean?"

"That's right—you don't know about my first real date with Rhys." Camile went on to explain.

Harper was wide-eyed by the time she finished the tale. "Wow," she said.

"Exactly," Nina agreed. "He didn't recognize her."

"That totally explains your fear and hesitation. I wouldn't have wanted to date him, either."

"Thank you. I was very confused. I knew I liked him, but how could I trust him after what he'd done? Then I got sick, and he was so amazing. You guys saw him in action—how could I not like him?"

Their somber, tandem head nodding made her want to cry all over again.

"Even after we sorted the date thing, I was still afraid. Ugh. Such a coward." Pausing, she placed a palm on her forehead to gather her thoughts. "But I liked him so much. And when Anne told me about the custody fight, I wanted to help. Her plan made sense, and she was so confident that it was the right thing to do. Ironically, by trying not to make his life worse, I made it much, much worse. Way worse than I could have ever imagined. I've actually, probably, done the worst thing anyone could do to him. If Willow gets taken away from him, I don't know what he'll do."

"So be brave now," Harper suggested. "Tell him how you feel."

"It's too late. He'd never believe me now."

Another knock sounded on her door. She had no idea who it could be.

"Do you want me to answer it?" Nina asked.

"Yes, please." She didn't have the energy to stand, much less greet anyone.

Nina got up, crossed the floor and opened the door. "Oh, Nina, hi," she heard Anne say. "Is Camile here?"

"In here, Anne," Camile called.

Anne came inside and rushed toward her. "Camile, I am so, so sorry."

"It's not your fault. Rhys is right. I'm responsible for my own part in this. I could have said no. I shouldn't have taken the money."

"And paid your rent with what? If you hadn't agreed, you wouldn't have fallen in love with him. Or maybe you would have, I don't know. What I do know is that my brother loves you, Camile. He's just upset right now."

"Pretty sure she's right," Harper said.

Camile tried to smile but those words hurt because maybe they were true. "It doesn't matter. Even if that were true, I wasn't honest with him, and he'll never forget that. He'll never trust me again. But I do have to make this better. Anne, we need to try to fix this before the hearing."

"I'm not sure that's possible. But what is

possible, and what I'm afraid of, is that it's going to get worse."

"Worse how?"

"I don't know. But if Heather found this out about Rhys, what else does she have? I'm afraid… I'm not sure what I'm afraid of, but she's angry and desperate. Rhys started this charity for veterans called The Other Front Line."

"I know that charity very well," Nina said. "It's wonderful. Aubrey and Eli support it, too. I had no clue Rhys was involved."

"Hardly anyone does. Rhys and the other guys try to keep their names out of it. They want all the attention on the veterans. But if this came out, it would look really bad for Rhys, damage his reputation, humiliate him publicly. The Other Front Line gets support from very important and influential people. What if she leaks all this to the press?"

"Oh no…" Another layer of apprehension to add to the situation.

"Maybe it's my PR experience, but I want to figure out what else we could be facing and be prepared. And what I don't understand is how this happened. I didn't tell anyone about our arrangement, not another living soul. Camile, do you have any idea how Heather found out? Did you tell anyone?"

Camile had just assumed that Anne had fessed up at some point, which meant… Cold reality settled into her. She'd only told one person.

"Laura."

"Who?" Anne asked.

Nina huffed an angry gasp. "I've never liked her."

"Neither did Rhys," Camile said. "And my best guess is that he told her so." She thought back to their lunch in Astoria and how curious Laura had been about Rhys and Willow, how concerned she'd seemed. She'd been digging for information to use against him, and Camile had played right into her hands. If she'd done this, given Heather this information, then Rhys was probably right that she'd sabotaged her thesis, too. But why would she do it?

Anne sighed. "No surprise there."

"I have to go to Portland. I'll go tomorrow morning."

"What are you going to do?"

"Confront Laura. Find out why. But listen, something else is bothering me." To Anne, she said, "This might seem like an odd question, but does Willow have a life-insurance payoff or a trust fund or money that comes attached to her along with custody?"

"Yes, both. Evan and Vanessa provided well for her. Life insurance funds and a trust. I think it totals a couple million. The trust can't be accessed until she goes to college. If she chooses not to go to college, she can't use it until she's twenty-eight."

"But not the life insurance?"

"That's just sitting there as far as I know. As her guardian, Rhys has control of it, but he's set every penny of it aside for emergencies and her future."

"Are Heather and Troy wealthy?"

"Oh, yeah. Troy has family money, and he's an executive with a pharmaceutical company. Heather is a dental hygienist. You should see their house—ten thousand square feet overlooking the Ashley River, gourmet kitchen, media room with a giant screen and a bunch of those reclining movie-theater-type seats, billiards table, tennis court, a pool. Her walk-in closet is as big as this apartment. I saw inside once and counted sixteen pairs of Manolo Blahniks. They drive matching sports cars. They live like royal-*tyyy*…" Anne dragged out the last syllable, then tipped her chin back and said, "Whoa. To borrow a phrase from Olivia, oh, my stars. Why did I not see this? You're thinking they're living beyond their means."

"I can't help but wonder…" Camile filled her in on her conversation with Heather at the cotillion. And then told her what Willow said at the beach about Heather's vacation promises and plans to "buy her anything she wants."

"Sounds like Heather plans on buying everything Heather wants," Anne said sardonically.

Camile looked at Harper. "This is where I was hoping you could help, Harper."

Harper smiled. "You want me to see what I can find out about them and their finances?"

"Yes, but how would you be able to do it? This can't have any negative consequences for Rhys."

Nodding, Harper reached for her bag. "Don't worry. I've got this. You'd be amazed what's out there in public records and free on the internet these days. I am so excited to be able to help, finally." She removed a notepad and a pen and handed them to Anne. "Anne, I need Heather's and Troy's full names, if you know them. Parents' names could be helpful, and siblings, birth dates or as close you can get. Pomona, South Carolina, right?" Heads bent together, the two continued to parse the relevant details.

"Well, I want to help, too!" Nina said. "I'm going to Portland with you tomorrow to talk to Laura. There's no way I'm going to let you confront that woman on your own."

Resisting the urge to tell her sister no, Camile sank back into the sofa cushions and answered with her heart. "Okay."

"Good. I know you're not going to like this idea, but I think we should ask Aubrey, too. If Laura is criminally insane or dangerous, we could use Aubrey's level head and her muscle."

Camile knew Nina was thinking about her and Aubrey's brush with a dangerous drug dealer a couple of years ago, so she nodded. The truth was, she wanted both her sisters with her. For the first time in years, it felt good to share some of her burden. Maybe Rhys was right; maybe a little help could be a good thing.

RHYS SWIPED THE security icon on his tablet alerting him that a visitor was requesting access. Heather's image popped on-screen. He thought fast. Probably not a good idea to let her in, especially without Anne here to play peacekeeper or Camile to keep him calm. Then he reminded himself that he couldn't rely on either one of them anymore. A combination of disappointment and frustration rolled through him. He felt like he didn't have any choice but to let her in. Was this how Camile felt about her life? About circumstances being outside of her control? He reminded himself that thinking about Camile would get him nowhere but more depressed. At least Willow was with her grandmother for the afternoon. His mom had picked her up this morning and taken her to

Portland to go shopping for school clothes. They planned to be back tomorrow afternoon.

Reaching out, he tapped the unlock button and watched the gate open. He went outside to wait for Heather on the porch.

"Where's Willow?" she asked after exiting her car, looking around and scaling the steps to join him.

"Shopping with her grandmother."

Heather nodded and looked out toward the ocean. "This place is amazing," she said softly, almost like she hadn't meant to say the words aloud.

"I agree," he said.

Then she addressed him with that tense, bitter harshness he'd grown used to. "Look, Rhys. I want you to know that I'm only doing this for Willow's benefit. A girl needs a strong female figure in her life."

"That's why Anne is moving here. Our parents only live a few hours away. You don't get much stronger than Bertie and Anne McGrath."

"But I'm Willow's closest female relative. She's my sister's daughter."

"She's my brother's daughter, Heather. And your sister wanted me to raise her if anything happened to them. Did you even read the will? You were sent a copy."

"Vanessa didn't know… She did that to

make you feel good after Evan died. She didn't mean it. She never imagined she was going to die, too."

This was pointless. "What are you doing here, Heather? My attorney advised me not to talk to you without her present. I'm sure yours did the same, so I'm assuming this is important."

"Troy. He convinced me to give you one more chance." Rhys thought back to his conversation with Troy at the cotillion, which hadn't amounted to much more than him trying to explain Heather's behavior. He'd seemed almost apologetic. But after Rhys learned that Heather had accosted Camile, he'd assumed it had been a ruse, a ploy to keep him occupied so Heather could bully Camile.

"I'll take my chances at the hearing. You can't prove these allegations about Camile." At least, Bailey didn't think so at this point. But if the judge called Anne to testify, likely it would all come out. He would not allow his sister to lie.

"Are you truly as naive as you seem? It's like you think that because you have this code of honor that you live by that everybody else does, too."

He'd heard this from Anne, and others, his entire life. But the simple fact was that they gave him too much credit. He wasn't taking some sort of high road; he just didn't know how else to be. Somehow, in the weeks he'd spent with Camile, he had learned to accept that another person's truth wasn't necessarily untrue if it wasn't the same as his. Even if Rhys knew they were wrong, it could be true to them. "Shades of truth," she called it. Most importantly, she'd helped him curb his inclination to correct that untruth. But he knew he'd never stop wanting to, and he'd never stop despising blatant dishonesty.

"I don't need to prove the allegations, Rhys. I only need people to believe them. If you don't sign the papers granting me custody of Willow by Tuesday, your story is going to be all over the internet. And we'll let the court of public opinion decide."

"What story?" he asked, even as the truth settled like a cold rock in his gut.

"About how the man behind The Other Front Line hired a prostitute to help him maintain custody of his thirteen-year-old niece."

"She is not a prostitute. Nor was she hired to be one. I don't care what people think about me," he said. "The judge's opinion is the only one I care about. I will swear under oath that I knew nothing about this, and that will be true. Anne will swear, too." Camile would be proud of him because he hadn't specified exactly what Anne would swear to.

"You might not care, but your prostitute will. And just so you know, that video of her freaking out in her taco suit will be part of the story. I'm not a writer, but I imagine it going something like this…" Placing a hand across her chest, she went on in a dramatic syrupy tone, "Desperate to find work after she failed her thesis and was fired from her job as a product promoter for a successful Mexican eatery, the mercenary yet clever dance instructor sought the highest paying job she could get in order to pay her student loans, mounting legal bills, and the settlement looming over her, et cetera."

"She didn't fail her thesis."

Heather scoffed. "She did fail. Initially." She pulled one shoulder up into a demure shrug. "If the story is inaccurate, I'm sure a retraction will follow. But you know how the media can be about checking their sources—it might be a while before it shows up in print."

"I will sue you for slander."

"It will be too late, won't it? Save yourself the humiliation, Rhys, and sign. Keep your charity and all its board members from being dragged through the mud. Your attorney has the paperwork. I suggest you get down to her office ASAP."

Careful to keep his features composed, Rhys watched Heather get into her car and drive away. But every beat of his heart pushed a fresh dose of terror into his bloodstream. Pulling his phone from his pocket, he tapped out a text to Anne. Despite his current feelings for his sister, she loved Willow, too. She had a right to know that their already desperate situation had taken a turn toward hopeless.

CHAPTER EIGHTEEN

UNSURPRISINGLY, LAURA WASN'T returning Camile's calls.

"If she thinks that's going to save her, she's wrong," Aubrey said early the next morning after picking up Camile and Nina at Camile's apartment. Aubrey had not only wanted to come along, she also insisted on driving them in her SUV for the long trip to Portland. They passed most of the time drinking coffee, munching on the healthy breakfast Aubrey had packed, and filling her in on the drama in Camile's life, including the details of Laura's betrayal. It seemed pointless to try to keep any of it from her now.

"Yeah, so," Camile said when she'd finished updating her about Bobby's lawsuit, "that's my life. I bet you're jealous of all my drama, aren't you?"

Aubrey's eyes briefly connected with Camile's in the rearview mirror. "Trust me, little one—it could be worse." Camile felt a warm glow inside at Aubrey's use of the childhood nickname she'd bestowed upon her practically at birth. Camile appreciated the show of support, even if she knew in her heart that it couldn't get much worse than losing Rhys.

A few moments of silence crept by as they neared the outskirts of Portland.

Then Aubrey announced, "Since we're sharing, Eli and I have an appointment with a fertility specialist next week." Her tone was all matter-of-fact like she was revealing an upcoming trip to the grocery store and not a traumatic and life-altering event.

"Aubrey...what?" Camile said.

"Yeah, we don't seem to be able to get pregnant."

Nina had swiveled in her seat and was gaping at her. "I didn't even know you were trying."

"I know. No one does, or did, until now. For me, it would have been an odd thing to announce. What if I didn't get pregnant right away? Unfortunately, my instinct was spot-on. Thank goodness, I didn't tell Mom and Dad we're trying. You know how much they're looking forward to grandchildren."

"You don't know that!" Nina said. "A lot of couples try for years before they get pregnant."

"True!" Camile chimed in. "A woman I work with at Tabbie's tried for eight years. She and her husband adopted a baby, and five months later she was pregnant."

They continued discussing the plans Aubrey and Eli had made, the steps they were about to begin. Camile felt a little twist of guilt as she realized how long it had been since the three of them had enjoyed any quality sister time. Her fault, she knew. At some point during the chaotic descent her life had undergone, she'd begun avoiding her confident, successful middle sister as well as her parents. She'd been too busy for Nina way too often for comfort. Nina just didn't allow her as much space to retreat.

Funny, how even people you thought you knew well could be struggling with issues and worries only they could see. Poor Aubrey. And here they were, her sisters, when she needed them most. Camile resolved to do the same. It was too late for her and Rhys, but she made a silent vow to be the sister, daughter, friend she used to be before she got stuck on this stupid treadmill of "when." When she got her life together; when she finished school; when she had a "real" job; when she got caught up on her bills. When her life was...*fill in the blank*. She'd used a lot of excuses. She was done with that. No more waiting until her life was in some perfect place or she'd accomplished some ambiguous goal so that she'd feel worthy. Life wasn't ever going to be perfect, and neither was she. And maybe if she quit trying so hard to be all of those things, she'd have more time to enjoy what she did have and to celebrate the accomplishments she'd achieved. These people loved her, and she loved them right back. A longing for Rhys burned at her core; she wished it hadn't taken losing him for her to see all of this. If only she had grabbed that brass ring when she'd had the chance.

They drove straight to Laura's condo in Portland. The lights were out, but Camile hopped out and knocked on the door. No answer. A quick peek through the side window into the garage revealed that her car was gone.

"I know she teaches a class at ten. Let's head to the university and see if we can catch her before class starts."

Because it was summer, fewer students were on campus, and that meant they easily found a parking space in the huge lot next to the tall steel-and-glass building that housed most of the social sciences department. Traversing the familiar cement and brick walkways, Camile tried to analyze how she felt about the place she'd spent so much time in during the previous seven years of her life, but she quickly discovered that she couldn't think past somehow fixing this situation for Rhys. And dealing with Laura. She was angry, too.

Setting aside her tangled emotions, she focused on the task at hand. She wondered how long it would be before Harper learned anything about Heather. She briefly considered texting and then decided against it, knowing Harper wouldn't delay when, if, she had news.

The three sisters settled on a bench with a clear view of the building's main entrance. Class time crept closer with no sign of Laura. Camile was nearly ready to give up when a different familiar figure approached the building: medium height, stocky build, close-cropped black hair with pretty gray-blue eyes. Camile thought Rob Bretz looked more like a hot collegiate athlete than the brainy sociology adjunct professor he was.

"There's Rob," Camile told her sisters. "A mutual friend of mine and Laura's. He might know where she is. I'll be right back." She jogged toward him, and she could tell the instant he recognized her.

Dazzling smile in place, arms up and out, he hurried toward her as if thrilled to see her. "Camile!" She stepped into his arms. Hugging her tightly, he said, "How are you? You look amazing."

Camile patted his back and stepped away. "Thanks, Rob. You are a very sweet liar. But look at you, you're looking pretty smart yourself there, Professor Bretz." She added a wink.

He laughed, gray-blue eyes sparkly and warm. She'd always liked how thoroughly his smile seeped into his eyes. "Congratulations, again, on a thesis job well done." Camile had sent him a text after she'd learned the news. His response had been immediate, enthusiastic and heartfelt. Like she'd expected from Laura.

"Thank you. I'll admit I was pretty thrilled to learn that I did pass after all." She added a little bow. "I wish I had time to take you out for coffee or lunch or something, but I'm looking for Laura. I know she has a class soon. Have you seen her?"

Rob cringed, his face twisting with distress. "Oh, wow… I guess you haven't heard, huh?"

"Heard what?"

"Camile, I don't know how to tell you this because I'm not sure exactly what happened, but Laura got arrested."

"Arrested for what?" Even though she thought she knew. Rhys's professor friend had said that because the violation fell under computer hacking laws, the matter had been turned over to law enforcement.

"There are rumors," Rob answered carefully. "No one seems to know for certain. But I can tell you that the cops arrested her here on campus early this morning. I saw them handcuff her and escort her from the building."

"Have you seen her since then? Did you go to the police station?"

"Me? No." He looked so startled by the question that Camile felt compelled to ask, "Aren't you two together?"

"Did she tell you that?"

"Yes. Right after I moved back to Pacific Cove, she said you guys had been spending a lot of time together and, uh, getting close."

"Ugh." Rob tipped his head and looked briefly at the sky. He sighed and focused back on Camile. "We did a small project together for Professor Vaughn. That's it. She wanted us to be more, but I wasn't interested. I thought it was strange when she told me because she knew how I felt about you. She's known since last year."

"Last year?" Camile thought about how hard she'd crushed on Rob. At one point, it had seemed like he'd returned her feelings. She'd been gearing up to ask him out when the chemistry between them suddenly cooled. Assuming she'd read the signals wrong, she'd been grateful she'd never ruined their friendship by making a move.

Rob peered at her. "Yes. I mentioned that I… liked you. I knew you guys were friends and I thought maybe you'd talked to her about me or whatever. But when I told her I was thinking about asking you out, she said you were involved with someone else. That you had a serious man in your life, but that you didn't like to talk about it."

"Unbelievable," Camile said with a shake of her head. No wonder Laura had seemed interested in Rhys. There was no romance between her and Rob. Camile felt her phone vibrate in her pocket. Pulling it out, she saw it was a text from Dr. Slater. "I'm sorry, Rob. I've got some unfortunate drama going on in my life, and I need to check this text." Camile read the message, confirming Laura's arrest. It also contained a heads-up letting her know the authorities would likely be contacting her soon. They had some questions.

Rob had been staring at the ground. When Camile slid the phone back into her pocket, he looked up and blurted, "She did it, didn't she? The rumor is true. She somehow made you fail your thesis."

"It's looking that way."

"I knew it. She's…off, Camile. The way she talks about you is weird. It's like she loves you and hates you at the same time."

Camile thought about how Rhys had Laura figured out in roughly five minutes while she'd spent years being her friend and hadn't seen it. *Some psychology major I am*, she thought wryly. Rhys was so much more insightful than he gave himself credit for.

"And you weren't involved with anyone else, were you?" Rob asked.

"Nope. I wasn't."

"So… If I asked you out now, what would you say?" It was endearing the way his cheeks tinged pink.

"Oh, Rob, I wish…" But she didn't wish because if Rob had asked her out, she probably wouldn't have moved back to Pacific Cove and she would never have met Rhys. "I would say that unfortunately, it's too late for us. I'm in love with someone." Even if Rhys didn't want her, even if he couldn't forgive her, Camile couldn't imagine being with anyone else. She had no idea how long it took a heart to heal, but she knew in her case, it would be a while. And Rob deserved to be with someone who could give him her whole heart.

Rob's smile was a mix of sadness and regret. Camile hated being the cause, but she wasn't, was she? Laura had done this.

"He's a very, very lucky guy. I hope he knows that."

"Thank you, Rob." Reaching out, she gave his hand a quick squeeze before releasing it. She turned to go.

"Camile, wait."

She faced him again.

"Be careful with Laura."

"Thanks, Rob. I will."

THERE WERE BENEFITS, Camile decided, to having a sister in the Coast Guard. Aubrey knew people in law enforcement. A few phone calls and she discovered that Laura had already been released on bail. They drove back to her house to wait. And it paid off when, in less than an hour, a car pulled up next to the curb adjacent to her building. Laura climbed out.

"That's her," Camile said, and, as they'd already planned, she called Aubrey's number. Aubrey accepted the call and left the line open so Aubrey and Nina could listen to the conversation from the car. Camile slipped her phone into her jacket pocket. Aubrey would be ready to intercede if needed, and Nina could call law enforcement if it came to that. Feeling like her heart was about to beat out of her chest, Camile exited the SUV and approached her.

"Laura."

She whirled around, and Camile could see the flash of emotion in her eyes, even though she couldn't quite identify it. "I don't have anything to say. My attorney has advised me not to speak with anyone, including you."

"You can't even tell me why? Laura, why

would you do this to me? I thought we were friends."

"Friends? How can you even say that to me right now? I hate this! I hate women like you. But I don't hate you. I wish I could, but I can't…" Shockingly, tears welled in her eyes. Removing a tissue from her pocket, she dabbed at her lashes.

Camile told herself not to feel bad but sympathy must have been evident on her face because Laura said, "Jeez, Camile, you're so *nice*. No one could hate you."

"But Laura—"

"All I'm going to say is that I didn't mean for all this to happen. Not like this."

"What did you mean—women like me?"

"You have everything! For three years, I've watched you get every single thing you want— everything I wanted—while barely even trying. And acting like you don't even care or that you even want it. While I worked and studied and played nice and batted my eyelashes like some kind of pathetic sycophant and got nothing!"

"Laura, what in the world are you talking about?"

Laura sniffled and glanced away for a few seconds. "See? This is exactly what I'm talking about. You don't even know how good you have it—how smart and funny and pretty you are. *Everyone* loves you, Camile! Including Rob, the guy I've been in love with since my freshman year." Laura paused to wave a hand up and down Camile's length. "Don't even get me started on that perfect little body of yours—how can you eat French fries with country gravy and four slices of pizza in one sitting and still look like a personal trainer? It's not fair.

"When I came to St. Killian's, I had one goal—to graduate at the top of my class, to be first in the psychology department. And I was there, a virtual shoo-in until you decided to transfer over from premed and steal my thunder. Who does that? If you're smart enough to become a doctor, you become a darn doctor!"

"Laura, I—"

"I'm not finished. Because then you hemmed and hawed around and finally decided to go on and get your master's degree like you were deciding which car to buy and not committing to your lifelong profession. Fine, I thought. Camile has to work and pay her own way through school—including dressing up and dancing around in those ridiculous costumes every weekend. She won't have time to be the best student in our master's program. I will. I'll have nothing but time to study. And I'll study harder and do more and be better, and the professors will see it. They'll read *my* papers out loud to the class, single me out, pick *me* to be their TA. They'll choose *me* to work on their research projects. And at the end of it all, I will get the grand prize—the adjunct professor job! But no, even with your crazy work schedule and your constant, pointless…dancing, you somehow managed to excel. We were neck and neck right up until the end. But when I read your thesis, I knew I didn't stand a chance. It was absolutely…brilliant. And I just… I snapped."

Camile stared at the woman she'd believed to be her friend and tried to decide how to handle this. She wasn't afraid of her, but she needed some serious counseling.

"Laura, I am so sorry. I'm sorry that you feel this way about me. I never meant to hurt you. I think I was too concerned with my own issues and trying to be my own version of successful to see that you were struggling, too."

With the heel of her hand, Laura swiped at an errant tear. "There were rumors about how you could hack into the university's cloud. I found a guy who would do it for two hundred dollars. He helped me, and it was so easy. I didn't know that it was illegal. It felt more like a prank. I thought you'd just have to fix it, redo it at the very worst. I made it easy to fix, too! I thought by the time it was all sorted, I'd already have the job, and I'd be dating Rob. And you could go on to be amazing at whatever you decided to pursue."

"You told Heather Dupres that I was working for Rhys, didn't you?"

"I did you a favor there. That guy might look like a Greek god, but he's a rude jerk, Camile. You are better off without him."

"Why would you do that? It's one thing to sabotage me, but why would you try to ruin his life? You don't even know him."

"Because I know he's the one who asked for your thesis to be reevaluated. My office is right next to Dr. Youngworth's. When I met him at the bowling alley, he gave me a weird vibe. That's why I left. The next day, I heard Dr. Youngworth talking to Dr. Sawyer from the English department. I heard his name and what he wanted, and I knew it was only a matter of time. If it weren't for Rhys McGrath and his feelings for you, I never would have gotten caught! We'd had lunch by then where you told me about your arrangement with his sister and the custody fight. It wasn't difficult to track Heather down."

Camile felt a fresh wave of frustration. "But why?"

"He ruined my life, Camile. It's only fair that I ruin his."

"Wow," Aubrey said when Camile finally climbed back inside the car. "That girl needs help. I mean serious, serious help."

Agreeing, Nina twisted in her seat to look at Camile. "That was intense. Are you okay?"

"Yeah, I'm fine. I think. For now, anyway. I'm glad it's over. I'm sure I'll be pondering all of that for a while, but right now, I need to call Anne and let her know what we found out." Camile couldn't help but wonder what exactly Rhys had said to Laura at the bowling alley.

"No need," Nina said. "Harper called. She tried to call your phone, but you were on your trip to Scarytown back there, so she called mine. We're meeting her and Anne back at your place. She says she is very optimistic and has lots to share."

"Heather and Troy are deeply in debt," Harper announced to the assembled cast of Camile, Anne, Nina and Aubrey. "Discovering the state of their finances was just as easy as I'd hoped. And don't worry, Camile, completely aboveboard. I even consulted my attorney to make sure Rhys can use what we found."

"How deep?" Camile asked.

"A few million dollars, not including their home, in which they are upside down and all tangled up."

Camile nodded. "This explains so much, but how can Rhys use it in the custody battle? The more I think about it, the more I realize that the court probably doesn't care that much about her financial situation. How could we ever prove her motive? Heather appears to love Willow. She would never admit that she wants custody of her sister's child for the money."

Harper handed her a file folder and added, "You could start by using this affidavit that a contact of mine—a good guy on my father's legal staff—got from Heather's BFF, Stacey. In her sworn statement, Stacey says that Heather regularly refers to Willow as her 'gravy train' and her 'golden goose.' And talks about how she'll spend 'Willow's money' once she gets it. Stacey also says that their friend McKinley has heard Heather use these terms numerous times, as well. My guy hasn't gotten McKinley's statement yet because she's been at a yoga retreat in Canada. She's willing to talk and she'll be back tonight. He'll be waiting."

Silence ensued for a long moment as they all stared in awe at Harper.

Finally, Anne said, "Harper, I love your guy so much. Who is he? I want to marry him."

CHAPTER NINETEEN

"RHYS, ARE YOU absolutely one hundred percent certain that you want to do this?" Bailey asked, zeroing in on Rhys with her signature laser-beam focus.

"Yes."

"You're sure there's not some other way? Do you want to discuss options? If you sign, you are stuck with this."

"Of course, there are other ways. I don't want to discuss options because this could drag on for years. This way, it's over and done."

"Fine. You're the one who has to deal with the…repercussions." With a resigned sigh, Bailey pushed the paperwork toward him. "The places where you need to sign have been marked with yellow sticky notes."

Rhys arranged the papers into a neat stack, picked up a pen and started signing.

"MOM, DO YOU know where Rhys is?" Anne asked into her phone as she paced in Camile's apartment. "What do you mean he's at the attorney's office?" Expression tight with anxiety, she listened to her mom's response. "Okay, thanks. I'll see you later." She tapped the screen and dropped her hands to her sides. "I can't believe this. Rhys told our mom that he had to go to the attorney's office and sign some papers. We didn't tell Mom about Heather's threat, so she doesn't realize what he's doing." Anne brought one hand up and placed it on her forehead. "Please don't tell me he's given up already."

Camile thought. Anne had been trying to get a hold of Rhys ever since Camile had spoken to Laura. If he was at the attorney's office "signing papers," it could only mean one thing.

"I can't imagine that he's given up. And I don't think he would make a decision like this without consulting you, Anne. He told you about Heather's threat. Despite everything, he loves you and values your opinion. It would be completely out of character for him. He'd consider it dishonest, don't you think?"

"Yes." Anne nodded, but she didn't look convinced. "Except—"

"Either way—" Camile picked up her keys and grabbed her bag "—I think we should hurry."

With Harper's pledge to get the proof they needed in hand as quickly as possible, Camile and Anne drove to Bailey's office. Luckily, Camile's apartment was much closer to the place than Rhys's house was. Minutes later, they were pulling into the lot. Anne let out a little yelp at the sight of Rhys exiting the office. Camile parked, and Anne was out of the car before Camile could get her seat belt unbuckled.

"Rhys!" Anne yelled. Camile hurried to catch up.

He spun around and faced them, blue eyes flashing with the same anger and sense of betrayal Camile had seen the day before. It was all she could do not to blurt everything they'd discovered, beg him for forgiveness and ask for another chance.

But Anne was already speaking, "What are you doing here? Please tell me you didn't sign Heather's agreement without talking to me first."

His answer was classic Rhys, his tone flat and controlled. "First off, none of your business. Second, you're lucky I'm talking to you at all. Which I'm only doing because, third, Willow is more important than my anger with you. No, I haven't signed Heather's agreement and I don't intend to sign it. You know I wouldn't do that without talking to you."

Anne glanced at the office and then back at Rhys. "You promise?"

"Making me promise is unnecessary, and you know it."

Anne heaved a relieved breath. "I do."

"Good. So, unless you have something important to say, I need to get going. I have things to do."

"We do have something important to say—some very, very important things. Can we go somewhere and talk?"

THE SCENT OF LILACS and all things Camile overwhelmed Rhys's senses the second he walked into her apartment. Memories followed and a bolt of longing hit him fast and hard. Stopping in his tracks, he struggled to get his bearings. Grinding his teeth, he hoped that whatever urgent news they had was worth this torturous sensory overload.

"You okay?" Anne asked him.

"No," he replied simply.

He could feel Camile's gaze on him, steady and concerned, but he refused to make eye contact. He ached for her hand, for the soothing comfort of her touch. He hated how much he still wanted her.

Nina pulled a chair from the dining room and set it next to the sofa. Patting it, she asked, "Can I get you some coffee or a glass of water?"

Rhys managed a small smile. "No, thank you." He walked over and sat.

Anne got right to the point. "So, lucky for us, Camile pays attention. Heather made some interesting comments at Willow's cotillion, and then Willow said some things, too. Combining them gave her this suspicion, which we've learned was spot-on. Rhys, I think we've got her. Thanks to Harper, we can prove it."

"Anne, what are you talking about?" Rhys knew he sounded cranky and impatient, but he didn't care. It was difficult being here so close to Camile.

"I know I'm not making sense, so I'm going to let Camile and Harper give you the details because I know you'll have questions."

He forced himself to look at Camile while she recapped her conversations with Heather and Willow. Then Harper spent the next few minutes detailing what her contact had discovered about Heather and Troy's finances. As he listened, Rhys felt hopeful for the first time since Heather had issued her threat.

He said, "This all makes so much more sense now. She and Vanessa weren't close. She never spent much time with Willow when Vanessa was alive. She and Troy have never even wanted to have children. I don't know why we didn't think of this sooner."

"Because they put on a good show," Anne answered.

Rhys glanced at Camile. "This is... Thank you. I'm incredibly grateful for your insight. And Harper, thank you, too. I don't know what to say."

Harper beamed. "Say that you'll text Heather right now and set up a meeting."

Smiling, Rhys removed his phone from his pocket and pulled up Heather's contact information. "Done," he said, after tapping out the message that would ensure that Willow would stay right where she belonged forever. Or at least until she went away to college.

RHYS AND ANNE left to go meet Heather. Harper and Nina stayed at Camile's.

"Harper," Camile said, "I don't know how to thank you. I hope you'll let me reimburse you for all these expenses."

"No, I won't. I did this because I wanted to. You and Rhys are both my friends. If I can't spend my money and use my resources on my friends, then what good are they?"

"Harper—"

"No," Nina chimed in. "Camile, she's right. Have you learned nothing throughout this whole ordeal? Your family and your friends—your real friends—love you and we want to help you when we can. That's what people who care about each other do. They help. End of story."

Camile knew she was right. She'd learned this extremely painful truth the hard way. If only she'd been honest with Rhys, then maybe he would see that she'd been trying to help. "Thank you."

"There is something you can do for me, though." Harper's smile was nearly as big as the one she'd given Rhys. "In the spirit of helping and all."

"What?" Camile asked. "I can't imagine there's much I wouldn't do for you right now."

"Okay, good. Let's go downstairs—I want to show you something."

Even though Camile kind of wanted to hole up and wait to hear from Anne and Rhys, she didn't argue. Finding a way to pass the time would undoubtedly make it go by quicker. Harper was already up and moving. A smiling Nina gave her an easy shrug, and they both followed.

Once downstairs, Harper led them into the largest classroom. "What do you think?" Arms up and out, she spun a circle.

Camile glanced around but everything appeared the same. "About what?"

"About my new building," she answered. "I couldn't bear the thought of no more dance classes—for us or the kids—or our adult students for that matter. Gia was ready to sell it to some business group and I had to make a decision. They didn't want to buy the dance business, so I offered to buy them both."

"Wow. Harper, that's amazing!" Camile was happy for her friend and relieved for the same reasons. There was also a tiny part of her that felt…

Harper stepped closer and placed her hands on the tops of Camile's shoulders. "I'm going to ask you a question. Don't think about your answer—just answer. Now, how do you feel right now?"

"Happy and excited, obviously, and, I'll be honest, a little jealous. No, not jealous—envious. But in a good way!"

"Perfect," Harper said on a relieved breath. "Because I want us to be partners. With my photography business, I don't have time to run all the aspects of a dance business, too. I understand if you've already made plans to move on, especially now that you have your master's degree. But there's no one I'd rather do this with than you, Camile. Be my partner. I've never known a more talented dancer or a harder worker than you. I just know that we could make this place amazing."

They could; Camile knew it. They'd talked and discussed and analyzed all the ways Gia could improve and expand. And this time, she didn't even try to squelch the yearning inside her. Partly because it was already too big, and partly because she was done doing things for the reasons she thought she should do them. That was one thing Laura had been right about; psychology wasn't Camile's passion. She'd stumbled into the discipline and she'd enjoyed learning about it, but working in the field had never felt like her calling. She could see now that was why, no matter how tough her class load or what she had going on in her life, she never missed her studio time. It was time to listen to her heart.

Nina was watching it all, wide-eyed and uncharacteristically silent. But Camile could see the hope and the tentative joy splashed all over her sister's face.

Camile said, "Yes. I'll do it. I've never wanted to do anything as much as I want to do this with you. Thank you, Harper. I won't let you down."

"I know." Harper enfolded her in a tight hug. "You never let anyone down, Camile."

"Not on purpose," she quipped, teary-eyed and joyful. And wishing she could share the news with Rhys.

FIVE DAYS. CAMILE hadn't seen or heard from Rhys since the day he and Anne had met with

Heather. An overjoyed Anne had returned to Camile's apartment three hours later with the news that Heather had dropped the suit. Just Anne. No Rhys. That was the moment Camile realized she'd been holding on to a sliver of hope that, if the situation with Willow was resolved, he'd somehow forgive her, and they would... But that hadn't happened. Nothing had happened and she needed to accept that it was over between them.

It had felt almost too good to be true when Bailey called that same afternoon to let her know that Bobby had dropped the lawsuit against her. The next day, she'd gone back to Portland so the police could interview her about Laura's hacking case. Laura was facing serious charges, the outcome of which was up in the air. Camile hoped she'd get the help she needed.

With most of her problems put to rest, Camile was free to concentrate on the studio. She still couldn't quite believe she was officially a business co-owner. Harper had her lawyer draw up the business agreement and in the days since, they'd spent countless hours planning, discussing, scheduling, and working up a marketing plan and all the accompanying details. And teaching dance classes. In her entire life, working had never felt less like work.

And now, here she was, waitressing her last

shift at Tabbie's. Camile watched Sam Garr—
wearing jeans that fit, she couldn't help but
notice—troop inside the café with a group of
three other guys and settle into a corner booth.

"Hey, Camile. How ya doin'?" Sam asked
when she approached their table with iced wa-
ters and menus.

"Better than average, Sam. How are you?"

"Not too bad myself."

Camile knew two of the other men, as well,
and she greeted them by name. "Jake, Wesley,
how are you guys?" Sam introduced the other
gentleman as "Logan" and she recognized him
from Rhys and Sam's almost scuffle after the
scavenger hunt.

She took drink orders, asked about family
members and made small talk. On the way
to the drink station, she checked on her other
tables, fetched an extra blue-cheese dressing
and a tartar sauce, returned an unsatisfactory
sandwich to the kitchen, and delivered a check.
Then she loaded a tray with Sam and company's
drinks and headed back to their table, where she
deposited two coffees, a soda and an iced tea.

"Thanks," Sam said. "Hey, so the latest
rumor around town is that your boyfriend is
going to be running Bobby's taco truck?"

Camile heard the words but the statement

sounded so ludicrous she needed to hear it again. "What are you talking about?"

Sam pointed. "Yeah, Logan here works at the machine shop across from the lot where a bunch of vendors park their rigs. This morning, he saw McGrath in the lot with Bobby. They shook hands and then McGrath drove off in the taco truck."

Camile stared at Logan and tried to process this information. Undoubtedly, a case of mistaken identity. "Are you positive it was him—Rhys McGrath?"

"Yes, ma'am. It was weird because I met Rhys last week. He's involved in a project with my brother, Brady. It hasn't been formally announced yet, but they're building a youth center here in Pacific Cove."

"Yeah, Camile," Sam said. "And if he is selling tacos, we're all buying. We heard about that charity he does, too—The Other Front Line. You know my oldest brother, Elijah, was wounded in Afghanistan. He knows a guy who got a state-of-the-art prosthetic leg from TOFL. For free."

Logan asserted, "Rhys is a good guy, not like a lot people around town have been saying."

"Yes, he sure is," Sam said soberly, his eyes locking firmly on to Camile's. "We're doing our best to set folks straight about that."

"My sister, Katie, works at Williams Realty," Jake said. "She put a post about the youth center on social media this morning."

Threads of joy, relief and sadness all wound together to form a thick knot right in the center of Camile's chest. The first two won out because Rhys deserved this. She delivered a huge smile to these men who were essentially telling her that they were now firmly on Rhys's side. Camile knew it wouldn't be long before people would be singing his praises all over town. She couldn't wait to tell Anne that they'd done it; the tide had finally turned.

"Thank you, guys. How about a slice of pie on me?"

Free pie was a hit. But while Camile went to retrieve it she revisited the first part of Sam's story because she couldn't wrap her brain around Rhys driving off in the taco truck. Bobby had dropped the lawsuit. Rhys would have no reason to talk to Bobby, much less drive his taco truck, unless… Camile delivered pie and refilled drinks. And then spent the rest of her shift alternately trying to decide how to proceed and cautioning herself about getting her hopes up too high.

CHAPTER TWENTY

AFTER WORK, CAMILE walked the short distance to her apartment while giving herself the pep talk of a lifetime. Before she could chicken out, she removed her phone from her bag and texted Anne: Are you home? If I drive out there can you unlock the gate and let me in without Rhys knowing? I need to talk to him.

In record time, she'd changed out of her work clothes. She perched on the edge of the sofa where she tried not to stare at her phone while she waited for Anne's reply.

She waited less than two minutes: Yes! A million times yes. It's about time. You two need to work this out. I am so over my brooding grump of a brother.

Camile responded: Thank you! But I don't want you getting too excited. I'm not sure this is going to work.

Anne's response made her chuckle despite her rapidly fraying confidence: Too late. Maybe wear your dance outfit? That always puts him in a good mood.

"CAMILE, HOW DID you get in?" Rhys asked roughly a half hour later, his gaze bouncing from the security screen to Anne, who was seated next to it, to Camile, and back to Anne. Ultimately, he directed his frown at Anne. "Never mind."

Anne stood up. "You can apologize to me later for that glare. Willow and I are going into town for ice cream. Do you need anything?"

Eyes on Camile, Rhys shook his head.

Silence built, crowding the space between them while Anne crossed the room. If Camile hadn't seen what she had outside when she'd pulled up, she might have bolted. The tension remained until they heard sounds indicating that Anne and Willow had gone out another door.

Then Rhys asked, "What are you doing here?"

"I wanted to talk to you."

"Why didn't you call or text?"

"I was afraid you wouldn't pick up or message me back. You didn't respond to my last twelve messages."

"That was before… Before things worked out."

"Fair enough," she said. "But this was too important to take a chance."

"I see. What is it?"

"Why is Bobby's taco truck parked in your driveway?"

He grimaced like he'd forgotten he'd parked it there. "It doesn't matter."

"It matters to me."

"Camile, I don't want to discuss this with you."

Confidence building, she walked closer. "Rhys, I know what that means, remember? I know that when you don't want to lie, you opt not to say anything at all. Is that what you're doing right now?"

A muscle ticked in his tightly flexed jaw. "Yes."

"Are you the one who made Bobby's lawsuit go away?"

"Camile, don't—"

"Answer me, Rhys, please." She could hear the edge of desperation in her tone and she didn't care.

"Yes."

A spark of hope flared bright and hot inside of her. Inhaling deeply, she tried to keep it tempered. Just because he'd done this for her didn't mean…everything. *Please, let it mean everything.*

"Why did you do it? How did you manage it?"

"Because he was suing you for a million dollars. He wasn't going to win but the legal bills and the stress would have crushed you. I found a way to make it go away and I did. Please don't give me the lecture about how you don't like people to help you. It's done and I can't take it back. The papers were signed."

"Papers," she repeated. "Is that what you were doing in Bailey's office when Anne and I found you in the parking lot that day?"

"Yes."

"So you did this when you were really angry and disappointed with me?"

"Yes, but—"

"Does that mean you still cared about me even after you found out about what Anne and I were doing?"

He winced a little and she knew he'd been dreading the question. But he answered it. "Camile, I've always cared about you. What you did with Anne didn't change that, no matter how much I wished it had. My feelings don't work like that. I don't give them away easily but once I do I can't just…shut them off."

"Rhys, I love you."

Squeezing his eyes shut, he dipped his chin and put a hand to his head like the words hurt him somehow. And that made her heart ache all over again.

Finally, with a troubled expression that she

couldn't read, he looked at her and stated, "That's not possible."

"Of course it's possible," she countered. "I'm in love with you. I've been in love with you ever since… I'm not sure when exactly, but definitely when you first called me sweetheart and took care of me when I was sick."

"But you said… I asked you to spend time with me and you refused. Then Anne offered to pay you and you agreed. The only logical conclusion is that your motivation for dating me was financial compensation. I know you cared about me on some level, but that's not enough for me."

"Fine, okay. You want to figure this out logically. Then think about this. Think about the fun we've had together. I hung out with you all day at the scavenger hunt, and then at the wine tasting. We even had a great time on that date two years ago before it ended so tragically. To me, you are irresistible. At the scavenger hunt, I told you that I didn't want to date you because my life was a mess—which wasn't untrue. Being served with Bobby's lawsuit seemed to underscore my point.

"But honestly, I was also terrified. You hadn't told me about the reason you left me on that date, and I had misgivings about getting close. Although I was already falling for you.

I didn't want to be, but I was. Right after that, Anne told me about the custody suit. She gave me the perfect excuse to be with you without having to act based solely on my feelings. I told myself I needed to help you. But I wanted to do it. Because I love you, and I love Willow. Then, after you kissed me and we started dating for real, I wanted to tell you, I needed to tell you, but Anne talked me out of it. For a good reason—Willow."

He was leaning against the cupboard, hands gripping the counter's edge on either side of his hips.

She moved closer. His eyes searched hers and she knew he was looking for the truth he wanted to believe. She hoped he saw it soon.

She tried to help him along. "I'll never lie to you again, Rhys, not even by omission, if that's what you really want? Think carefully before you answer, though, because a little fudging of the truth might be a good thing once in a while."

He scoffed at that and shook his head.

"No, I mean it! Like when you ask me if I think your jeans are too tight when you know you've put on a few pounds or if I want to spend the *entire* day at the military history museum—I will tell you the truth."

He still didn't respond, so she took one more

step. It put her right into his space, and the sharp intake of his breath gave her a tremendous amount of satisfaction and a boost of confidence.

"Can I kiss you?" she asked, her eyes searching his. "Because I really want to kiss you right now."

"Yes," he said.

"Yes what? I'm not sure which question you're answering right now."

"Yes." His voice was a gruff whisper fraught with emotion. "I want you to kiss me." He swallowed, and added, "But what I want the most is for you to love me."

Camile felt her heart clench so tightly inside her chest that for a moment she couldn't breathe. She said, "I want to spend the rest of my life doing both of those things. You can trust me, Rhys. You know you can." She slid her arms around him and pushed onto her toes to give him the kiss he wanted. Before she could manage it, he picked her up and turned with her, setting her on the counter where he'd been leaning.

One side of his mouth curved up as he said, "There, now you can kiss me properly."

Clutching his shirt, she pulled him in close between her knees. "You got it," she whispered, just before her lips found his. She kissed him and tried to convey all the meaning behind the words she'd already spoken. His arms went around her, and there was a hint of desperation in his embrace. Camile felt that, too, and then soon, thankfully, all the misery of the last week spent without him fell away. And she reveled in how much better it was without all the worries and distractions between them.

Rhys relaxed, too, and eventually he loosened his hold just enough to pull back and look at her. "You love me," he whispered, and this time it was a statement, not a question. "Camile loves Rhys," he added with a grin that nearly stopped her heart. Truly, the man was just completely gorgeous. "No one has ever loved me before. Not in a romantic way, I mean."

"Rhys—"

"Shh." He placed a finger over her lips and then removed it. "Don't tell me it's not true. I don't mind because I've never wanted anyone's love before, until you."

"Oh my…" Leaning in, she rested her forehead against his chest. "There's something to be said for this honesty of yours."

"I'm glad you think so."

She pulled back to smile at him. "But, see, I know better than to ever ask you how I look in my skinny jeans when I've been eating too many of your cookies and muffins."

Rhys did his confused scowl. "Camile, you can always ask me that. It won't matter to me. I will always love the way you look as long as you look at me with the same love in your eyes that's there right now. I hope you can see it in mine because I love you, too. And I don't want you to ever doubt my love for you. No matter what happens or how either one of us looks."

"I…" Camile let out a little squeak and fisted both her hands in his shirt. "Rhys, that is so… romantic. Are you trying to kill me with these truths of yours?"

Looking extremely pleased with himself, he kissed her again.

"Okay, so now that we've cleared up the important details like how much you adore me and how much I love you, will you please tell me how you got Bobby to drop the lawsuit?"

"It was a simple matter of figuring out what he wanted," Rhys explained without explaining.

"He wanted to sell his taco truck?" she asked with a doubtful head tip.

"No, he wanted money and revenge."

"So, what, you gave him money?" That didn't sit well with Camile. Despite the misery of it all, a part of her was looking forward to thoroughly exposing Bobby for the weasel she knew him to be.

"Of course not. I also wanted something."

"Which was?" she prompted.

"Vengeance."

"Vengeance?"

"Yes, for the way he treated you. For the way he treats women in general. And for Howard. I don't have a staff at my disposal like our friend Harper, so I hired a private investigator. In addition to false advertising of his taco filling, Bobby has a history of sexual harassment. The PI found several women who were willing to testify—on tape. I told him if he didn't drop the case immediately, I'd compile a YouTube mash-up of these women's stories that would put your taco trashing to shame. I told him if he signed over his taco truck to a women's charity and agreed to sensitivity training, the worst he'd have to contend with is a lawsuit from one or more of these women."

"I'm guessing you were similarly as direct with Laura that day in the bowling alley?"

"I was. I won't tolerate anyone speaking dishonestly about the woman I love."

"Wow." Camile chuckled. "I'm glad you're on my side."

"Yes, you are. And I'm glad you're on mine. If it wasn't for you and your suspicion about Heather, I'd still be fighting for Willow."

"That's true." Camile did feel good about that.

"I love you. Will you tell me you love me one more time?"

"No, I will not tell you one more time," she answered with a trace of drama in her tone. Bringing her hands up, she wound them around the back of his neck. "In the spirit of that Rhys McGrath honesty that I've come to cherish, I will be telling you at least a million more times."

"You do realize that means you'll have to tell me you love me fifty times a day for roughly fifty-four point seven years? Or a hundred times a day for—"

She cut him off with a quick kiss, and then pulled back enough to whisper, "I guess I better get started then, huh? I love you, Rhys." And then kissed him again, and repeated, "I love you."

EPILOGUE

As she stood in Nina's driveway, Camile did a quick inventory of vehicles and knew that everyone else had arrived. Her stomach took a nervous dip while she waited for Rhys to walk around the cab of his pickup and join her where she stood waiting for him.

"I've been thinking," she said when he approached. She slipped her hand into his.

"About what?"

She liked how he stayed right where he was, holding her hand and looking at her like he wanted to hear whatever she had to say. He always did that—treated her like she was the most important person in the world. Even when what she had to say was about where she'd like to go hiking or what flavor of ice cream she wanted to order.

"Possibly my dad is not as bad as I've made him out to be." Camile had been on edge about this encounter for days, alternately venting to Rhys about her dad's strong opinions and expressing her excitement at seeing her parents after such a long separation. Bottom line, she was nervous about how her dad was going to react to her business venture. "Everything I said about my mom is true, though. She is lovely. Genuinely, one of the kindest people you'll ever meet."

"So you take after your mom," Rhys said in a decisive tone.

Before them stood Nina's lovely old farmhouse, and inside, her family waited along with Anne, Willow, Harper and Kyle, Mia and Jay, and some other friends. The faint sound of Marion barking reverberated through the cool evening air. After spending weeks towing their RV around the United States visiting relatives and national parks, her parents were back in Pacific Cove. Nina had invited everyone out to her place to welcome them home and to celebrate Camile's thesis triumph. Her sister loved to entertain. She'd been planning this for days, and while Camile appreciated it, it all felt like a bit much. Nina had called and texted enough times now that Camile feared she'd gone overboard where the "celebration" was concerned. Nina and Rhys had even been exchanging texts. Camile's business partnership with Harper and her relationship with Rhys both felt like achievements more worthy of celebration.

"You are sweet," she said as they started toward the house. "And that's true in that I have much more in common with her than I do my dad. My dad is… I don't think I've exaggerated how opinionated he is, but he is a good man. He's one of the most generous human beings I've ever met. He's just very set in his ways when it comes to certain things."

Together they scaled the steps of Nina's wide front porch. Marion barked again but the pitch had changed and Camile knew the dog now recognized that it was her. That made her smile. She'd like to have a dog someday. For now, she was thrilled with the new cats in her life. Rhys and Willow had just adopted two adorable kittens from Lucky Cats, and they were tons of fun.

"Don't be surprised if he says something about me that you don't like."

Rhys frowned at her. "What do you mean? Like what?"

"Like about the dance studio or my 'useless' degree."

"I don't think he'll do that."

"Don't be too sure," she said. "Now that I think about it, you guys sort of have that trait in common. He's honest, too, although his opining is more deliberate. You don't have to ask to get it."

"That's a quality I can respect."

"I know. It's just... Don't be nervous," she said nervously.

He lifted her hand and brushed a kiss across her knuckles. "I'm not."

The door swung open. "Hey, guys!" Aubrey and Marion greeted them, Aubrey with smiles, Marion with jubilant tail wagging. Aubrey stepped aside and waved them forward.

Rhys gave Camile's hand an encouraging squeeze and she immediately felt calmer. She glanced up at him. He smiled. Why wasn't he nervous? What was going on here? How had it happened that he was the one reassuring her? Shouldn't he be the nervous one? He was meeting her parents.

She didn't have long to ponder these thoughts as they were inundated with hugs and greetings. Willow and her friend Jenna hurried over to show Camile the photos they'd taken earlier of the kittens. School had started a few weeks prior. There'd been a minor amount of drama for a girl Willow's age; she'd joined band and already found a bestie in Jenna.

Chatting with Nina, Camile saw Rhys's mom stroll out of the kitchen.

"Rhys, your parents are here? How wonderful! You didn't tell me they were coming." She was getting a little embarrassed. This was definitely excessive for a thesis party. It wasn't like she'd earned her doctorate degree or even landed some cool job in the psychology field.

Camile looked for her mom and found that she was heading right for her. Across the room, her dad waved. But not at her, she realized as Rhys returned the gesture.

"Why is my dad waving at you like he knows you?"

"Because we've met."

"What? When?"

"Kyle introduced us yesterday" was his specific yet puzzling answer.

"How is that possible? They just got home yesterday. I haven't even seen them yet."

"So go greet them," he encouraged. "They're anxious to see you. I'll tell you about it later."

That was when she noticed the banner hanging across the wall in the dining room. Congratulations, Camile. It was surrounded by big, colorful paper flowers. A matching cake sat in the middle of the table. It was pretty except... the writing was slightly off center. Odd. And completely unlike her perfectionist sister.

"Camile, honey, congratulations!" her mom said, enfolding her in a tight hug.

"Thanks, Mom. It's so great to have you guys back."

"We're happy to be back—especially your father. I don't think I'm going to be able to get him away from Pacific Cove again in the summer."

Camile chuckled. "He does love his ocean, doesn't he? I'm surprised he agreed to this trip in the first place."

"Yes, I do," her dad said from over her shoulder. "But I love my girls more. That's what I was really missing."

"Hey, Dad." Camile slipped her arms around him, comforted by the feel of his strong arms and familiar scent. Despite her anxiety, she loved her parents and she knew they loved her.

He loosened his hold but kept his hands on her shoulders. "I'm so proud of you."

"Thank you." Camile braced herself for the inquisition.

It didn't happen. Instead, she spent a few minutes laughing at their travel tales and catching up. Rhys brought her a glass of lemonade.

Her dad said, "I'm so happy for you, honey. I think you've found your niche with this dance studio."

"Me, too," Camile answered cautiously, waiting for him to qualify the statement.

"I was telling Rhys last night about how your mom and I went to one of those acrobat-type shows while we were in Vegas. You know, with the ropes and trapeze things and gymnastics and dancing?"

"Yeah, I know the ones you mean." *Here it*

comes, she thought. She almost wished he'd just get it over with.

"Those people are extremely talented."

"Yes, they are."

"Like you."

What?

"The whole time, I kept telling your mom how great you'd be at that."

"Um, thanks, Dad." Who was this man and what had he done with her father?

"What could be better than having all three of our girls settled here in Pacific Cove? That's a father's dream come true. Especially when our grandchildren get here."

"Brian, let's not rush things now," her mom scolded in a whisper that had Camile wondering if Aubrey had shared her pregnancy challenges. "It'll happen when it happens."

Rhys leaned in and said close to her ear, "Camile, can I borrow you for a minute?" The question made her smile. She remembered asking him the same thing that night at the mayor's fund-raising dinner. The night he'd kissed her, and she'd learned the truth about their date, and everything had changed.

She was about to steal his response when Aubrey's voice stopped her; there was something about her tone.

"Uh-oh," her sister said from where she stood in the dining room. "Shoot!" The exclamation was accompanied by an odd sound, like paper ripping. "I knew we should have used tacks," she said frantically as she scrambled to reach the wall where the banner hung.

But it was too late. The flowers had peeled away on one end and were falling. The crowd quieted as the last one fluttered to the ground. Camile squinted to read the newly revealed message: Congratulations, Camile and Rhys!

"Oh no…" Nina cringed and raised a tense, fisted hand. "Rhys, I'm so sorry."

Camile looked at him.

"It's quite all right, Nina. Or, at least, I hope it will be." From his pocket, he removed what was clearly a ring. A ring! Camile felt her heart flip and then proceed to do its own happy dance right inside her chest.

Rhys, bless him, gave her a little shrug and made the best joke ever: "Leave it to me to make an unintentional public spectacle of your proposal. At least there's no danger of me calling my fiancée by the wrong name. I love you, Camile. Will you marry me?"

Across the room, Anne busted out a laugh. Nina joined in. Harper, who stood nearby, snickered behind her hand. Willow was grinning.

Camile faked a scowl. "Is this why you've already met my parents?"

"Yes, I went over to their house last night so I could meet them first."

She looked at Nina and pointed at the banner. "So this excessive celebration isn't actually about my thesis?"

"No. Well, I mean, everyone is excited for you and all but—"

"I'm assuming you're going to add Rhys's name to that cake, too? That's why the bad frosting job?"

"Guilty." Nina lifted the frosting tube she held in acknowledgment. "Rhys was going to take you outside and ask you. Text me with the yes. Then we were going to do the big reveal when you came back inside."

Camile looked at Rhys again.

The amusement in his expression and the unmistakable love in his eyes had her melting all over. "I was hoping this would be our engagement dinner."

"Now *that* is a reason to celebrate." Beaming, she stepped into his arms where she whispered, "Yes, Rhys, I will marry you. And you can borrow me forever."

* * * * *

For more great romances from acclaimed author Carol Ross, visit www.Harlequin.com today!